YOUR CHEATIN' HEART

YOUR CHEATIN' HEART

Nancy Bartholomew

HarperPaperbacks
A Division of HarperCollins*Publishers*

🔥 HarperPaperbacks
A Division of HarperCollinsPublishers
10 East 53rd Street, New York, NY 10022–5299

This is a work of fiction. The characters, incidents, and dialogues are products of the author's imagination and are not to be construed as real. Any resemblance to actual events or persons, living or dead, is entirely coincidental.

ISBN 0-06-101409-5

Cover illustration © 1999 by Barbara Gordon

First HarperPaperbacks printing: February 2000

Printed in the United States of America

Visit HarperPaperbacks on the World Wide Web at
http://www.harpercollins.com

❖ 10 9 8 7 6 5 4 3 2 1

For Grandma Alice, who held me close,
loved me unconditionally, and always said,
"Life ain't hard, honey. You make it hard."

And for Papa Lee and Mama Becky,
who believed in family and believed in me.

YOUR CHEATIN' HEART

1

The day I married Vernell Spivey, it rained. I should've taken that as an omen. When his brother, Jimmy, pinched me on the ass as I was headed for the vestibule of the church, I should've seen that for what it was, too. However, I was young and pregnant and too tenderhearted to start a war between brothers on what was allegedly the best day of our young lives. I figured it was Jimmy's way of welcoming me to the family.

But then, when I was nine months pregnant with Sheila, too big to do more than waddle to the kitchen table and sit, Jimmy professed his undying love for me. He came over when he knew for certain Vernell would be at work, and gave me a speech that had obviously been rehearsed.

"Maggie," he said, "it ain't no use us denying it. I have wanted you since the day I met you, and I can tell by the look in your eyes that the feeling is mutual."

What I was really feeling was a sudden gas pain brought on by Sheila flipping over inside my womb. Tears flooded my eyes, and for a moment I was bent over, clutching the edge of the table for support. I was speechless.

"Let it out, honey," he said. "It'll be for the best."

Somehow I didn't think so.

There was a kernel of truth in what Jimmy was saying. As I sat at the kitchen table, clutching my belly and wishing like hell for a swig of Alka-Seltzer, I had to admit I found Jimmy attractive in a good-old-boy sort of way. He was tall and dark, with deep brown eyes that always looked lonely and left out. I'm a sucker for men like that.

"Maggie," he said, reaching out to touch my stomach tenderly. "I'll love your baby like it was my own. We can tell Vernell together." I cried out as Sheila kicked again, and Jimmy took it for a shriek of fear. "Aw, he'll be upset for awhile, but he'll get by. Vernell's always got an eye for the ladies." Didn't I know it. Already Vernell had shown his ass, chasing women that worked with him.

I tried to straighten up, if only for a moment, and give Jimmy the true picture. "You just want me 'cause I'm Vernell's wife, Jimmy," I said. "That's how it's always been with you and him." Jimmy started to protest. "And honest to Pete, you aren't my type."

In addition to being in Vernell's family, which

was one strike against him, Jimmy had no ambition in life. He wanted it all handed to him. If we'd run off, it wouldn't have taken any time at all before I was the breadwinner and Jimmy was out bass fishing.

"Aw, come on, sugar," he said, his deep voice dropping almost to a whisper, "you know that ain't it." He reached his hand out again, letting it rest on my forearm briefly before he started gently stroking it. I had to admit that between his soothing voice and warm touch, I was starting to feel sleepy and maybe a little sexy. Nobody'd made me feel that way in months.

Vernell picked that moment to suddenly appear for lunch, bursting through the back door, letting the screen slam loudly behind him, and staring at the two of us.

"What?" he said, his voice pitched to a high, anxious squeak. "It ain't time, is it?"

Jimmy jumped like a scalded yard dog, and I favored Vernell with a withering glare. Vernell had not asked out of concern; he'd asked because his chief aim at this point in our lives was to avoid the labor and delivery room at all costs. He'd increased his hours at the mobile home lot, volunteering to deliver every home he sold, personally, no matter what the distance. He couldn't fool me.

"No, Vernell," I said. "Jimmy here was just professing his undying love and asking me to run off with him."

Vernell laughed, not noticing that Jimmy had turned heart-attack red and started gasping for breath.

"Yep, Vernell," I said, "strange as it may seem, pregnancy has not lessened my desirability to some men."

Vernell laughed again, but this time it had a strained quality as he took a quick glance over at his brother.

"Aw, don't worry, boys," I said, "I'm not about to take either one of you too seriously." I stood up and headed for the refrigerator. Then it happened. My water broke. Vernell's worst fear was realized and Jimmy's declaration of love forgotten.

From that day forward, Jimmy continued to wage his campaign of love, but from a safe distance. He'd pop up unexpectedly, sit in my kitchen like a lost soul, sighing and hoping I'd take pity on him and ask what was wrong. I never did. I knew that if I waited long enough, Jimmy'd tell me.

"Vernell's on my back again," he'd moan. "He wants me to take over the mobile home business so's he can start a satellite dish company. You ever hear tell of such a ridiculous speculation?"

Famous last words. Jimmy got forty-nine percent of the mobile home business and Vernell got the gold mine. I have to admit, Vernell did work like a dog to get the satellite business off the ground. I can't help but wonder how much quicker his rise to the top would've been if he hadn't been pursuing and sleeping with the lovely Dish Girl, Jolene.

Jimmy finally married, but he didn't see that as cause to leave me alone. "Well, hell, sugar, you're married, too."

When his wife, Roxanne, turned out to be the

queen bitch of the universe, content to lay on the sofa all day, watching soaps and eating Chee-tos, I felt sorry for him. Even Jimmy didn't deserve the treatment she gave him. Always yelling, calling and checking on him all over town if he was two minutes late. No wonder I sometimes found him sitting at my kitchen table, even with no one home.

Of course, now that would all change. Jimmy'd played on my sympathies and irritated me for the very last time. Thanks to him, I was sitting in the Greensboro Police Department, staring at a possible charge of murder one and ruing the day I'd ever met up with the Spivey clan.

2

On Vernell's fortieth birthday, he came home drunk and announced he didn't love me anymore. He went on to say that he had to be alone to find himself and that he knew he was put on this earth for a purpose.

"What's her name?" I asked.

"Aw, now ain't it just like you to think this is about a woman!"

One year later, he married Jolene Hayes, the Dish Girl from his Satellite Kingdom commercials. Blond, twenty-six, and stacked. I figured Vernell, North Carolina's self-proclaimed King of the Satellite Dish, had found his higher calling.

Then my sixteen-year-old, Sheila, pitched a fit because I took her driver's license away on account of her bad grades and a certain long-haired, nineteen-year-old, dope-dealing musician she'd been sneaking behind my back to see.

"I'm going to live with Daddy," she stormed, "and you can't stop me. He won't be so mean to me!"

I packed her bags. I drove her to Vernell's New Irving Park mansion, pulled up in the circular drive, and said, "Don't let the door hit you in the ass on the way out! You're here for the rest of the school year. We'll just see how lovely life is with Daddy!"

Then I went home to my College Hills bungalow, marched inside, and went to bed for three days. Even though I'd done the right thing by calling Sheila's hand, it hurt so bad I could scarcely catch my breath. I cried for my baby and the fifteen years I'd lost to Vernell Spivey.

I called in to the beauty shop I co-owned and told Bonnie to open without me and cancel all my appointments, even with the regulars. Then I ate, everything in the house that had a hint of chocolate, every french fry and greasy chip, and every chemical-laden snack cake that didn't have mold on it. I was pitiful.

On the third day, I got up out of bed, staggered into the bathroom, and addressed myself in the mirror.

"Maggie," I told myself, "you are a pitiful waste of God-given talent and womanhood." I stared back at myself. "Look at you! Going all to pieces because your daughter decides to go try life with Daddy! She ain't dead, and frankly, she's been a royal pain in the derriere these past few months." I leaned in closer to the mirror, staring at the woman I'd become. My curly red hair hung in a sleep-tangled mat, my green eyes were red-rimmed and bloodshot, and I was getting pimples from eating chocolate and grease.

"Girl, Mama didn't raise no fools and she certainly didn't raise a whiner. It is time to take the bull by the horns and get a life!" I remembered something else Mama used to say, too: If you tarry on fate's highway, you'll become life's roadkill.

Mama was right. My future was awaiting me, and somehow I knew it would mean a big change. I just didn't know that it would also mean big trouble.

Six months later, I found myself. I turned the day-to-day management of the beauty shop over to my partner, Bonnie. I told her I'd still come in and do my regulars, but she was in charge. Then I took half of the money Vernell reluctantly forked over in the divorce settlement, and claimed what I knew was my rightful place in the world.

Ever since I'd gotten pregnant with Sheila and had to marry Vernell, I'd been pretty much playing it by the rules. My crayon never strayed outside of the lines. But I decided that taking the bull by the horns meant pursuing the one dream that I'd always kept buried in the back of my head. Maggie Reid, thirty-six-year-old divorcée and mother of one, co-owner of the Curly-Que Beauty Salon was about to become Maggie Reid, girl singer for the Drivin' Wheel, the house band at Greensboro's leading country and western bar, the Golden Stallion Club.

I was born to sing. But like Mama always told

me, a caged bird can't sing if it's living with a gilded lily. With Vernell across town shacked up with a Barbie doll and Sheila going for the Miss Spoiled Rotten Award, I figured there wasn't much I had to lose.

It's not like I had no experience. I'd sung all my life, one way or another. That's how me and Vernell met. He was dancing with some girl right by the stage at a high school dance. When he swung her around, he looked up at me as I was singing in my little band, and he winked. The rest was history. Bad history.

So, I thought, go for it, girl. What've you got to lose? All my life I'd stood by and watched the parade. It was finally my turn. And that's how I wound up on stage at the Golden Stallion, standing in front of a microphone, ready to make my mark on the world of country music.

I won't ever forget that first night. The auditions were open to the public, with every drunk, bouncer, deejay, and wanna-be cowgirl putting in their two cents worth about who the new lead singer in the house band ought to be.

I remember hearing them call my name over the P.A. system, and someone giving me a little shove. Next thing I knew, I was under the bright lights, walking across that stage like I owned the place, and praying I didn't make a fool of myself by tripping over the cables and wires that criss-crossed the floor.

The band members looked at me. The lead guitar player, a cute fella with a small black beard, nodded and said, "Count it off and we'll come in behind you." He could've said, "Hey, my name's Jethro and we're the Beverly Hillbillies," for all I heard. I was too nervous to think.

I stepped up to the mike, my heart somewhere up around my ears, and looked back at the band. "Fake it 'til you make it," I whispered to myself. "One, two, one, two, three, four." I gave them the count, the pedal steel started to whine, and the rhythm guitar slipped in underneath as I began to sing "Your Cheatin' Heart."

I spent the first verse just trying not to wet my pants with fear, wishing my knees would quit knocking. On the second verse, I began to look out past the lights into the audience and sing to the house. After all, I was going to be a Country Legend. I had to act like a Somebody.

I sang my heart out and as I did, something started to change in me. For the first time in maybe ever, I felt strong deep down inside. I made eye contact with every lonely-looking man I saw, even the cute ones. I unhooked the mike from the stand and started walking and singing. By the start of the third verse, they were mine.

Somewhere in the middle of the third verse, I fell in love. A tall, lanky man was moving through the throng of dancers, his eyes locking onto mine and pulling me to him. He kept right on coming until he stood at the edge of the rail that rimmed the dance floor. He wore a white straw western hat and tight, faded blue jeans. His face was deeply tanned and laugh-lined, like he worked outside for a living. And he had a thick, cowboy mustache, the kind that makes women think about kissing.

He stood there, arms folded, smiling up at me like we were old friends, sharing a secret, an intimate, under-the-covers secret. I looked straight back at him, smiled, and let the music tell this man we had a common destiny. When the song ended, I had a new job and a future.

There was only one casualty that evening. By the time I'd finished singing and talking with the band, my blue-eyed cowboy had disappeared. I looked for him, not in an obvious way, but short of going into the men's room, I was pretty thorough. He was gone, but the gift he'd given me remained. I knew now there was life after Vernell Spivey. I had a new job and prospects on the horizon.

For the next five months it no longer mattered that Vernell was basking in the artificial sunlight of TV cameras, hawking satellite dishes and becoming rich. It even stung a little less that Sheila was now attending the Irving Park Country Day School and hanging out with girls whose first names always sounded like somebody's last name. Life had dealt me an inside straight, and I was happy.

That is, up until the day when fate, in the form of the Greensboro Police Department and Jimmy Spivey, conspired to ruin my life and take away my newfound happiness.

3

Maybe it wasn't entirely Jimmy's fault that I was sitting in a little eight by six cubicle, counting the cracks in the linoleum. After all, I was the one who had mouthed off to those cops. But they deserved it. They came busting in and interrupted me at a very crucial point in my tribute to Tammy Wynette.

Cletus, the Golden Stallion's doorman, tried to stop them. See, he ain't afraid of nothing or nobody. He spread his big, beefy legs, folded his two-by-four arms across his chest, and glared at them with his black, beady eyes. That look'll stop an overnight trucker lit up on speed and spoiling for a fight. But it didn't faze the Greensboro Police Department's finest.

I could tell from the way they were staring and pointing in my direction that it was me they were after, and they weren't looking for autographs. What in the world did they want?

"No," Cletus said, still trying to stop them.

"Step aside," the older one seemed to say. The younger one, hungry for his nightstick, started fingering his belt. Cletus bristled and the older one shot his partner a look.

"We ain't after making no trouble," the older cop said, or something like it. He raised his hands as if placating Cletus and gestured toward me. "We just want Ms. Reid."

"She's singing," Cletus must've said.

"Cain't help that," the cop said, and pushed right on by him.

I saw them coming and it ticked me off. Jake the Snake, local to the Pagan Motorcycle Club, and known to tip big-time when he's loaded, was just about to approach me when he saw the cops and scuttled away like a frightened crab. Any other night, the cops would've been glad to find him, but these two were looking straight at me and they didn't look happy.

The younger one walked right to the bottom of the stage where I was singing "Stand By Your Man," and started yapping like a terrier.

"We need to talk to you," he said.

I ignored him and kept right on.

Sparks, the pedal steel player, was eating the whole scene up with a spoon. That's 'cause he's only five-feet-two with his boots on. He has an authority problem. Sometimes short men are like that. Sugar Bear, on rhythm guitar, was about to pass out. He figured the cops were after him and the ounce of pot he had stashed in his guitar case. Harmonica Jack was tracking a cutie at twenty paces and never even stopped blowing his harp to acknowledge the law's presence.

Cheryl, the waitress with the fewest brain cells and the largest cup size, actually wandered up to the cops and asked if she could take their order. When they said no, she got all miffed and said, "Well, there's a two drink minimum, ya know!"

I was laughing, but couldn't nobody tell. I'd turned my back and dropped my head down like Tammy Wynette used to do right before she'd turn back around with a tear rolling down her cheek. It's all in the timing. In the world of country music, not a teardrop falls without it bein' planned for maximum effect.

I held the last note until the audience started hooting and whooping. That's when the two cops rushed the stage.

"Ms. Reid?" the older one said, as if he didn't already know.

"In the flesh," I answered.

"We need you to come down to the police station with us." He sounded just like a TV show. Who knew they really talked like that?

"Well, am I under arrest?" I asked, and the small crowd of Nosy Parkers standing at the foot of the stage began to snicker. That made the young cop's trigger finger get itchy again. Somebody should've told him early on that being a police officer isn't a popularity contest.

"No, you're not under arrest. You got trouble at your house, and the detectives wanted us to come get you."

Now I had something to worry about.

"What is it? Did someone break in?" The cops stood there, like big park statues, all stony and grim.

"Tell me!" I demanded. "I got a right to know what's wrong before I just go busting out of here."

The younger guy couldn't contain himself. "Not in a murder case you don't," he said.

I thought the older cop was going to take him outside and whip him. He started turning red in the face and his gray flattop started to glow white against his skin.

"They'll explain it all once we're downtown," he said, trying to act like there wasn't nothing out of the ordinary going on.

"Wait a minute," I said, a tiny pilot light of fear suddenly cutting on in my heart. "I got a sixteen-year-old daughter. She lives with her daddy, but she's got a key. She wasn't . . . I mean . . . she's not . . ."

Flattop caught on. "No, nothing like that."

"Yeah, this one's male," his partner said.

"Shut up, Dave!" Flattop yelled. "Jeeze!"

"Cuff her?" Dave asked hopefully.

"For pity's sake, no."

At the mention of handcuffs, the crowd—my fans—turned ugly. They moved in close and there was a hostile smell to the air.

"Aw, now," I said, lifting my hands out in front of me, "he just don't wanna risk me running out on him." I laughed and winked at the crowd. "See, ain't every day a cute redhead rides in a big old squad car!"

The young cop colored, more of a purple than his partner's ruby. "Shucks," I said, stepping forward and linking my arms through the officers'. "Two boys cute as y'all? Why I'd be honored to go riding!"

I pushed them forward, toward the front door. The young one started to resist.

"Listen, big man," I hissed under my breath, "there's two of y'all and a houseful of them. A wise man knows when to shut up and run low."

I looked back over my shoulder at the uncertain mob. If I'd raised my finger, or so much as whistled, they'd have come running.

"Toodaloo, boys," I said with a laugh. "Looks like I got a few fish to fry. See y'all tomorrow night!" *I hope*, I breathed to myself. I had the feeling I was headed for big trouble. As usual, I was right.

4

Police departments are set up to intimidate the guilty, and Greensboro's was no exception. Someone had hung a rubber chicken on the doorknob to the interrogation room where I sat waiting. The symbolism was not lost on me. I was beginning to feel like the sacrificial bird at a Sunday supper.

I sat in a hard plastic chair, considering my options. The right thing to do was to walk. But since I'd been personally escorted to the station, I'd be walking out in the middle of the night, hoping to catch a taxi. Greensboro is not New York City. The cab drivers here go home at a decent hour.

Someone was dead in my home. Who? It had to be someone I knew. Otherwise, they wouldn't have made such a big deal about bringing me downtown. A chill ran over me. They were gonna make me look at the body! No! They couldn't do that. I couldn't look at someone I knew, maybe even loved or cared about, dead.

In an attempt to distract myself, I stared up at the two-way mirror that took up most of the wall across from me. Was that a tiny flicker of movement? I stood up and walked around the battered metal table, standing right in front of the mirror. This time I was sure I saw movement.

"You know, I'm thinking if you're man enough to stare at me from behind the safety of a two-way mirror, you're man enough to walk in and look me in the eye." I was guessing, of course, but a woman wouldn't skulk around like that. At least I wouldn't. "Why don't you come in here and tell me what's going on?"

The movement stopped. I slowly returned to my chair and started thinking again. Who was dead in my house? Why didn't the police take me there to identify the body? Was it someone I knew? An intruder, or someone I cared about?

Behind me, the door swung open. I jumped, startled as it banged into the wall, and turned around.

"Well, it's about damned . . ." The words faded on my lips. Standing in front of me was the blue-eyed cowboy from the Golden Stallion, just as I remembered.

"It's you," I said, kicking myself for pointing out the obvious. To make matters worse, I stood up, knocking my bag off my lap and onto the floor, the contents scattering everywhere.

"Let me help you," he said, his voice a deep, silky baritone.

We both knelt down, with me trying to grab up every little embarrassing item that women carry in their pocketbooks. He handed me my lipstick, his fingers briefly brushing mine. A shock ran up my arm. We were only inches apart.

"I'm Marshall Weathers," he said, a smile creeping out from underneath his mustache.

"Maggie Reid."

"Oh, I remember."

My heart was pounding in my ears. I focused on my purse, punching the flap closed and trying to calm down. Then I noticed the gun and the badge.

"You're a cop?"

"Yep."

We both stood at the same moment. I came almost up to his shoulder. "Then you know what's going on." He nodded. "Then why am I here? Who's dead?"

"Why don't you have a seat, Maggie," he said. He stepped past me, taking the chair across from mine.

I stood, gripping the back of the chair with one hand and slowly putting my purse down on the table with the other. "Who was it?" I asked slowly.

"His license says James Spivey. Do you know him?"

"Jimmy!" I cried. My legs weakened and I sank down into the chair. "Oh, no!" The tears came, tightening my throat. Not Jimmy!

Marshall Weathers sat there quietly, waiting for the initial shock to pass, I guess. Then he reached into his pocket, pulled out a clean, white handkerchief, and passed it to me.

"I'm sorry," he said softly.

"What happened?"

"We got an anonymous nine-one-one call from a public phone booth, saying there had been shots fired in your house and that someone was hurt. When the patrol officers responded, with the ambulance and EMS people, it was . . ." His voice trailed off and our eyes met.

"You mean someone shot Jimmy? In my house? Like a burglar?"

Weathers shrugged his shoulders. "At this point we're not sure. There doesn't seem to be any sign of forced entry."

"Oh, that doesn't mean a thing!" I said. "My house is so old, all you need do is slam your fist upside the front door lock and the thing'll fall open. Just about everybody close to me knows that."

Weathers sighed softly. "Well, we haven't looked all through the house and premises. I'll need your permission for that to happen."

"Sure," I said, "do it."

Weathers whipped a form out of his pocket and passed it over to me. "Just sign right there."

I didn't even read it. My eyes blurred with fresh tears as I scrawled my name across the paper and shoved it back.

"All right," he said, "this'll get us started." He pushed back his chair and started for the door, then stopped, as if he'd had one more thought. "You own a gun?" he asked.

"Yes, I do. A Smith and Wesson thirty-eight. My ex gave it to me." I hated the thing, but Vernell had insisted.

"Where is it?" His tone was even, almost as if this were an afterthought, but I knew it wasn't. I watched enough TV to know. A little tingle of fear ran down my spine.

"I keep it in the closet, just off the kitchen. It's kind of my closet and the pantry. See, my house is so tiny, and well, they didn't leave me much space to put things, so I have to make do. I mean, my bedroom used to be a sunporch! That's why the back door opens right into it."

I was running on like a faucet as Weathers listened patiently, waiting for me to drip to a stop.

"Where in the closet do you keep it?" he asked.

"What?"

"The gun," he reminded.

"Oh, that. In a basket full of cookie cutters, on the top shelf."

If this seemed strange to him, he didn't let on. He merely wrote it down on a piece of paper and shoved it in his pocket.

"Okay," he said. "Wait right here. I'm gonna send this out to your house and let them get on about checking everything. I might have a few more questions for you. You want some coffee or something?" he asked. He was halfway out the door, his mind already on the murder scene. I don't think he even heard me say no.

I was alone again. Waiting. But now I knew. Jimmy was dead.

I'd lost track of the time, my mind drifting back over the fifteen years of my marriage and all the different memories I had of Jimmy. But when Marshall Weathers walked back into the room, I knew in an instant that something was wrong.

He was staring at me, as if trying to reach inside me for something. He was sizing me up. His eyes, deep blue lie detectors that darted across my face, seemed to be trying to take a read of my personality.

"When was the last time you saw your gun?" he asked.

"I don't know. It's not like I make a habit of checking all the time. Maybe two weeks ago?" My stomach tightened and I found myself fumbling with the flap of my purse. "What does it matter?"

"Well," he said, drawing the word out into one long sigh, "it wouldn't matter so much, except we can't find it."

"Well, that's funny. I haven't touched it. Nobody lives there but me. Where could it have gone?" I looked at him. He was staring right back at me, the lie detectors in full swing. "You mean, the guy who killed Jimmy could've stolen it?"

"Did you have it hidden real good?" he asked. He was rocking back in his chair, lifting the front legs up off the floor, just like a teenaged boy.

"Well, I thought so. It was at the bottom of that basket full of cookie cutters."

He brought the legs of the chair down, hitting the floor with a sharp snap.

"Maggie, Jimmy was shot with a thirty-eight–caliber gun, just like yours."

"So you think the killer somehow dug through my cookie cutters, found my gun, and killed

Jimmy?" I asked. "That doesn't make sense."

Weathers spread his hands out, palms up, on the table. "Exactly," he said. "It just doesn't make a piece of sense."

"So, it must've been another gun." I leaned back away from him, edging myself backward on the chair and feeling the cold metal slats dig into my spine.

"Thirty-eights are a dime a dozen," I said.

He shook his head again. "True, but then, where is *your* gun, Maggie?"

My head was starting to spin. Where *was* my gun? What did all this mean?

"I don't know," I said.

Marshall Weathers pushed back away from me, his hands resting on the edge of the desk, pushing his chair back on its rear legs again.

"I gotta be honest with you, Maggie, and I'm probably not supposed to tell you this, but I will 'cause I think I know what kind of woman you are. But if it turns out that Jimmy Spivey was shot with a thirty-eight–caliber gun, in your house, with no sign of forced entry, well, it's gonna start looking bad for you."

I was so afraid that I felt tears beginning to well up and close off my throat. This wasn't happening to me. It couldn't be. Weathers was watching me, noting my reactions, waiting for my response. I couldn't say a word.

"Maggie, why don't we do this: Tell me everything you did from about seven o'clock on tonight." He slipped a notepad out, flipped it open, and sat ready to write down my every word.

"I left home to go to work at around seven o'clock. That was early on account of something I do every night before I go in to the club."

"What would that be?" he asked, looking up for a moment.

"Well, I ride over to where my daughter, Sheila, lives and just kind of drive by the house. You know, just to check, see if she's home. When it's dark, sometimes I can see inside. That bimbo Vernell's married to keeps the house lit up like the Statue of Liberty."

"You just ride by and then go on to work?" He looked up quickly, making eye contact, and holding it. My stomach got that warm, electric tingle that let me know he was looking straight through me. I shivered deep inside.

"Well, not exactly. I drive by, and then I circle back around and park across the street. There's a big tree out in front of the house across from Vernell's palace. The limbs hang down so far you can almost hide under them." I hated admitting this. It was my secret ritual, my way of watching my baby. I knew it was as pathetic as it sounded.

"How long were you there?" he asked.

"Maybe twenty minutes, maybe a little longer. No one was home, so I sat there hoping she might come in."

"Did she?"

"No."

"Did anyone see you there?" Again he looked up, watching me.

"I don't think so. They live on a cul-de-sac. There weren't too many people home and not much traffic." Damn, I was hanging myself.

"Then what?" he asked.

"Then I drove on to work, got there about eight, and that was that until your men showed up."

"You've got people who can vouch for you the whole night?"

"Yep, except for going to the ladies' room, I was there all evening, in plain sight of everyone." I was feeling much better. I was at work when Jimmy got killed, so I wasn't going to be a suspect after all. "So, you see, all these questions were for nothing. I couldn't have killed Jimmy. I was at work."

Weathers was still staring at me, a disappointed look in his eyes. Slowly he closed the notepad, capped his pen, and folded his hands on top of the book, just like a schoolmarm. Then he unclasped his hands and brought them up to rub his face.

"Oh, Maggie," he sighed, "we've got us a problem. The medical examiner is fixing time of death somewhere between six and eight P.M. That don't let you out." The trip-hammer started in my chest again. I had begun to feel like a caged animal. "It'll get more specific after the autopsy and after we figure a few more things out, but right now, I can't count you out. It sure would help if you knew where your gun was."

"But I don't," I said, my voice sinking to a half-whimper.

At that moment, the door sprang open and a young officer beckoned for Weathers.

"Excuse me a second, Maggie," Weathers said, standing. "I'll be right back."

He stepped to the edge of the doorway, his back

to me, listening to the young officer's report. What were they talking about? How could this be happening to me? What in the world would make the police think I had anything to do with Jimmy's death?

When the officer left and Detective Weathers walked back across the room, I could tell that his manner had changed. I could see it in the way he strode over to the desk, his back stiff, his shoulders straight and his movements terse and economical. He didn't sit down. Instead he placed his hands on the side of the desk near me and leaned over, inches from where I sat.

"Maggie, would you like to start over?" he said, leaning in a little, staring deep into my eyes.

"Not particularly," I said. "We need to be about catching the person who killed my brother-in-law, not wasting time going over the same little details. I don't have anything more to add."

"Oh, I think you might." His tone was almost hostile.

"No, I don't." The McCrarey temper, my mama's temper, began to simmer somewhere deep inside me. How dare this man think I was a liar?

"Miss Reid, I could arrest you right now. In fact, I need to go ahead and advise you of your rights. You have the right to remain silent," he started, droning on rapid-fire until at last he stopped. "Do you understand your rights as they have been given to you?"

"Yes," I said, "but no, I don't understand what in the world you're trying to do to me. I am an innocent, law-abiding citizen, and I haven't done one thing wrong."

A muscle in Detective Weathers's jaw started to twitch, his face had a dusky red undertone to it, and he seemed to be barely reining himself in.

"Perhaps you can tell me," he said softly, "how your brother-in-law's credit card came to be in your possession?"

"I don't have his credit card," I said. What was this?

"It was in your car, on the floor of the passenger seat. How did that happen?"

"What were you doing in my car?"

"You signed the search warrant." He was smug.

"I want a lawyer," I said quietly.

"Maggie," he said, straightening up. "You don't want to go and do that. Why, if you call a lawyer into this, I won't be able to help you. Your options will be limited."

That's when I lost it. I could feel the fire burning up from my gut, creeping across my throat, singeing my ears. I'd had a belly full of manipulation and fear and it was time to set some things straight. Unfortunately, my temper's never been better than a rabid dog treeing a coon in hunting season.

"Listen," I said, "all my life I've let men run over me like lawnmowers over fall leaves, but them days ended three years ago, and you aren't about to start it back up now. When I tell you I don't know anything about Jimmy's death, I mean it. When I say I want a lawyer, well, son, I mean that, too. You may haul riff-raff and convicts through here like lambs to slaughter, and your scare tactics may work with them, but, buddy, not with me. You're running a twenty-four-hour sucker lot and I ain't buying, because while I was born in the dark, I wasn't born yesterday. I know my rights and I know what I want. I want a lawyer."

Weathers didn't say another word. In fact, he was out of his seat so fast, I flinched, thinking he was about to come for me. He was gone, the door slamming behind him and leaving the rubber chicken dancing at the end of its rope.

I must've sat in that hardbacked metal chair for an hour, alone, with only the cooling coffee and a rubber chicken to keep me company. I didn't say a word. I tried to not even look anxious. If real life were like TV, then there was a hidden camera somewhere. Finally, Weathers came back, slammed a phone down on the metal table, plugged it in, and shoved it in my direction.

"Make your call, Ms. Reid," he said.

I pulled the phone a little closer, my heart pounding. Who was I going to call? Not my divorce attorney. She didn't handle criminal cases. Not Vernell. Not Sheila. Not Bonnie at the Curley-Que. She had enough on her with six kids and running the shop. The simple fact was, I had no one to call.

I sat there with my hand on the phone, not wanting Weathers to know I was in a bind. As Mama always said, pickings are slim when your mouth plants the seeds of pride. I slid the phone back in his direction. The time had come to take action.

"You know," I said, "I'm not gonna make that call just now. Instead, I'm gonna do you a favor." I pulled my purse onto my lap. I wasn't a lawyer, but I'd watched enough TV to play one.

Weathers snorted. "You're going to do me a favor, huh?" His eyes were lasering through me, sparkling. Beneath the angry exterior, he seemed secretly amused.

"Yes, I am. See, you don't have enough to charge me with murder. If you did, you'd have a D.A. in here." No discernible reaction from him, so I went on. "Jimmy was a good man. I don't know what's going on, or who wants to make me out to be a killer, but I do know one thing: If you don't find his killer, I will. So, I'm going home right now, and you can't stop me. I'm closing in on twenty-four hours without sleep, and I don't function like that."

I stood up, slinging my purse strap over my shoulder. "I'll talk to you later, if you let me leave. But if you jam me up, I'll have my attorney here in a New York minute, and then I won't say another word to you."

I turned around, headed for the door, and left. I couldn't believe he hadn't tried to stop me. I glanced up at the wall clock in the investigators' room, it was almost five A.M. It hit me as I reached the door of the main office that I'd gone and sowed the seeds of pride once more. How was I going to get home? Before I could stop myself, I'd whirled around and glanced down the corridor at the door to the interview room. There he stood, leaning against the doorjamb, a half-smile edging his face.

"Need a ride?" he drawled. His eyes slid over my body. He didn't try and hide his interest.

"Don't go to any trouble," I answered. I just couldn't help myself.

Weathers walked slowly toward me, the smile never leaving his smart-aleck lips.

5

MARSHALL Weathers left me in the parking lot of the Golden Stallion Club. I stood next to my battered white '71 VW and watched him drive away. As sure as I stood looking at his taillights fading off into the early Greensboro morning, I had not seen the last of him. And there wasn't going to be a damn thing I could do about it either.

I reached for the door handle and noticed for the first time that black fingerprint powder smudged the door handle, the steering wheel, and most of the interior of my car.

"Good, great, all I need," I said into the cold morning air. "Why don't you just put one of those fluorescent orange stickers on the car and say murder suspect?" The Golden Stallion parking lot was empty, except for the cars of those customers who had been unable or unwilling to drive home alone last night. Beer bottles littered the broken asphalt lot. The building, normally outlined in bright neon lights, looked seedy and exposed by breaking daylight.

I slid into the driver's seat, stuck the key in the ignition, and cranked up the car. It would take the entire ride home for the heat to begin kicking in, and even then, it would be minimal. I drove a VW because it was a personal symbol to me. Before I got married, I'd owned a white Beetle. It was my pride and joy, earned with every penny I'd saved since childhood. Vernell wrecked it one night when he was drunk, not long before we got married. Another omen I'd overlooked.

I puttered out onto High Point Road, driving down the commercial strip that gradually disintegrates the closer you come into town. It took me all of the five-minute trip to Mendenhall Street, until I drove up my block and saw the crime scene van still parked in front of my house, to realize that I couldn't go home.

A Channel Eight news van was parked just down the street from the crime scene van. They wouldn't be the only buzzards swooping down for a good look. And how long would it be before the phone started ringing and the neighbors started to gather? How long before the Spivey family saw fit to start their own fact-finding mission into Jimmy's death? I needed some place to hide, somewhere no one would look for me.

I put my head down and kept right on past my house. I must've driven in circles around UNCG's campus, winding across Spring Garden Street and down Tate Street, pausing in front of A Cup of Joe before realizing that even it wasn't open. One by one, I ruled out my friends. It didn't take too long, either. Since the divorce, I hadn't made the effort to get out and make new friends. Bonnie, my partner, was the closest to a best friend I had, but she was a single mom with six kids. And I sure couldn't afford to fritter money away on a hotel, not unless I went back to cutting hair full-time.

I don't know exactly how I arrived at the conclusion that I should go to Harmonica Jack's. Maybe I just happened to turn onto his street. It could've been because the band rehearsed in his huge, echoing, loft apartment. Or perhaps I knew, instinctively, that he was the least likely to make a pass at me, and even if he did, he would take no for an answer. Whatever the reason, he was my last shot.

Jack's loft was in a very transitional part of Greensboro, in the heart of the historic district, across the train tracks from the upscale renovated lofts. Jack really lived in a converted warehouse, retrofitted, by himself, for human habitation. It was a work in progress. He had no doorbell or front door, only a loading dock. Whenever we came to rehearse, we banged on the loading dock garage door, a battered metal contraption that worked on pulleys.

In the still-early morning, I pounded and the door sounded like a yard dog chasing an alley cat across garbage cans. It took quite a bit of pounding on that door to rouse Jack from what could only have been a few hours of sleep. I heard clattering from deep inside the building, swearing, and finally the groan of the pulley system, working to open the loading-bay door.

"What in the name of sweet Jesus," he groused, the door only halfway up. I bent down, peering up under the door.

"Jack, it's me, Maggie. I know this is a hell of a time to bother you, but I . . ." The tears that I hadn't known were coming, came. "Sorry," I said, rubbing my sleeve against my eyes and trying to get the control back. "I don't mean to get like this. I haven't had any sleep and . . ."

Jack popped the door up, anchored the chain on a cleat on the doorframe, and pulled me inside.

"Maggie," he said, his arm around my shoulders, "it's all right. Come on in." He released the chain with one hand, his other still resting on my shoulder. The door slid quietly back into place. He led me across plywood floors to a dilapidated sofa which rested in front of the warehouse's sole heating system, a pot-bellied stove. "Take a load off," he said, pushing me gently down into the sofa's soft cushions. "I'll make us some coffee."

He turned and walked to the makeshift kitchen which seemed to consist of a microwave and a hot plate. He looked no different fresh out of bed than he did most nights at the club. His wiry blond hair stood out in wild tufts around his head, and he was smiling, a soft, gentle smile I'd never seen him without. Jack was a hippie in a generation that no longer recognized them. He'd missed his era.

He wore wrinkled, wide-legged jeans and no

shirt; his feet were bare. His chest was smooth and for the first time I realized that he was too thin. He'd been away from his mama long enough to get scrawny and not long enough to learn how to tend to himself properly. He probably wasn't more than twenty-six or -seven, but his face looked younger.

He could make coffee, though. Just like I liked it, strong and black. Mama always said, "Weak coffee, weak character," and she was probably right. Jack didn't seem to lack character.

"Now," he said, settling into the arm chair next to me, "what happened with the cops?"

I told him, skipping the details. When I got to Jimmy, a tear or two started leaking down my cheeks and Jack handed me a wrinkled napkin for a tissue. He didn't say much, just listened, sipping his coffee, his eyes slowly widening.

"That stupid detective seems to think I killed him," I said. "I was there for hours and hours, saying the same thing over and over, but he wouldn't listen."

"So you've been there all this time?" he asked.

"Yeah. Well, there and driving around trying to figure where to go. I can't go home. I didn't know where else to go and . . ." I broke off, refusing to give in to my feelings. "I'm going to get the creep that killed Jimmy. You watch me!" The coffee sloshed dangerously in its cup when I saw myself, facing down Jimmy's killer, a gun in my hand.

"Maggie," Jack said, standing up in front of me, "here." He grabbed one of my hands, took the coffee mug from the other, and pulled me up from the couch. "Come on." He led me from the room, up a roughly framed set of steps and into the huge loft that overlooked the downstairs and functioned as his bedroom.

"You haven't slept in more than twenty-four hours. You gotta get some sleep." He led me over to his unmade waterbed, pushed me down onto the edge, and proceeded to take my boots off. "Here," he said, pushing me back against his pillow and covering me with the thick quilts that layered the warm, squishy bed. His voice was as soft as the little waterfall by the old home place. "You go to sleep. We can talk when you wake up."

Patting me on the shoulder as if I were his little sister, he sank down onto the frame of the bed.

"I gotta call Sheila," I muttered, half attempting to get up and grab the phone.

"No, you don't. Call her later," he said, and I wondered if he knew who Sheila was. He reached over to the bedside table and picked up one of the harmonicas lying there.

"Maggie," he said, his voice the softest whisper, "listen to this. I thought I'd play it behind that song you wrote." He began to play and I closed my eyes, working to listen. Now and then I struggled to open my eyes, but it was no use. My mind was following Jack's tune, deeper and deeper into the darkness.

6

In my dream I was floating on a yellow raft somewhere in the Caribbean. The warm waves gurgled beneath me and felt warm. I flipped over, onto my stomach, and looked at the water below me. It was so clear that I could see the sandy bottom, fifty feet away. Brightly colored fish swam by as I watched, floating in and out of a clump of black seaweed. As I watched, the seaweed swayed with the movement of the water, then left the sea floor to float toward me. The black weeds changed shape and became Jimmy's body, arms and legs swollen pink logs, the eyes eaten away.

I screamed, instantly awake, panting, struggling to sit up and unable to move. For a moment, I couldn't remember where I was. Then it all came flooding back. I was in Jack's house, on his waterbed, and Jimmy was dead in my house. I tried to hop out of the bed but I couldn't. Whenever I moved, the waterbed seemed to surround me, resisting my attempts to leave.

I finally settled for rolling to the edge, grabbing the wooden frame, and sliding off onto the floor. I could hear soft music coming from the floor below, and smell the faint trace of old coffee.

"Jack?" No answer.

I grabbed my boots and walked to the edge of the half-framed wooden stairway. There was no sign of Jack anywhere.

I had no idea what time it was, but from the way the sun hit through the trees, touching the window, I guessed midafternoon. I needed coffee and I needed a plan. I wandered in a stupor into the designated kitchen area of the big open room and started searching for coffee. A note from Jack and a garage door opener lay beside a dirty white carafe.

"Gone to see Evelyn. Here's your opener. Make yourself at home. There's coffee in the carafe. It'll be all right. Jack. P.S. Sparks wants us at the club early. 8 P.M."

I glanced at the clock on the stove. Three o'clock. I reached for a broken-handled mug and poured the still-hot coffee.

"All right, girl," I said into the empty warehouse air, "what was it Mama always said? If you keep your chin up, your mouth won't bring you down." Something like that.

I reached for the phone and tried Sheila's private line at Vernell's palace. No answer, just her cheery voice instructing me to leave a message.

"Sweetie," I said, "it's Mama. Honey, pick up if you're there." No answer. "Sheila, when you get this, call the shop. We need to talk." Before Vernell and Jolene poisoned my baby against me.

I jammed my feet into my cowgirl boots and took a few quick swigs of coffee. First things first. Stop by the Curley-Que and cash a check. Then on to the house to grab enough clothes to get me by for a few days. I had a purple denim and rhinestone outfit hanging in the back of my closet that I'd been saving to wear for New Year's Eve at the Golden Stallion. I figured that tonight called for something special, something that made me feel good about myself no matter what people said about me. In a town the size of Greensboro, Jimmy Spivey's death was gonna be big news. People would be flocking to the club, just hoping to get a good look at the woman the police were surely labeling as their prime suspect.

Somewhere out there lived Jimmy's killer. He knew and I knew that I hadn't killed Jimmy. The cops didn't care. They had their suspect. I crammed the garage door opener into my purse and headed out. The metal grated against the track, screaming in protest as I opened the garage door. It was clearly up to me to find Jimmy's killer.

Big doin's were happening when I walked into the Curley-Que. It was Saturday afternoon, our busiest time of the week. The 'Que hummed with activity. The air was filled with the familiar stink of ammonia covered over with perfume, and every-where you looked women sat patiently in pink smocks, waiting to be beautified.

The two new girls we'd hired when I went to full-time singing were doing customers. Bonnie was apparently heading off a crisis. She stood facing me, but unaware of my entrance. Her entire attention was focused on a short, white-haired woman.

"What do you mean, Maggie's not here?" the woman was saying. "Maggie always does me."

"I'm sorry, Neva," Bonnie said calmly, "not today. Your appointment is for next Saturday."

"Cain't be," Neva said, her voice a petulant whine. "My granddaughter's coming to take me to early church in the morning. I know I made my appointment so's I could have fresh hair when I went."

Bonnie touched her arm gently, as I'd seen her do many times with her children.

"Honey," she cooed, "I'll do you. It'll be fine."

I stood watching for a moment. Neva Jean Riddle would never stand for it.

"Nope," she said, stamping her tiny foot. "Maggie knows just how I like it. She knows about my cowlick and ever'thing." From where I stood, I could see Neva's jaw working a plug of chewing gum.

Bonnie's face was slowly flushing, and she pushed a strand of brown hair back over one ear. I could almost hear her thinking, *Maggie don't pay me enough for this.*

"Neva," I cried, stepping up and tapping her

on the shoulder. "Let's get a smock on you, sweetie. I'll be right along. Isn't your granddaughter coming to get you tomorrow?"

Neva whirled around, a relieved smile on her face. "There you are! This 'un said you wasn't coming." She gestured toward Bonnie, who stood gaping, looking at me as if I were a ghost.

"Well, sweetie, it isn't your regular day, but I'm here, so let's get to work."

Neva toddled off toward the changing room and Bonnie practically flew toward me.

"What in the world are you doin' here?" she demanded. "And where have you been? Did you not see the paper? I've called your place a million times!"

The busy shop had come as close to a standstill as possible, given the whirring dryers. Everyone was slowly looking up, drawn like soda crackers to soup by their curiosity.

"Keep your voice down," I said.

"Whatever for?" she asked. "It ain't as if there's a soul left on this earth that don't know what's what. It's on TV, it's on the radio, and it's all over the paper. The phone's been ringing off the hook with folks looking for you."

"Like who?" I asked, catching sight of Neva out of the corner of my eye, emerging from the dressing room swathed in a faded pink smock. I motioned to Lotus the shampoo girl to go ahead and do Neva, then turned back to Bonnie.

"I don't know. They aren't leaving names whoever they are."

"Bon, the police think I killed Jimmy. My gun

is missing. Someone put Jimmy's credit card in my car. Someone's trying to make me out to look like a killer. I'm not a killer!"

Bonnie's face softened. "I know, honey."

"I'm going to make the police believe me."

Bonnie nodded.

"But I can't go home right now. I'm staying with one of the guys in the band until things calm down and Jimmy's killer gets arrested."

Lotus was slowly leading Neva back to the shampoo station. Bonnie's customer was shooting her impatient looks from the chair where Bonnie had temporarily abandoned her. Time was running short.

"Listen, Bon, I need a cash advance, about two hundred dollars."

"Well, Maggie, shoot, you don't have to ask. It's your business."

"I know, but can we spare it?"

Bonnie grinned and looked around the packed Curley-Que. "You ever seen us do this much business on a Saturday?" I had to admit the place did seem more crowded than usual, even for a Saturday.

"I reckon we'll make two hundred extra today alone," she said. "Just keep in touch, all right?"

I nodded. No sense worrying Bonnie. Jimmy's killer had gone to a lot of trouble to set me up. I figured it had to be someone I knew pretty well, someone who knew how to get into my house and get to my gun. I wasn't going to waste a lot of time telegraphing my next moves.

I wandered over to Neva and started my routine. She was a pretty simple job, curl and comb-out, then once every three months, a trim. I got into the rhythm quickly, winding little pink curlers around her thinning white hair.

Neva seemed to be the sole resident of Greensboro who had not heard about Jimmy, so she prattled on about her children and her grand-daughter Felicia. It was the sort of one-sided conversation that required only a nod or a murmured "uh-huh," so it took me by surprise to hear another voice impatiently calling me.

"Mama, Mama! I'm talking to you!"

I dropped the curler I was holding and turned to see Sheila standing right behind me, her brown eyes pools of concern.

"Sheila! Baby, are you all right? I would've called you, but I didn't want to talk to your daddy."

Sheila's eyes were rimmed with dark circles and bloodshot. The poor kid must've been worried sick. I pulled her to me and hugged her tight. Her head folded onto my shoulder and her arms wrapped around me. In her chunky high heels, Sheila dwarfed me, favoring her daddy's side of the family for height. At least she had my red hair.

"Mama," she whispered into the side of my neck, "everybody says you killed Uncle Jimmy."

I pushed her back off my shoulder and looked her square in the eye. "Well, every one of them is wrong. I didn't." I narrowed my gaze, focusing on her tell-all brown eyes. "Did your daddy tell you that?" I asked.

"No, ma'am," she said softly, her eyes darting

away from mine. Someone close to her had.

"Jolene!" I said.

The eyes sunk down to the floor. That scheming bitch. Poisoning my own daughter against me!

"Look at me, young'un" I said, tipping her chin up with one hand. "Have I ever once lied to you?"

"No, ma'am," she replied softly.

"Then why would I start now?" Neva had fallen asleep in the chair. From across the room I saw Bonnie watching us, a worried expression on her face.

"You wouldn't, Mama."

"That's right, I wouldn't." I forced myself to smile and look her straight in the eye. "I don't know how Jimmy came to be at the house, or what happened after he got there. I'm just sick about the whole thing, especially Uncle Jimmy's death."

Sheila's eyes welled up with tears. "Me too, Mama," she said, her face turning paler as she spoke. The child was making herself ill.

"Now, Sheila, I don't want you to go worrying about me. The police will get things all sorted out. They'll find Uncle Jimmy's killer."

Sheila didn't say anything, which worried me more than anything she could've said. When I caught up with Jolene the Dish Girl, there was going to be hell to pay.

"Sweetie, you look terrible. Does your daddy know where you are?"

"No, I'm supposed to be at home, but I couldn't stand it, Mama. I had to know what was going on."

"Well, baby, scoot on back to that brick palace, hold your head up, and remember what your Grandma always said in times of trouble: a clear conscience and a pure heart will lead the brave to truth and the guilty to justice." Neva snorted softly in her sleep.

Mama'd never said any such thing. It was more like Mama to say, if you spend all your time chasing honey, you'll likely end up with your head in a sticky mess and your butt in a sling. It was one thing for Vernell to marry a prize bimbo, but it was another for her to slander my good name to my own daughter.

I scribbled Jack's phone number down on a piece of scrap paper and stuck it in Sheila's hand. "Here's where I'll be if you need me, baby," I said. "Let's just keep that information between me and you, all right?"

Sheila nodded and I hugged her close again. "This ain't nothing I can't handle, baby. You go tend to your daddy. He'll need you close for awhile."

"All right, Mama," she said, her voice the little girl voice I remembered from years ago. I was gonna pay Jolene back for making my daughter doubt me—that day would come—but first, I had business to attend to.

I put the finishing touches on Neva's do, sent her to change, and then walked up to the counter to draw two hundred dollars from the till. The salon was in a frenzy of Saturday activity when one of the girls shoved the cordless phone into my hand.

"For you," she said, breezing past. I started to

hang it up without answering. After all, it was probably a reporter, but on the other hand, you just never knew.

"Maggie Reid," I said.

The voice that answered me was muffled and indistinct, neither male nor female, young nor old. "Say your prayers," the voice rasped, "I'm coming."

The line went dead. After a few moments, someone took the receiver from my hand. Bonnie.

"Maggie, what in the hell is wrong? Who was that? A reporter? You shouldn't have answered the phone!"

The salon noise covered the sound of my heart, muffled Bonnie's voice, and saved me from answering. After all, what could she do, call the police? And what would they do? Believe me? When they'd believed nothing else I'd said?

I grabbed four fifties out of the drawer, mumbled something, and ran out the door. The caller'd said they were coming. Well, they'd have to find me first.

7

The house was dark when I pulled up in the backyard. I would be cutting it close to get my things, change, and still arrive at the Golden Stallion on time. I ran up the stairs to the back door and into my bedroom, ducking under a piece of yellow tape that identified my house as a crime scene. If I'd gone in the front door, it would've taken no time at all for nosy neighbors to come rushing over, wanting to know every detail of Jimmy's demise. And if Jimmy's killer was out there looking for me, then coming in through the front door would've been an advertisement for target practice. At least this way I could sneak in and get out.

I pushed the door shut behind me. I stood still in the darkness, getting my bearings before I moved toward the bedside table and reached for the lamp. My bedroom looked just as I'd left it, with a few exceptions. There was black fingerprint powder over almost all of the surfaces, the door, the phone, the dresser. Little things were out of place, a figurine moved, a chair slightly off-kilter with the rest of the room, pictures hanging at a half-tipsy angle.

I made myself go through the house, turning on as few lights as possible, looking for the spot where Jimmy died. I found it in the living room. Jimmy died on my grandma's rag rug. An ugly, brick red stain covered the center of the cheerfully colored rug, destroying it forever with blood and memory. I would throw it out when I came back to stay.

I stood still for a moment, staring down at the rug, saying a silent prayer for poor Jimmy. I started to kneel down, my fingers reaching out to touch the spot. As I bent forward, the front door exploded open with a resounding crack, like gunfire.

I jumped backward. Jimmy's widow, Roxanne, stood framed in the doorway. Even at only five feet, her two hundred-pound body blocked out all but a thin halo from the outside streetlight. She looked like a darkened angel, but the sounds emanating from her mouth were anything but angelic.

"You!" she gasped. "Why aren't you in jail?" She staggered forward into the living room, her terry-cloth slippered feet squarely planted in the middle of the dark blood stain. She wore a wrinkled pink floral housedress and a green plaid coat that might have been her bathrobe.

I wasn't sure what to do. Roxanne's brown eyes glowed with a feverish intensity, her fat fish lips were drawn together like purse strings, and her mousy brown hair stood out from her head like a fright wig. She looked more dangerous than usual.

"You are responsible for my Jimmy's death," she pronounced in a raspy voice that seemed to originate from deep within her chest. "He wouldn't have had to die like a sorry yard dog if he'd been able to stay away from you! I warned him time and again, but no, he had to keep sniffing around you!"

I didn't move, but I didn't look away either. If she sprang at me, I'd run back through the house and out my bedroom into the backyard.

Roxanne looked down just then and gasped, jumping quicker than I would've thought her mighty frame could move. "Agggh!" she squawked. She had realized where she was standing.

"Roxanne," I said, trying to keep the panic out of my voice, "why don't you . . ."

"Shut up," Roxanne snarled. She took a step closer to me and I tensed up, preparing to make a run for it. "Now you know how it feels," she said, a slight smile crossing her crazed face.

"What are you saying, Roxanne?"

"Years," she said slowly. "For years I watched you two. Neither one of you knowing I was there." Her voice drifted off and her eyes glazed over. I took a tiny step sideways, toward the dining room archway.

"Now you won't have him, ever!" she said, her eyes focusing on my face. "But I'll have him!"

"Roxanne, I don't know what you're talking about," I said slowly.

"Shut up!" she screamed, startling me into jumping. Roxanne may have looked like two hundred pounds of couch potato, but I knew from Jimmy that she was as strong as a bull. Roxanne harbored a secret desire to be a pro wrestler on the newly created women's circuit.

"You think I didn't know about you and him?" she said. I started to speak, but she rushed on, ignoring me. "You were planning to run off with him, weren't you? You done lost one rich Spivey brother, now you was aiming for the other. Well, it didn't happen, did it?"

I gave up. Roxanne was out of her mind with grief and nothing I did or said would change how she felt about me. I took a small step toward the dining room, but she grabbed me, whipping my arm behind me and pushing me off balance against the edge of the mantelpiece.

"I ain't done with you," she said. She was bending my arm painfully up behind my back. Her breath reeked of stale liquor.

I brought my foot up sharply, biting into Roxanne's fleshy shin. She shrieked and dropped my arm. I slipped away from her, leaving her moaning and massaging pink skin that was rapidly turning purple.

"Jimmy's dead," I said, and Roxanne's attention returned to me. "And yes, I loved him, but not in the twisted, sick way you think. He was like a brother to me!" I was breathing hard, my heart pounding against my chest.

"He didn't love me!" Roxanne yelled. "He never had the chance, not with you and his mother always there to tell him how wrong I was!" Roxanne had it all twisted to suit herself. "The two of you must've had a high old time, thinking dumb Roxanne didn't know, thinking you could just run off and leave me in the lurch!"

A dangerous glint came into Roxanne's eyes and I knew she was seconds from attacking me again.

"Mrs. Reid?" a voice said, and Roxanne whipped around, instantly on alert to the intruder standing in the open front doorway.

"Keith," I said, pushing past Roxanne and walking over to the door. Sheila's wanna-be boyfriend, the one I'd prayed thousands of times would somehow be banished from this earth, was staring from Roxanne to me, disbelief written all over his twenty-year-old, acne-pocked face. Maybe he was shocked by the scene he'd come upon, but more likely he was shocked by my warm reception.

"Is this a bad time?" he squeaked, looking for all the world like a tall, scrawny rat.

"No, son," I said loudly, "Sheila's aunt was just leaving." I glared at Roxanne, trying to look like I wasn't afraid when in reality, I knew Keith and I rolled into one couldn't have taken her.

Roxanne was making up her mind. She eyed Keith up and down, taking in the saggy, ripped blue jeans, the metal dog collar around his neck, and the tattoo of a dragon that sprawled up and down his forearm.

"I've done all I needed to do here," she said,

lowering her head and charging toward Keith and the open front door like an angry bull.

Keith scampered out of the way, letting her pass and fade off into the night.

"She looked upset, huh?" he said, dodging me as I rushed up to slam the door. I had hoped he would've stayed on the outside, but he jumped into my tiny living room like a dog avoiding a lick with a broom.

"No flies on you, son," I said. "It was her husband that was killed here."

"Oh." He nodded, his eyes following the floor to the blood stain. He had to have known about Jimmy. He only lived three doors down. But maybe he was stupider than I gave him credit for.

"I heard that woman yelling at you," he said finally. "I was just walking by, you know, and I, er, thought you might be in trouble or something. So I just came on up." He looked at me expectantly, like maybe I was going to tip him, or worse yet, decide to like him.

"Thank you," I said, trying to keep the edge out of my voice. "I'm fine." Did he really think that coming to my rescue with Roxanne would make me suddenly decide that a twenty-year-old unemployed skater/musician/dope dealer was a suitable boyfriend for my seventeen-year-old daughter?

Keith was walking around the living room, his eyes rooted to the floor, as if maybe he'd lost something. Always his attention returned to the blood stain. I didn't have time for this. I was going to be even later for work if I didn't get my clothes and get out of here.

"Keith," I said, "if you don't mind, I'm kind of in a hurry. I've gotta go to work." I moved toward the door, but for some reason, Keith moved toward the dining room.

"Keith? The door's this way." Mama would've hated my manners, but then, I think if the situation had been reversed, she might've taken the same course.

"Oh," he said absently, still wandering into the dining room. "You know, Mrs. Reid, I believe you've changed the furniture around in here."

"No, Keith, I . . ." But Keith was suddenly overtaken by a fit of coughing.

"Water," he gasped, collapsing into one of my dining room chairs.

"Oh, for pity's sake," I muttered. "Come on."

I swept by him and on into the kitchen. He followed me, coughing up a storm, his face reddening. I ran the tap, filled a glass with water, and shoved it into his outstretched hand. His fingernails were too long and they were dirty. What had Sheila seen in him?

I ducked into the walk-in closet that was just off the tiny galley kitchen. Maybe if I emerged with my outfit and started turning off the lights, he would take the hint and leave. He followed me, sipping on his water, his eyes darting around the room like a nervous cat.

"So, Mrs. Reid," he said quickly, "Sheila says you're the lead singer down at the Golden Stallion."

"That's right," I said, my face buried in the clothes rack.

"Well, that gives us something in common."

"How's that, Keith?" I said. I'd grabbed the purple denim outfit and was heading out into the kitchen when I stopped, staring at Keith. He had moved past the kitchen and the closet and was in Sheila's bedroom, down on his hands and knees, peering under her bed.

"Did you lose something?" I asked. He jumped, startled by my sudden presence, banging his head against the iron bedpost.

He jumped to his feet, his face beet-red. "I, uh, um, well, to be honest, Mrs. Reid . . ." I went on triple-guard when I heard that phrase. Mama used to say, sure as shooting, when a fella said "to be honest", whatever followed was sure to be a lie.

"To be honest?" I prompted, as Keith seemed at a loss for words.

"Oh, yes, ma'am. To be honest, I was just trying to check around. You know, just to make sure you're all right and there's no intruders or nothing like that."

"Keith, don't try and bullshit me. You and I have never gotten along. So why are you here?"

"Well, I . . ." Keith's head dropped down to his chest. "Well, to be honest, Sheila asked me to."

I might have known. Sheila was worried about me. A wave of emotion swept over me and for a brief moment I found myself warming to the scruffy kid. He was looking out for Sheila by looking after her mom. Just as quickly, I remembered that this was the same boy who was on probation for drug dealing.

"Keith," I said, moving through my room and opening up the back door, "I am fine. There are no bad guys in my house. Whoever shot Jimmy is long gone, and you need to leave because I'm late for work."

Keith finally took the hint, reluctantly. He wandered through my bedroom and out onto my back stoop. I practically slammed the door behind him. I turned and ran back through the kitchen and into the bathroom. I just had time to apply another coat of makeup and hit the trail, if I wanted to make the first set on time.

In the bathroom, I found the real reason for Keith's frenetic search, at least that's what I found myself assuming. The little garnet and diamond chip ring that Sheila wore on her left hand was lying by the side of the sink. It had been a present from me to her on her fifteenth birthday and it hadn't been lying on my sink two days ago. As far as I knew, Sheila hadn't been to my house in over three weeks.

I picked up the little ring and slipped it into my pocket. An icy finger of fear and worry prodded at the base of my throat. When had Sheila been inside my house? And had she sent Keith over to look for her ring?

The doorbell rang as I stepped out of the tiny bathroom, startling me. Now what? As I made my way toward the living room, it became apparent that the nightmare was continuing. Red and blue lights moved like strobes across the wall, reflections of the two police cars that lined the narrow street in front of my house.

"Oh, great!" I sighed. "Now what?"

I pulled open the door and found myself face-to-face with Heckle and Jeckle, the two officers who had been sent to escort me downtown the night before.

"Ms. Reid?" the younger one said. It was more of a statement than a question.

"Officer."

"Detective Weathers wanted to speak with you," he said.

"Well, why didn't he pick up the phone?" I asked.

The older officer decided to take over. "I think he tried, ma'am. He just wanted us to stop by, make sure you were in. He's on his way over."

I peered around him at the two patrol cars, their lights flashing.

"Where's the SWAT team?" I asked.

He never answered my question. In fact, he didn't speak until Weathers's brown Taurus pulled up behind the patrol car. The officers left the porch and walked to meet him, probably relieved to be away from me.

There was no smart-aleck grin this time. Weathers looked angry. I watched the officers confer with him, speaking in low tones, gesturing back toward the porch where I waited. The neighbors had begun to gather, standing out on their porches craning their necks, or flat-out wandering to the edge of their walkways.

Detective Weathers left the two officers and started walking toward me. I felt a shiver run through me, like somebody walking across my grave.

"Where have you been and why didn't you call me back?" he demanded. He was wearing faded jeans.

They could've been the same tight jeans he'd worn the first night I'd seen him. The denim shirt he wore made his eyes sparkle, even in the near total darkness.

"I am right where I'm supposed to be," I answered. "And I can't call somebody back if I don't know they called."

"You don't check your messages?"

"Well, you know, with all that's gone on, I just plumb forgot." No apology from me.

"From now on," he said, "I don't want you to sneeze without letting me know."

He was wearing a new pair of cowboy boots, lizard skin, Tony Lamas if I didn't miss my guess. His belt buckle was large and silver. He caught me staring at it and arched an eyebrow. My stomach did its little flip, and I found myself responding to the man behind the badge.

"Listen," I said, "I am not your property. I have a life and I intend to lead it. Now, you and I both know that I've got a job and I work regular hours. If you want to haunt me, come right on down to the club. Looks like you were headed there anyway. As for my personal life, and where I go and with whom, well, buddy, I ain't never punched a clock for nobody and I won't start with you."

We were off to a good start. He took two long strides and was up the steps and by my side in a heartbeat, his jaw twitching and his eyes glowing with anger.

"Now see here, Ms. Reid," he said, "I cut you some slack when I let you go last night and—"

I interrupted. "You did no such thing." *Let me*

go! If he'd held me, I would've known it. I would've felt it. I would've . . . Stop it, I argued with myself, *he's just a cop.*

"I could've held you, don't let's be mistaken about that. If you want to play games, I'll make your life a living hell, lady. This is a murder we're dealing with, not some little dating game charade. I want to know where you are and with whom, at all times."

I turned and started to walk back inside. I'd had all I could take of this bozo. I was going to work.

He followed me. I could smell him. I could almost feel him breathing down my neck. "I want to talk to you," he said, "downtown."

I whirled around to face him. "Look, Detective, I told you I'd go over this all again and I will . . . tomorrow. Right now, I'm going to work."

I didn't give him a chance to say anything. I marched off into the kitchen, into the walk-in closet, grabbed my purple denim outfit off its hanger, and started back to my bedroom. I needed space. I needed to keep my head before my body got involved and I lost my cool and started acting like a damn woman. But he was right behind me.

"If you don't mind?" I said, waiting for him to move. He didn't budge. I took another step closer, until I was inches from his flint-hard face. "I'm going in that room," I said, gesturing toward my bedroom, "and I'm going to change. I think it would be carrying things a little far for you to accompany me." *How long has it been? When was the last time a man . . . Stop it!*

"I'm thinking we're going to have that talk tonight," he said, clearly angry. For a second I wondered if he really could hold me. I decided it wasn't worth testing him.

"All right," I said, "let's make a deal. I'll get changed and we'll talk for a little while." He said nothing, which I took for an okay, so I closed the bedroom door and started changing.

I intended to honor my end of the bargain, I really did. But that was before I looked at the clock and saw what time it was. Sparks had called an early practice and now it was five minutes 'til eight. If I had to stick around and talk to the detective, I'd miss practice, and maybe even be late for the first set. I couldn't do that. My band, the Drivin' Wheel, was my job, my dream.

I pulled off my jeans and slipped on my skirt. There was only one thing I could do. I picked up my purple suede boots, tiptoed to the backdoor, and quietly twisted the handle. I let myself out into the chilly fall night and eased down the stairs, sneaking out of my own house, just like a rebellious teenager.

For the first time in twenty-four hours, I felt good. I allowed a small giggle of triumph as I gripped the door handle of my car and started to open the door.

"Not this time," Weathers said, a strong hand clamping down on my shoulder. He seemed to have materialized out of nowhere.

I gasped, jumped about six inches, and felt his strong hands twisting me around to face him. I was pinned against the VW, Weathers's strong arms on either side of me, his face inches from my own.

"Maggie, why do you keep lying to me?" he asked, his voice menacingly soft.

"I just have to get to work and it's late," I answered.

"Nice try, but I don't think that's it." He wasn't moving. He had me trapped, and the only way to move would've been to try and wriggle out under his arms. Something he knew I'd considered, because he brought his elbows down and moved in still closer.

To anyone passing by, we would've appeared to be lovers, embracing. He was so close that I could feel his breath on my cheek and smell his cologne. It felt intoxicating, the smells, the sensations, my fear, all snowballing into a reaction I felt powerless to control.

"Trust me, Maggie," he breathed. "Talk to me." His voice was hypnotic. "Trust me."

I snapped out of it, jerking my head forward. "There's nothing to tell," I said. "I have to go to work. You can follow me, or ride with me, but I have to go!"

"What did Jimmy do to hurt you, Maggie?" he asked softly.

"Nothing, I'm telling you!"

Weathers was staring at me, his eyes burning into mine. He wasn't ready to let me go, not just yet.

"Maggie, I know he did something to you. People like you, they don't just take a life unprovoked. Let me help you, Maggie."

"Damn it! No!" I cried, stamping my stockinged

foot on the cold ground. "I didn't shoot Jimmy!"

"Shhh," he whispered, his voice a warm caress. "Where's the gun, Maggie?"

"Listen to me," I said, "if I was gonna kill someone, I sure wouldn't do as sloppy a job as this. Believe me, if I were to kill you, there wouldn't be a trace left behind. And right now, I'm giving homicide some serious consideration. If you don't clear away from me and let me go, I'm liable to take matters into my own hands. Trust me, you won't like that, Detective."

He pushed back slowly, dropping his arms to his sides. "I'm not through with you, Maggie. I know you've got something you're not saying. You don't lie well." Well, he was right on that count. I wasn't one to go long without talking, but he was dead wrong about everything else.

"You can trust me, Maggie," he said softly. "I want to help you."

For one split instant I let his voice get to me, reaching deep inside, starting up a bank of feelings I hadn't let out in years, but just as quickly I boxed it back up. I could trust him, sure I could. Like Mama always said, if you put your faith in a bucket but let someone else do all the toting, you'll come up empty-handed every time.

The only person who could help me was me. I would have to find Jimmy's killer on my own. The police didn't believe a word I said. My daughter was living in the midst of a nest of vipers. And I was the number one suspect in a murder investigation. The way I saw it, it certainly fell to me to put things to rights.

Now I knew two other things that I hadn't known an hour ago. One was that Detective Marshall Weathers was dangerous. If I didn't watch him, he'd lull me into admitting all kinds of things, only half of them true. The second thing I'd learned frightened me even more: Sheila was involved somehow in this whole situation. No matter what else happened, I had to help her, even if it meant that the police thought I was guilty of a crime I didn't commit.

8

Every night before I go on stage, just before the band strikes up the tune that the regulars all know as mine, I get sick. I rush for the ladies room, shove my way into a stall, and break into a cold sweat, my stomach churning like Mama's old Sunbeam electric mixer. I am just sure that I am going to throw up, but I never do.

This little ritual has not changed in all the months I've been singing at the Golden Stallion, and so I do not look for anything to be different in the near future. I figure they wrote the line "You gotta suffer if you want to sing the blues" just for my benefit.

When the band starts the set, they always do so without me. They play one song, then break into Maggie's tune. Out I come from the restroom, my lipstick fresh, my hat on straight, and a smile on my face. The second I set foot on that stage, my stomach problems vanish, my life outside of the club fades away, and I am there, live, and ready to steal your heart.

It was no different the night after Jimmy died. I ran up the five steps to the stage, grabbed the mike from Larry the stage hand, and strutted out to the middle of the stage. I threw my head back, let my free hand swing out to my side, and started to croon my signature song: "He Was Just a Lonely Cowboy till I Lassoed Him with Love."

Right in the middle of the third verse, I whip out a little lasso and make a big show of roping in one of the young studs who wanders a little too close to the stage. It's kind of expected now, so a whole crowd of them come down front, shouting out my name and trying to get me to reel them in.

Tonight was no different from all the others, except that the man I lassoed bore a strong resemblance to my ex-husband. Of course, it couldn't have been him. Vernell Spivey wouldn't have been caught dead in a club like the Golden Stallion. He had a reputation to uphold.

Nowadays, Vernell frequented the Guilford Country Club. I don't know how he got a membership, because they don't normally let uneducated country bumpkins in. I guess he must've had some dirt on somebody, or else paid a wad of nouveau riche bucks to smooth his entrance. Whatever, once he learned about me and the Drivin' Wheel, old Vernell had increased motivation to stay away from the Golden Stallion.

So, it couldn't have been him. Besides, the

Vernell Spivey I knew didn't drink hard liquor. At least, I thought he'd given up the hard stuff three years ago. But Vernell came by his lyin' easy, and many's the time he'd pulled the wool over my eyes. This man in front of me was blind drunk. He was wearing a powder blue polyester cowboy suit, with fancy white cording on the lapels and down the sides of his pants, another thing that Vernell would never do. Vernell was vain as a peacock. Once he learned about rich folks and Ralph Lauren, Vernell made the switch and, to my knowledge, never looked back at man-made fiber. Of course, in his heart of hearts, I knew Vernell and his roots were country, West Virginia country.

But, doggone, that sure looked like Vernell, with his dull brown hair, his pencil-thin mustache, and his little pot belly.

"Eee-haw!" he yelled, as I threw the noose around his shoulders. "She got me!!"

The band was playing, I was singing, and at the same time roping this strange man toward me. My mouth was singing about the lasso of love, but my mind was saying something completely different. Something I really did not want to hear. My brain was saying, "This here's your ex-husband, and honey, he's lookin' volatile."

Sure enough, there was an ugly, snakelike look in Vernell's beady eyes, a look I'd seen all too often in our marriage. I looked over at the band, hoping for help. Sugar Bear was the biggest, but he was picking out a solo and totally unaware that he was even in the Golden Stallion. Sparks was sitting at the pedal steel, lost underneath his white ten-gallon hat, and too short to be a match for Vernell anyway. Jack was watching me, but he was also tracking yet another cutie who was waving to him from the edge of the dance floor. The situation was too complicated to communicate to a man whose mind was divided by female attention.

"Maggie," Vernell said, his voice slurred with liquor. "The most horrible thing has happened." Sugar Bear was picking out his instrumental, so I could speak, but only for a moment. I roped Vernell closer, which took some doing as his body didn't or couldn't cooperate.

"Vernell Spivey," I said, in my no-nonsense, mother tone, "now you listen to me. This is not the time nor the place to get into this."

Vernell looked up at me, his brown eyes narrowing and his bushy eyebrows furrowing so close together they looked like one continuous shaggy line of displeasure.

"The hell it ain't," Vernell blustered loudly. "He died in your house. I'd say you got some 'splainin' to do." Vernell was clearly out of his mind. I wasn't sure, at that moment, that he even realized we were divorced.

The young studs on the fringe of the floor were catching on that our dialogue was not exactly friendly. A few of them moved closer, their testosterone spoiling for a good fight. I looked up for Cletus the bouncer, but he was working the door and momentarily unavailable. I gave up all pretense of singing, and Sugar Bear took over with an instrumental.

"You and Jimmy," Vernell stuttered. "You and

him was . . . was . . ." Vernell's face was taking on a green hue and I remembered right quick why Vernell had knocked off drinking. It didn't agree with his liver.

"Me and Jimmy was family, Vernell, and that's all there was to it."

"You and Jimmy was dogging me in my own house!" he thundered. That brought the dance floor to a standstill and set Cletus into action.

"Well, if that ain't the pot calling the kettle black," I stormed, unfortunately into my live mike.

"But kin, Maggie, you was doggin' me with my own kin."

As if that somehow made the sin worse. I gave Vernell a pitying, down-my-nose look.

"Vernell, I would no more be unfaithful to you with a member of your family than fly to the moon. But all that's really neither here nor there, 'cause we're divorced! You left me and married a bimbo!"

This clearly threw Vernell for a loop.

"Naw!" he cried, falling back a step into Cletus's outstretched arms. "Naw!" A confused look crossed his face, then pain, and finally tears. "Cain't be."

What was wrong with him? Had Jimmy's death sent him into such a tailspin that he no longer remembered anything? Was this a form of post-traumatic stress or amnesia?

The band had picked up that their lead singer was out of action and was doing its best to rock the audience away from me and back out onto the dance floor. I crouched down at the edge of the stage and motioned for Cletus to move Vernell up closer.

"Vernell, I know Jimmy's death was a terrible shock—" I said, but he interrupted me.

"Jimmy and me, we always take care of our own, Maggie. I take care of my family."

"I know you do, Vernell." Yep, he took care of me all right. Ran out on me and his baby girl, but those support checks rolled in, right on time, every month. Of course, they quit coming the day Sheila moved in with Vernell and his lovely Dish Girl. There was caring and then there was care. Vernell maintained his family, but he didn't care squat about us when he left.

"Come on," Cletus grunted, and started to lead Vernell away.

"Keep your hands off me!" Vernell shouted.

When Vernell was younger, he was bad to drink. Young and wiry, he'd been mean as a snake when he got liquored up. Soon as he sobered up, he'd forget everything that'd happened. Most of the time, he'd deny he'd ever been drinking, just block out what he didn't want to remember. Looked to me like Vernell hadn't changed much, even though I thought he'd quit the hard stuff over ten years ago.

Cletus let his eyes go flat and hard. His grip tightened on Vernell's arms and I could tell by the pinched look on Vernell's face that it hurt. Vernell had to face facts, he wasn't a young buck anymore and Cletus would take him if he had to.

"Maggie," Vernell said, his attention once more on me. "I done drove my ducks to bad market but there's no undoing it now. I got to lie down with the dogs and take my lumps."

"Vernell, what on earth are you saying?" I didn't like the way he was talking, or his tone. Something about it frightened me.

"Be careful, Maggie. There's all kind of danger in this world. There ain't always gonna be somebody looking after you. You're a woman alone. Yep," Vernell said, the green tinge to his skin suddenly turning ash white. "You never know when life'll sneak up on you and eat your lunch, sack and all." Then he clasped a hand to his mouth. "Aw, gawd," he moaned. "I'm gonna be sick!"

That got Cletus moving. With one beefy hand on Vernell's collar and the other on Vernell's waistband, Cletus propelled Vernell away from me and over to the men's room.

I straightened up, looked out at the crowd who by now had returned to dancing, and shrugged my shoulders at the young studs. Poor Vernell, I thought, but I couldn't quite get my heart into the sentiment. There was something different about him, and it wasn't just the clothes and the liquor. Something had changed and Vernell the Entrepreneur had vanished, leaving behind a shadow of the man I'd once known.

9

Jack noticed the long scrape down the side of my car first, then the flat tire. We had walked out of the Golden Stallion together, the energy necessary for performing quickly draining away and leaving in its place a bone-weary fatigue.

"Shit!" he swore. "What is that?"

My right rear tire lay flat on the ground, a gash torn vertically across the rubber, just below the rim. I stood there, trying to get my brain to accept the image. Then I saw the scrape down the passenger side. Narrow and jagged, it cut through the paint, leaving an ugly metal scar.

I looked around at the cars nearby. They were untouched. Why me? Why my car? What was going on here? "I'm coming," the voice had said. Was this it? The beginning?

I didn't say anything. Maybe I was afraid to open my mouth, afraid of the sounds that would come out into the cold, fall dawn. Instead, I gently lowered my guitar case to the asphalt and walked to the hood of the Beetle. Jack was squatting down by the tire, his fingers rubbing against the fraying rubber, swearing under his breath. Slowly and methodically, I pulled the tire kit out of the trunk, then unbolted the spare and began carrying it.

"I'll get that," he said, moving quickly to take the dirty tire out of my hands.

"No, don't!" I tightened my grip and practically shoved him aside in my hurry. I didn't want any help. I needed to feel as if there was something I could do, one thing I could still control in my crazy universe. I could change a damn tire by myself!

I knelt down, pulled out the tire iron and placed it over the first lug nut. I gave it a mighty wrench. When it didn't move, I stood up and jumped on the iron arm, demanding that it give. Slowly the lug turned.

To his credit, Jack never moved, never said a word. He stood there in the frosty morning air and watched, now and then stamping his feet against the cold. *My car*, I thought over and over. *My car, my car, my car. My house, violated. My gun, stolen. My grandma's rug, ruined. Jimmy, dead. My daughter. What about my daughter?*

I rocked back and forth on my heels, not just loosening a lug nut, but rocking to soothe away the tears that bit the edges of my eyelids and cut a pathway down my cheeks. *My baby. My baby. My baby.*

Once, when Sheila was four, I went to pick her up from preschool. It was raining and I was a little early, so I parked and walked up to the door to get her instead of waiting in the carpool line with the other mothers. I opened my giant yellow-flowered umbrella and held it with one hand, taking her pudgy, warm little-girl hand in my other.

I knew, even before she reached my side, that something was wrong. Don't ask me how. She didn't say a word to let on. She even smiled when I stretched out my hand to her, but it was a small, tight smile. Her eyes were huge and her shoulders stiff. We walked about twenty feet down the sidewalk, just past the edge of the line of vans and station wagons waiting to claim their children.

"How was your day, honey?" I asked softly.

"Mom," she said, a small tremor leaking into her lispy-lilty voice, "Will doesn't want to marry me. He said we can't be engaged 'cause his cousin Barbara is going to marry him." With that, all pretense of composure left her, and she began to sob, deep wracking gulps that shook her tiny body.

I stopped still on the sidewalk, in the rain, and knelt down by her side. "Oh, honey," I said, pulling her to me. "I'm so sorry."

We knelt there in the rain, half-hidden by my sunny yellow umbrella, crying. Sheila sobbing because her heart was broken for the very first time, and me because I couldn't save her from the pain of finding out for the first time that life can be terribly cruel and unfair.

I was having that same kind of feeling all over again as I stood by the side of my damaged car.

Jimmy's killer had done this, I could feel it in my bones, but try making the police believe that. No, if they didn't believe I hadn't killed my brother-in-law, they sure wouldn't believe this wasn't just random vandalism. The slashed tire was off, the spare securely attached. But everything in my world was changing. I stuck my hand inside my skirt pocket and fingered Sheila's little ring. What was going on here?

"Here," Jack said, gently taking the tire iron from my grimy hand. He tugged gently, and I let it slide out of my grip. He carefully packed the tire kit, tied it together, and then placed it and the slashed tire into the trunk.

I walked around to the driver's seat, slipped behind the wheel, and stuck the key into the ignition. Jack picked up my guitar, slid it into the backseat, and arranged his lanky frame in the front passenger seat. I turned the key and the car abruptly lurched forward and stalled. I'd forgotten to push in the clutch.

"Damn it!" I swore, stabbing my foot at the pedal. I reached for the clutch and tried to jam it into first gear, but Jack stopped me.

"You're all right," he said softly, his hand resting firmly over mine. "Now just stop a second. Let go of the clutch and breathe." He leaned back against his seat, letting his shoulders drop, watching me. I took a deep breath impatiently and started to jerk my arm back toward the gear shift.

"That's it," he said, gripping my arm and closing his eyes. "Now like this." He took a deep, New Age breath, holding it, then exhaling. "Breathe."

I did it. I leaned my head back against the headrest, closed my eyes, and took a long slow breath. My shoulders relaxed and I felt a tiny bit of tension leave me.

"Again," he said softly, "that's it."

I couldn't believe it. Here I was, deep breathing in my car at three in the morning, after some maniac had slashed my tire. The worst part was, it was actually working.

"You're fine," he said. "You can do this."

Damn straight, I thought, *I can do this. And I can find the sorry dirtbag who did this, too.* I leaned forward slowly and started the car.

"Who's Evelyn?" I asked.

He laughed and looked out his window. "That Evelyn," he said, "she's quite a gal." He reached forward and switched on the radio, pulling out his harmonica to play along with the country station.

He played for a moment or two and then I felt him watching me as I drove. "You know," he said, "you're thinking it's all related, but it might not be. The universe is funny that way. Full of coincidences."

He went back to his harmonica, not waiting to hear what I thought about the matter. I glanced over at him a few times, but his eyes were closed and he seemed lost in the music. In his world, events probably were coincidental; they probably followed some Zen kind of philosophy or Quaker kind of lifestyle. That was him. In my world, everything meant something. Like Mama always said, don't matter if the glass is half full or half empty, it'll still stain your skirt if it spills.

I listened to him playing, my head jumbled up with ideas and thoughts. I was barely paying attention, but I did notice one thing. Someone was following us, and they had been ever since we'd left the Golden Stallion.

"Hey, you missed the turn," Jack said, as I drove right by Elm Street and turned right onto Church. Still there.

"It may be coincidence," I said, "but a car's been following us since we left."

"Get out!" He sounded more impressed than worried.

I drove over to Lee Street and headed back toward the Coliseum. Still there. We were definitely being followed. I whipped into a parking lot at Lee and Elm, then swiveled around to see what would happen next. The car drove right on past, a Jeep Cherokee, not new, but not more than a few years old. It moved too fast for me to see who was driving or even catch a plate number.

"Damn! That tells me a hell of a lot," I said.

Jack stared after the car and back over at me. "Are you sure we were being followed?" he asked. "Maybe it was just—"

"Coincidence?" I said, interrupting. "I don't think so."

I let my foot off the clutch and pulled back out onto Elm, made the quick turn into the parking lot behind Jack's loft, and slid the Beetle into a spot under the only light in the lot. If someone wanted to hurt my car further, I would at least make it difficult.

Jack hauled my guitar out of the backseat and

aimed his garage door opener at the back of his building. I scanned the parking lot, looking past it back to Elm Street. We were surrounded by buildings and alleys. A hundred people could be watching us, from almost anywhere, and we wouldn't see them.

Jack stood on his loading dock, waiting. I gave up trying to figure out who was lurking in the bushes and headed for the warmth of the woodstove.

"Want something to drink?" he asked. He was pulling a Rolling Rock from the fridge and twisting off the cap. The garage door was slowly descending, closing us in. Suddenly Jack's place seemed small and foreign.

"No," I said, starting to turn away, but then changing my mind. "Yes, maybe I will." I am not a drinker. Not like Vernell and the Spivey clan, but the situation called for something. I just wasn't sure what.

Jack busied himself pulling out a second beer, draping it with a graying dishtowel, and twisting off the cap. If he sensed my discomfort, he didn't show it. Instead he walked over to the sofa with both beers and sat down in front of the woodstove.

"What a night." He sighed and took a swig from his bottle. "You look worn out."

"No," I lied, reaching for the beer to hide behind. "I'm always keyed up after we play. Changing that tire didn't even wear me out." I took a huge swig of beer and choked. Mama said lies'll choke you, but it was the beer.

"Really?" he asked. He was sitting on the

couch, shoes off, his legs drawn up Indian-style, looking at me as if I were the strangest thing he'd ever seen. "So, you're wide-awake, not sleepy at all." His voice had taken on an almost hypnotic drone, and I felt myself struggling, just the way a child fights a nap in the afternoon.

I pinched the inside of my leg, hard, and sat up straight. "Nope," I said, "not at all. Why don't you go on up to bed and when I get tired, I'll just turn out the lights and sack out right here." I said it in my most motherly, matter-of-fact voice. A voice that I hoped said, "We both know I'm almost old enough to be your mother, but in case you didn't believe it, I'm not interested."

"Man." He sighed, a snorty kind of laugh escaping into the space between us. "You are one uptight woman."

"I am not uptight. I am telling you I'm not tired."

Jack leaned a little in my direction. "You were telling me that you didn't want me getting any ideas about us having sex."

I almost jumped backward. My cheeks flamed up, my heart pounded a little, but I held my ground. "Well, so what if I was? I mean, here you are, an attractive young man, and I come bursting into your place, looking for somewhere to stay. Well, how does it look? I wouldn't blame you for thinking it!"

He sat up straight, staring right into my eyes, smiling. I didn't see anything to smile about.

"Maggie, let's get a few things straight, okay?" I sat still. I was about to be on the receiving end of a lecture; I could feel it in his tone. I tried not to look at him with Sheila's impatient adolescent face. I hated lectures as much as she did.

"You aren't that much older than me. Lord, yes, you are damned attractive, but I don't prey upon women in trouble. I don't have to." *Yeah*, I thought, *you've got Evelyn*, and I felt foolish, but also more comfortable.

"Now, here's the deal," he said. "This couch is old. It's rump-sprung. You can sleep here if you want to, but I've tried it before and you wouldn't get any rest. I'm going to sleep in my waterbed, like I always do, and I'm suggesting you do the same."

I knew it! The alarm bells went off again. I stretched my hand along the cushion and wiggled a little bit, testing his statement. It was uncomfortable, but I still didn't think it was right to just crawl into bed with a man I hardly knew, New Age or not.

"It's a queen-sized bed," he said, taking another swig from his beer. "I sleep on my left side and I don't snore. And Maggie," he said, reaching over and covering my hand with his, "I won't touch you. Not on purpose, that is." He was laughing and looking at me. I felt foolish. "Keep all your clothes on if you need to. I won't, but you can. All I ask is that you take off those pointy-toed cowgirl boots. I'll even lend you a T-shirt."

I took a huge swig of beer. In fact, I about guzzled the whole thing, and then I looked him right straight back in the eye.

"You'd better not be telling anything but the God's honest truth," I said.

He held up his fingers in the Boy Scout salute.

"On my honor, I will try to do my duty . . ."

"Trying ain't good enough, Jack."

"Don't worry, I promise." He finished his beer and stood up. "Now, you are tired, aren't you?"

Truth was, I was so tired I was seeing and hearing things. I nodded and followed him up the winding stairs to the loft.

He lent me a T-shirt, long enough on me to come to mid-thigh, and a toothbrush. It was strange and awkward, figuring out who went first in the tiny bathroom and dressing and undressing in there, using his faded towels, smelling the patchouli oil and other scents that filled his space.

When I emerged from the bathroom, the bedroom was in almost total darkness, except for the skylight over the bed and one small candle by his bedside.

"You get the right side," he said in the darkness.

Clumsily I half fell into the waterbed, rolling up against him before I could stop myself.

"Oh my God!" I gasped, as my skin brushed up against his. He was totally—and I do mean totally—naked!

"Jack, you're . . . you're . . ."

"Well, I told you I was taking my clothes off."

"Yes, but I thought you meant you were changing into pajamas."

"Never wear 'em," he said calmly. Then he rolled slightly away from me. "That better?" He chuckled. "You are so uptight!"

"I am not!" I was edging, the best way I could, over to the wooden rail and as far away from his hot skin as I could move.

"Maggie, the human body is just a trapping for the soul. The world makes way too much of it."

I did not think I was doing any such thing.

"Maggie, it's just skin and parts. Take a deep breath and relax."

"You know, Jack," I said, fuming, "I've about had it with meditating reality away. If I breathe deeply, I will still know that I am lying in bed with a naked man!"

He chuckled a sleepier chuckle. "It's all relative, Maggie."

"What would Evelyn say about all this?"

There was a deep, prolonged sigh from the other side of the bed. "I'm sure, in her way, Evelyn knows all about it." He shifted a little in the bed, pulling the quilt a little farther up on his shoulders. The moonlight drifted through the skylight and touched his shoulders and made his blond hair seem to glow. "Go to sleep, Maggie," he murmured. "You are new to the world in many ways."

I lay there, listening, my body rigidly clinging to the far side of the bed. Slowly his breathing deepened. He was actually asleep. I stayed vigilant, thinking maybe it was all some kind of weird meditative state, but soon he began to snore gently. I clung to my edge of the bed for as long as I could, but eventually I fell asleep.

At some point in the night, I woke up suddenly to find my head nestled up against his shoulder and one of his hands resting on my arm. I was barely awake, and didn't move, because for that one moment I felt safe again.

10

Jack was gone again when I awoke. I don't know how he did it. I usually sleep light. Motherhood does that to you. Any sound in my house and I'd have been up and investigating. Vernell used to swear that if Sheila so much as turned over, I'd be down the hall, in her room, and checking her breathing. But for some reason, when Jack woke up and left, I'd slept through it.

I wandered downstairs, looking for coffee, and found the carafe waiting for me with a note attached.

"Evelyn waited around to meet you, but you were sleeping too hard. I'll be back later this afternoon. May need a ride to work. Hope you slept well. Jack."

I reached for a cracked mug and poured steaming hot coffee into it. A Starbucks bag lay empty on the counter. Mocha Java. I'd have to run by the Barnes and Noble at Friendly Center and pick some up for him. I wandered across the plywood floor, spotting a CD player. Music. That's what the morning called for, music.

I was not surprised to find that Jack had strange taste in music. He had a mishmash of artists I'd never heard of, along with some that I could recognize. At least he had Emmy Lou Harris. That fact redeemed him somewhat in my eyes. But I settled for a Jesse Winchester oldie. "Brand New Tennessee Waltz" floated out into the room.

I whirled around, singing softly and sipping coffee. I drifted up the stairs with my second cup of coffee and took a shower. The shower was one area where Jack seemed to have spared no expense. I stood in the stall and let two showerheads cover me in a warm spray. It was wonderful. Even his soap smelled good, like leather and spices.

By the time I'd dressed and let my hair fall around my shoulders in damp ringlets, I had a plan. A visit to Miss Sheila and then Vernell. One of those two, if not both, knew something they hadn't told me. I thought of the dark circles under Sheila's eyes when she'd come to the Curley-Que. A mama knows when something's wrong, and in hindsight, I could see there was more to Sheila's anxiety than worry about me.

I sat on the edge of the one clothing-draped chair in Jack's room and pulled on my boots. Sheila'd probably be at her after-school job at the bagel shop by now. Vernell would be at the satellite dish shop or at the mobile home lot, supervising the crew. That is, if he wasn't at the funeral home.

I ran down the stairs, added more coffee to my mug, and pushed the garage door button. Slowly the door began to edge upward, revealing a pair of new lizard-skin Tony Lama boots. I sighed. This was not going to be my day after all.

The garage door slid further up, revealing Marshall Weathers in all his glory.

"Sleep well?" he asked. He was smiling, but he didn't mean it. I could tell by the cold glint in his eyes. "Your boyfriend left about an hour ago. You didn't feel like breakfast?" There was a hard edge to his voice. Despite myself, my body started to respond.

"He's not my boyfriend," I said, my voice squeaking a little and making me sound like a guilty teenager.

"Well, I don't know what else to call him," he said. "The boy brought you home to his place. All the lights went off a half an hour later, just that little bit of candlelight coming from the bedroom. What else would you call him? I suppose you slept in separate rooms?"

"Yes," I snapped. "As if it were your business!"

"Everything about you is my business right now," he said. He was looking past me, into the living room. He was taking in the couch, the two beer bottles sitting on the coffee table in front of the woodstove, the coffee mug standing in the sink. He wasn't missing a trick, but he was looking hardest at the couch. It showed no signs of having been slept on.

"You followed us last night!" I said, the knowledge infuriating me. "That was your Jeep?"

"Might've been." He took a step closer on the loading dock. "You gonna let me in, or do you want to have this conversation out here?"

I took a giant step forward, over the doorsill, and pushed the garage door opener again. The squeaky wheel started to grind and the rusty door started rolling back down.

"Here is fine," I said. "It's not like *I* have anything to hide. I can talk out in the open. *I* don't have to skulk around in the bushes, spying on folks. You must have a lot of time on your hands, Detective, if you've gotta go following innocent people around! You don't have a love life? You've gotta go speculating on mine instead?"

He shook his head, like maybe I didn't get it. But his neck was slowly turning red. "This is gonna get us nowhere," he said. He looked at my cracked mug of steaming coffee and seemed to sigh slightly.

"Maggie, why don't you leave that there and come take a ride with me."

"Why, are we going downtown?" I stressed the word *downtown*, just like they do on TV.

"No, I was actually figuring we'd go over to Yum-Yums and get us a couple of hot dogs and milkshakes." The cold glint in his eyes was gone. He'd lost the anger and that astonished me. Somehow he'd just let it go, or stuffed it away in a box. He now seemed genuinely friendly.

"Hot dogs and milkshakes?" My stomach

growled in agreement. I figured I owed him. I'd run out on him twice. It wasn't really that much of a choice anyway. If I got all snippy, then we'd end up downtown in his office. My stomach growled again, louder. I'd never get lunch at the police station.

He didn't wait for my answer. He assumed and started walking toward his brown Taurus.

"Where's the Jeep?" I said, following him.

"Home." He walked around to his side of the car and unlocked the door. This was not a date. This was still, underneath the friendly exterior, business. *A gentleman would've unlocked your door,* Mama's voice said inside my head.

He did wait for me to fasten my seat belt before he spun out of the parking lot and onto Elm Street. He picked up his radio, spoke into it briefly, then turned the volume down. He didn't say another word until we drove into the Yum-Yums parking lot.

Even at three in the afternoon, business was booming. There were a lot of police vehicles there, which surprised me because Yum-Yums is right by the UNCG campus. I'd always assumed it was just a kid hangout.

"Hungry?" he asked.

"Starved!"

He looked like he wanted to ask another one of his sharp-edged questions, but stopped himself. I hopped out of the car and followed his determined progress across the lot. Yum-Yums is a small storefront operation, with a few tables and stools outside and rows of hard plastic booths inside. It is old, settled in its grime, and full of good smells.

"All the way," he said to the guy who ran up to take his order. "And a chocolate shake."

"Just catsup, please," I said, "and a diet Coke."

He turned then to look at me. "No shake?" he said. "They've got the best ice cream in town. That's why folks come here."

"Not me," I said. "Gotta watch my figure."

He didn't move his eyes from my face. "I don't see why you'd think that," he said. "Nothing wrong with your figure."

I felt my face flush. I grabbed my hot dog and headed for the nearest booth, forgetting the soda, which he carried over. He slid in across from me and took a long sip of his milkshake.

"You missed out," he said, "best shake in town."

"You come here a lot?" I asked, studying him, trying to see a chink in his armor.

"A right good bit." He wasn't going to give up one single detail about himself if he didn't have to.

I stretched and took another shot at it.

"You grow up here?"

"Uh-huh."

"Where'd you graduate?"

"Smith. In 1978, since you're gonna ask that next." His blue eyes were twinkling. He was enjoying himself.

"I'm just making polite conversation! So you grew up over by the mill, huh?"

Weathers was chewing, his gaze circling the room, sweeping the customers and always returning to watch the entrance. He was making me nervous, like maybe he expected an armed robber or something.

"Your parents still live there?" I asked. The mill area had changed over the years, with older mill couples leaving and younger couples moving in. It was an innocent question, but instead his neck turned red and his jaw started to twitch.

"How about another hot dog?" he asked, abruptly sliding out of the booth and standing where he could tower over me, keeping me boxed into my side of the booth.

"No, thanks, I'm about done."

"Uh-huh," he said, then leaned down close to me, his hands resting one on the table and one on my seat back, fencing me in tighter. "Maybe you can think up a few more questions for me while I'm gone," he whispered. "Maybe you'll ask the ones you're afraid to ask."

He turned around and left me sitting there. The questions I was afraid to ask. *Are you married? Do you want me the same way I want you? Do you feel it, too?* I could feel my face growing redder by the second. Damn him! How could he read me like that?

He acted as if he'd never said a thing when he returned to the booth. We ate in relative silence. I kept waiting for him to start with his questions, but he seemed comfortable just to be sitting and eating. Plenty of police officers stopped at the table, saying hello, offering a friendly comment. Weathers mainly grunted, sometimes said a phrase or two, but didn't offer them a seat or try to draw them into conversation. It was clear he had other things on his mind.

It all came to a crashing halt when he finished his meal. Suddenly he leaned forward, looked right in my eyes and started with the questions. Not the questions I expected either.

"How'd you feel when you and Digger Bailey broke up?"

I choked on my last bit of hot dog and felt my face flame. How in the hell had he found out about that?

"How'd you find out?"

"Hard work," he answered, a small, smirky grin playing across his face. He was pleased with himself.

"Hard work and nosiness!" I stormed. "What right have you to go hunting up my past? Who did you talk to? How did you . . . ?" I lost my voice, my throat closed in, and I couldn't speak. How did the sonofabitch find out about Digger?

"I'm just doing my job," Weathers said, his voice calm, his face never betraying the kind of emotions I knew were written across mine.

"Digger doesn't have a thing to do with this!" I could feel the people behind us listening. They'd stopped talking and hadn't moved in their booth for minutes.

"Digger hurt you," he said softly. "I just wondered how you felt about it."

No two ways about it, Digger had hurt me. Digger hurt me publicly and in ways that I could not put words to because I was ashamed. Ashamed at my foolishness and ashamed at my stupid youthful belief that I was invincible.

"You must've been angry at him," he said.

"Angry?" Yes, I had been, but only later, years later. "No, I wasn't angry."

"Then what?" He was watching me with a sad look on his face. I couldn't stand that. I didn't want someone to feel sorry for me.

"Maggie, he left you and the whole town knew about it. He married someone else while you were off buying a wedding gown. Why weren't you mad?" Tears flooded my eyes and I couldn't see. "Come on," he said, standing up. "Let's go outside and sit in my car."

Why had I ever agreed to eat lunch with this man? Why did I agree to answer his questions? Maybe because I was still chasing the cowboy who'd come and smiled encouragement as I did my audition. Marshall Weathers was not that man. Oh, he lived in the same body, but he was not the same man.

I climbed into the front seat and tried to pull myself together. Digger was years ago. It just hurt me to know that Weathers had been nosing around in my hometown and had managed to find out the one thing I'd hoped everyone would've forgotten by now. Someone, probably more than one someone, remembered me for being left behind.

"I figure Digger was a real creep," Weathers said. "If I'd been your big brother, I'd have set him straight on a couple of counts."

I ignored him. I didn't want to talk about Digger anymore, even if Weathers was on my side.

"Why are you following me?" I asked, wiping at my eyes and blowing my nose.

"Because it's my job."

There was no smile to accompany that answer. He was stating a fact. He had a job to do and that's all he could see, his job. I was a case number, a suspect.

"Why don't you look for the real killer? Why do you keep hounding me?"

Weathers turned in his seat and looked at me. "Maggie, I haven't accused you of anything."

"Oh, come on, you might as well have!" How could the man stay so calm? And why did I keep staring into his eyes?

"You're all I've got to go on right now, Maggie. I haven't accused you of anything. I haven't called you a suspect, have I? I'm just covering all my bases."

"Then why aren't you haunting Jimmy's widow? And why haven't you checked up on anyone else the way you've done me?"

"What makes you think I haven't?" he asked.

I didn't have a thing to add to that. We just sat there for a few minutes, watching people come in and out of Yum-Yums. Eventually, he leaned forward and started the car. The interview was almost at an end. I could make it back to Jack's place without anymore forays into my past.

We drove in relative silence and I relaxed a little. When we pulled into Jack's parking lot, I had my hand on the door handle and was almost out the door before he could roll to a stop.

"Thanks for lunch, I guess," I said, jumping out of the car and leaning down to look in on him. I was pushing the door closed when I heard him, and by then it was too late to stop the door from flying out of my fingers and slamming on his last words.

"Maybe we'll talk about Union Grove sometime," he said. The car began to roll and I was left standing in the broken gravel parking lot, staring after him. Now how in the hell had he found out about Union Grove?

11

Don't fish with a skunk, Mama used to say, it'll only raise a stink and you'll come home empty-handed. Mama was right. There I stood, empty-handed and staring after a Grade A skunk. Union Grove! "Ask me what you really want to ask me, Maggie." The words kept circling around in my head like buzzards. If Weathers had his way, I was done for. I just knew it. But then, Marshall Weathers didn't know what I was capable of doing. And if I had my way, he wouldn't find out until I was ready.

Know where your enemy keeps his dirty underwear and you'll have won the war, Mama said. It was time to follow the smell. I ran inside Jack's place and called Bonnie down at the Curley-Que.

"Maggie?" she said, all breathless and worried. "Are you all right?"

"No, Bonnie, I'm not," I said, "but I'm sure

gonna be! Listen, didn't you go to Smith High School?"

"What?" Bonnie hadn't expected this.

"Smith. Did you go to Smith?"

I was pacing around Jack's living room, staring out the window, unable to sit still.

"Yes, I went to Smith. Graduated in '80. Why?"

"Good," I said, "then you're just the help I need."

"Maggie, I don't see what this has to do with ..."

"Did you know a Marshall Weathers?" I demanded.

Bonnie sighed. "Know him? Know him! Just about every girl in the school knew him! Driving a sixty-eight Mustang convertible, football, track, softball, and women! That boy was a hundred miles of fast, bad road. Liked to kill his poor ole mama with worry! You know she goes to my church, don't you?"

I leaned back against the wall facing the window and stared out at the parking lot, a smile edging its way across my face.

"He's come a long way, that ole boy has," Bonnie sighed. "He's a big detective now, down at the ... Hey, he isn't the ... ? Aw, Maggie. ..."

I could hear the beauty parlor sounds in the background, the whoosh of blow dryers, the chatter of the customers, but above it all I heard a tiny little giggle.

"Maggie, you watch out now, girl! He ain't like Vernell, not at all!"

"Bonnie," I said, "how's about me and you going to church Sunday?"

Bonnie sucked in her breath. "You are a wicked woman!" she said. "I'll meet you there about quarter to eleven."

"Thanks, Bon, I owe you. Big time!"

I hung up the phone and started humming a little. Okay, so he knew more about me than almost anyone, but the tables were turning. Soon I was gonna be sitting in the catbird seat. Union Grove! How in the hell had he found out about that?

It was years ago. We'd sworn ourselves to secrecy. Which one of them had talked? Well, they were weak. A bunch of girls, women now, mothers, bored, with too much time on their hands and too little attention. I could easily see them giving in the face of Weathers's thousand-watt charm. Hell, if I stayed around him too long, I'd give, too. But that was never going to be an option. I'd see to that. I hoped.

Women, girls really, Boone's Farm apple wine, and the feel of a spring night our senior year of high school. That's what was really responsible for Union Grove. We were just young girls, with the sense of power that comes from blossoming bodies and not enough freedom to know a risky situation. And it was all my fault, as usual.

It was before the Digger Bailey fiasco, before I knew how badly the world could wound you. I wasn't scared of nothing, not my alcoholic father, not his wild-assed family, not my teachers, and certainly not boys. That's how come when we heard the senior boys had rolled toilet paper around the statue of Robert E. Lee that stood in front of our high school, we knew we had to show them the proper way to pull a senior prank. I was the organizer.

"That was a pitiful display," I said to my girl-friends the next day. "How juvenile. How imma-ture!" The others were nodding right along. We were all piled up in my VW, down at the end of Shannon Able's driveway, smoking cigarettes and drinking Boone's Farm apple wine. "They're just little boys. We're women!"

"Yeah," they chorused. "Women!" Evella Lynn threw back her head and uttered a long rebel yell, and the rest of us whooped and tossed our ciga-rettes out the open windows.

"Let's do something really, really bad. Some-thing that'll let them boys know that we're women!"

Well, the more we drank, the more the idea of besting the boys appealed to us. No idea was too outrageous for us! Finally a plan gelled. We would leave our mark on Union Grove High School, all right!

The next night, Friday, actually early Saturday morning, the six of us met at Evella Lynn's place.

"Evella, you got the paint?"

"Yes, ma'am!" she cried, brandishing a bucket of bright blue latex.

"Darnelle, you got gloves?"

"Check!"

We went through the list, swigging our Boone's Farm at record speed, then heading out in Evella Lynn's brother's pickup, bound for the school. Lacy was the only one who had doubts. She always was the sissy, and as I thought on it now, would be the most likely to have ratted us all out to

Weathers. She was just sure we'd be caught.

Evella killed the headlights when we were still a mile from the school, throwing the truck down into second gear and forcing it along almost at a crawl.

"Shush, y'all!" she said. "Listen out!"

We all shut up and listened, little thrills of anxiety gnawing at us all. We heard nothing. Union Grove, home of the Blue and White Lions, stood in the middle of a cow pasture, surrounded by a small football stadium and an Olympic-sized pool that served in the summer as the community swimming hole.

We ran the truck up around back of the school, then up over the curve to the northeast corner of the old brick building, right under the principal's window. Evella killed the engine and handed me a roll of masking tape.

"Knock it out, big girl!" she cried softly.

I taped the window, and then, just like in the *I Spy* TV show, I knocked the pane out with a gloved fist and pulled the taped pieces out of the frame. No jagged edges. No clinking sounds. No mess. In a few moments the six of us were inside Mr. Slovenick's office, painting away and drinking our sweet summer wine.

We painted his floor, his desk, his chair, his phone, his papers, even his flag, bright Lion blue. We covered the walls and the ceiling and when at last we were finished, we had almost as much paint on ourselves as we did the room.

"I know what let's do," I said. "Let's go swimming! Naked!"

That was our mistake.

We ran old Evella's truck right down to the chain-link fence and used the roof of the cab as our ladder to scale over. We didn't plan how we'd get back out from behind the fence. We didn't consider that the swim team would meet on Saturday. We just knew the pleasure of swimming alone and naked in the school pool. The untouchables.

The water turned bright blue from the paint, just like the pictures you see of the Carribean. The sun began to slowly edge its way up over the southern Virginia hills, and there we were, on top of the world. We were laying out on top of the concrete, drying off, when we heard the car in the distance and knew it was headed for the school. After all, where else would a car be going at six A.M. on a late spring Saturday, down the one road that led only to the high school?

"I told y'all!" Lacy shrieked. "I told you!"

We jumped up, the naked six of us, all running in different directions, all panicked except for Evella, who calmly started to scale the fence, butt naked, her fingers and toes grabbing hold of the mesh as she worked her way up and over the fence. By the time we'd come to our senses enough to start climbing, she'd crawled into the car and cranked the engine. We dropped down into the cab like fat, overripe apples hitting the ground, and in an instant Evella had popped the clutch and was skidding her way across the pasture.

There was only one way out. We were going to pass the car and sure as shooting, we'd be recognized.

"Hide, y'all," Evella screamed. "Lie flat in the bed!"

We squished ourselves flat against the bedliner of the old truck, huddling in one blue-tinged mass of naked girl flesh. Evella was gonna take the fall. She couldn't drive and hunch down under the windshield. So, she went out like Evella.

"It's Dickie!" she screamed back through the cab window. Dickie was the president of Beta Club, the smart kid club, and manager of the swim team. Towel Boy, they called him.

Evella pushed the accelerator to the floor and sat up straight, blue and naked, her big breasts pushed up against the steering wheel. As she passed Dickie, Evella let out a mighty Indian war whoop and kept on going. Evella really wasn't afraid of nothing or nobody.

We hightailed it back to Evella's, borrowed her clothes and took showers, hoping to clean up before the cops came to arrest us. For surely they were hot on our tails. But the cops didn't come that day. Or the next. It wasn't that our crime went unnoticed. It was more the way little Dickie related it to the police and the press.

"Oh, my gawd! Oh, Lord," he moaned to the reporter who wrote up the big front page story, "Union Grove High School Mauled By Blue Man." "It was the biggest, meanest-looking man I ever did see!"

"Man!" Evella raved after school on Monday. "I ain't no man!" But of course she couldn't say it out loud.

"We were robbed!" I said. "They think a man did it!"

"But what about our clothes, back at the pool?" asked Lacy, who I believe trembled the rest of her senior year.

The clothes were never mentioned. Not in the paper. Not around the school. Nowhere. However, a few years later, the most peculiar thing did happen. Evella married Dickie. Little shrimpy Dickie and big old Evella. The rest of us always wondered if somehow he'd found out, taken our clothes and decided to cover for us, or realized later that the "man" he'd seen was really Evella. We never knew, but rumors circulated as always. Dickie and Evella live in a blue house, drive blue cars, and mostly wear blue clothing. But I'm sure that has nothing to do with the year the Union Grove Blue Man struck.

If Weathers had gotten to the bottom of that story, what other distorted ideas did he have about me? How would I ever convince him that I could be trusted, believed to tell the truth? How could I convince him that I wasn't a murderer? And how would I ever make him believe that someone was coming after me? And maybe not just me. I felt my stomach seize up and a wave of nausea swept over me. What about Sheila? Was she safe? What if the killer had been after us and only happened on Jimmy?

I had to get to my baby. I had to find some answers before we found ourselves in real danger.

12

I sat out in my car for a minute and watched Sheila through the glass front of the bagel shop. This was not the Sheila I knew, the headstrong teenager who stomped out of my house and all over my heart a mere eleven months ago. Sheila had evolved into someone else.

The girl I watched had straightened her curly red hair and now wore it slicked back in a ponytail, just like the other girls in the upscale Irving Park shop. She'd toned down her makeup so she'd look "natural" like the others, not like a vampire runaway. I had to admit it was a positive physical improvement, but at what cost to my little rebel's freethinking spirit?

The Bun and Bagel was no redneck, lard-cake bakery. There wasn't a bun in the place that smacked of squishy white bread and Vienna sausages. It was wholesome, a quality I much dislike in my baked goods. Give me a hunk of greasy yellow cornbread with bacon drippings any day of the week.

Sheila saw me coming and seemed to cringe.

"Pretty uptown little shop," I said, stepping up to the counter in front of her.

"Hey, Mama." She smiled weakly. But like every child with something to hide, she didn't meet my eyes. This was made all the easier by her bagel cap. Designed to look like a bagel, it slid down lopsidedly onto her forehead, giving Sheila the appearance of a drunken angel.

"I need to talk to you, honey. Tell your boss you need to take a little break."

Sheila looked frightened. "Now?" she asked. "I can't right now, Mama. I'm working and we're swamped."

I looked around. There was one customer in the store, a woman in a fur coat, being waited on by another girl. I looked back at Sheila, raising my Mama-don't-buy-that eyebrow.

"All right." She sighed. "Mary Catherine, I'm taking a break for a second." She used a chatty little tone I'd never heard before, and pitched her voice an octave lower than usual. It was her version of an upper-crust accent, and it cut me to the quick. What was happening to my baby?

Sheila flung her cap down onto a stool and brushed past me, headed for the door. She walked past the storefront and around to the side of the tiny brick building where the girls inside couldn't see her. She was fumbling in the pocket of her bagel apron, her hand closing around a telltale rectangle.

"When did you start smoking?" I asked.

Sheila looked guilty. "I only smoke every now and then," she said. She looked up at me, and for a second I saw the Sheila I knew. "I know, I know. It's bad for me. It might even kill me one day if I do it until I'm as old as you and Daddy. But I'm only smoking now and then."

I couldn't believe it. Sheila'd always been so health-conscious. A sudden memory of her rushed back. It had been only a few months back, on the porch with Jimmy. She'd been getting onto him for smoking. What had changed her?

"Why are you smoking? Do all your new friends smoke?" That's what it was. Sheila wanted to fit in more than she cared about her health.

"No, Mama." She sighed. "Don't hardly a one of them smoke." She had lapsed back into her deep, country accent.

"Well then?" I stood waiting for an answer, forgetting all about my true agenda.

Sheila just shrugged her shoulders. If none of her fancy friends smoked, then who was she hanging around with who did? The image of Jimmy tossing his cigarette out into my front yard returned. He'd laughed at Sheila's earnest attempt to make him quit.

"That's not why I came to see you," I said. I reached into my pocket and pulled out the tiny garnet and gold ring. "Look what I found."

I watched her face carefully. Mama used to say the truth was like a doorbell. She'd never elaborate, but I always took it to mean you shouldn't go poking at it and running away. The truth has a way of catching up with a body. I didn't want to see Sheila's face mirror a lie, but that's what happened.

She swallowed, groped for her cigarettes, let go when she remembered that she was facing her mother, and then tried to smile. It was a pathetic performance to a mother. It might've fooled a stranger, but not me.

"I wondered where I'd left that!" she said, reaching out to take it. I folded my fingers over the ring and snatched my hand back. "Hey!" she cried, trying to look puzzled and hurt.

"Not so fast," I said. "How'd you lose it?"

Sheila shrugged her shoulders again. "I don't know! God, Mama, if I knew how I lost it, it wouldn't be lost!"

"Young lady!" I started, then thought better of it. "Let's fish or cut bait here, Sheila. Is this what Keith was looking for in my house?"

"I don't know what you're talking about!" she insisted.

I leaned back against the cold brick of the wall and watched my daughter lie to me. How had we come to such a place? Hadn't I been tucking her in bed, her arms wrapping around my neck, her "I love you" echoing in my ears, just a little while ago? When did this adolescent demon take over her body?

"I haven't seen Keith in weeks!" she cried. "And it's all your fault!" I watched her thinking up her next lie. "I probably dropped it in your car, or in my room the last time I was over."

"When was the last time you were over?" I asked softly.

"Three weeks ago, you know that." Somewhere

in the middle of that statement, Sheila saw the trap, realized there was nothing she could do to help herself, and continued on into it.

"Sheila, I found this ring next to the bathroom sink. It wasn't there before I left for work the day your Uncle Jimmy died."

"Well, I don't how it got there then," she said, her voice weakening, her eyes fixed on the traffic out on Battleground Avenue.

"There was a two-hour window of time between when I left for work and when the police say your Uncle Jimmy was killed. Now if you were in the house, I need to know about it. Honey, you might have seen or heard something that will help the police find Jimmy's killer."

Sheila's eyes widened, and her face paled. "Me? What makes you think I know anything?"

She was lying. Don't ask me how I knew, but she looked straight at my face and continued to lie. "I wasn't there. I don't know how my ring got there!" Her voice took on a distinct edge of hysteria, and her neck had flushed a bright, beet red that clashed with her hair. "I don't know anything about who killed Jimmy. I didn't hear a thing! I didn't see nothing!"

I reached out for her arm, but she jumped backward, her eyes widening and her breath coming in short little gasps.

"Honey, calm down!" But she couldn't, or wouldn't.

"What is it, Sheila?" I asked. "What's wrong? Talk to me, baby."

Sheila moaned and started to walk past me.

"No, Mama. It's nothing. I gotta go."

"Sheila!" I reached for her, and she let me stop her.

"Mama, I told you, I don't know anything about Uncle Jimmy." This time she looked me in the eye, but her look was far scarier than her lies. She was looking through me. "No matter who asks me, no matter what they try and do to me, I won't say any different, to anyone. I don't know anything! I didn't leave my ring at your place." Her voice was low and deliberate, as if she were a zombie, delivering a rehearsed line. "You can just keep it! I never want to see it again!" The edge of hysteria was creeping back into her voice.

Her eyes softened for a second. "I love you, Mama," she said, "no matter what happens, no matter what anybody says. I love you." A tear slid over her eyelid, running through her artfully applied makeup and leaving a pale liquid streak behind.

My heart was racing, breaking in half at the same time. I grabbed for her but she was gone, almost running back into the shop.

I would've gone in after her if I'd thought it would've done any good, but I knew better. Sheila was like me, stubborn. If my back was against the wall, I'd come out swinging. My gut instincts told me that my little girl was cut from the same cloth. It would be pointless to go after her.

I started back to the Bug, tears blurring my vision. If I'd had any doubts about my decision not to pursue Sheila into the shop, they were wiped away as a large panel truck rolled into the parking lot. Vernell Spivey was impossible to miss and the truck he drove made it a certainty that he'd be noticed, even on a foggy day.

Vernell drove a two-ton panel truck with a satellite dish mounted up on top. The truck was painted bright florescent orange with the words SATELLITE KINGDOM spelled out in huge black letters. VERNELL SPIVEY, THE SATELLITE KING was written in slightly smaller letters on the driver's side door. A painted profile of Jolene the Dish Girl, pointing to a huge dish—her largest attributes almost overshadowing Vernell's product—adorned the side of the truck.

As I watched the truck glide across the parking lot, drifting inevitably toward my little Bug, I saw Vernell's latest addition to his advertising campaign. I knew then that the Vernell Spivey who had come to the Golden Stallion dressed in a powder blue polyester leisure suit was not just a passing apparition. Nope, Vernell was having some kind of personality transformation, and from the looks of it, this was serious business.

The satellite dish mounted on the top of his truck had been painted with a tableau depicting Jesus, his arms outstretched and a tearful look on his face. At the very front of the truck, on the hood and just below the longhorn steer horns, Vernell had mounted a set of loudspeakers. I did not take that small detail in until I heard the music and Vernell's voice flooding the air around me.

"Wait right there, sister," he crowed. "I bring great tidings from the land beyond." I froze as organ music blared. Behind the windshield I could see Vernell, a microphone in his hand and a wild look in his eyes.

I stood absolutely still, hoping against hope that he hadn't been speaking to me. Anyone within a ten-shop radius of Vernell's truck also stopped, frozen like possums in the middle of a south Georgia highway. My eyes were drawn to the satellite dish. It was a darn good rendering of Jesus. The arm that extended out from the dish, curving back in toward the center, had been painted gold, probably in an attempt to look like some stick Jesus was using in his work. I couldn't figure it out and didn't want to know.

Vernell, for his part, was clambering down out of the truck, which he had stopped just behind my Volkswagen. I could only imagine Sheila's reaction inside the shop. She was probably trying to pretend she didn't know us. I could hardly blame her.

Vernell still wore the leisure suit, although it was now much the worse for wear. His ruffled shirt had lost a few buttons and the suit was stained with paint. Vernell wasn't looking any too sober, either. Even though it was approaching the traditional cocktail hour, it was apparent to me that Vernell's happy hour had begun long before noon.

His hair was mussed, he sported a black stubble of a beard, and his eyes were bloodshot.

"Maggie!" he cried. "I was jess looking for you." He slurred his speech slightly. This was another serious sign. Vernell could hold his beer. He even did a pretty good job with liquor. But when he'd crossed the line, Vernell began to lose his capacity for speech. He could still walk, and many folks would think he'd had a few, but no one knew how much liquor it took to make Vernell appear drunk. I knew. He'd at least finished a fifth of the hard stuff, probably Jack Daniel's.

"Come here, you! I gotta talk to you!" He'd made it to my side, but now seemed to sway slightly.

"Sit down, Vernell," I said, pulling him down to the curb that ran alongside Sheila's store. He didn't have much of a choice once I got the momentum swinging downward. He sank like a sack of potatoes.

"Maggie," he said, his whiskey breath coating my face. "Jimmy's dead."

"I know, Vernell, remember? You came to see me last night."

Vernell looked confused. "I did?"

"Yeah, Vernell, you did. You were liquored up, just like you are now." *And just like you always were,* I thought.

"Maggie," he said again, paying no attention to what I'd said. "I saw him!"

"Who, Vernell? Saw who?"

Vernell shot me a look like maybe I hadn't been paying attention. "Jimmy! He come to see me last night!"

Poor Vernell. Now he was slipping into the d.t.'s.

"Honey, Jimmy's dead."

Vernell gave me that look again. "Don't I know it!" he said loudly. "Of course he's dead! How else could he've found himself and received his true gift?"

"Vernell, how long have you been drinking?"
Vernell was bad to go off on these kind of binges.
Every three months you could count on it, and in
between then if he was under stress. Jimmy's death
must've set him off good.

"Listen to me, Maggie. We're gonna be partners, you know. You gotta listen."

I sighed and prepared to give Vernell time to
talk until he ran out of gas. It was the only way
when we'd been married, and it was obviously the
only way now.

"You listening?" he asked. I nodded. "Good
then," he said, and we were off to the races.
"Jimmy came in a vision, Maggie! He was all
dressed in pink robes!"

"*Pink?*"

"I know what what you're thinking," he said,
nodding. "It's supposed to be white. I told Jimmy the
same thing and he said, 'That's what all you people
left behind think! Don't a one of you know, 'cause
you ain't dead!'" Vernell went on. "Well, I couldn't
argue with that, especially not when he told me what
the Lord wants me to do! The Lord is working in my
life, Maggie. He has a great vision for me, and dawg,
if it ain't an inspired business vision to boot!"

I was starting to have a bad feeling, a way-
down-deep-in-the-pit-of-my-stomach bad feeling.

"Lookee up there," Vernell said, pointing to the
satellite dish. "Jimmy says, 'Vernell, the Lord wants you
to spread his message. Vernell, paint the dishes.' I said to
him, 'Paint the dishes, what kind of talk is that!' But
Jimmy explained it all. He said if I painted the dishes in
His likeness, then one and all would receive him."

I didn't know whether to laugh or cry. I just shook my head.

"I know, I know," Vernell said, seeing my reaction. "I told him I couldn't even draw, but Jimmy said I had the gift now. He even told me what kind of paint to use, so's we wouldn't affect the transmission. Latex. Get that? Latex. Jesus even knows about paint!"

"Vernell," I said, trying to interrupt, but he went right on.

"So look, Maggie! It's a damn good likeness, don't you think?"

I looked back over at the truck and nodded wearily. It was a damn good likeness, all right.

"And best of all? This'll sell. Why, do you know I took sixteen orders right here today? In Greensboro? Why, honey, we'll spread the word all over the world."

I didn't like the way Vernell kept saying *we*.

"What's Jolene think about this, Vernell?" I asked.

Vernell shook his head and spat out into the parking lot. "Jolene don't know shit!" he pronounced. "She thinks the best thing I can do is take you to court."

"Me? Vernell, hello, we're divorced. Why're you gonna take me to court?"

"On account of what Jimmy did." He looked over at me as if to say "The jig's up."

"Vernell, I told you Jimmy and me were never any more than friends, and not even good friends."

"Not that! Although, that's probably why he done it. Maggie, Roxanne's the one who found it!

You couldn't hide the truth away from us forever!"
I was trying to get a word in, but Vernell was on a
roll. "Sure, I was madder than a coot owl when
Roxanne told me, and she's still fit to be tied, but
eventually I had to accept it. We've gotta work
together. And you know what?"

"What, Vernell?"

"Maybe it's God's way of working a miracle in
my life." Vernell started to cry.

"All right! All right, Vernell Spivey, I've pitied
you and babied you enough. Now you reach down
in your drunken soul and you pull yourself
together. I want to know what you're talking
about, and I want to know now!"

Vernell raised his tearful eyes and reached his
hand out to touch my arm. "Maggie, Jimmy's done
left you his share of the business, you and Sheila.
Don't you know?"

I shook my head in disbelief.

"If I recall correctly, Roxanne said he left a
copy of his will at the house and he said half of
everything him and me co-owned was for you, and
half for Sheila, on account of how he told you he'd
take care of the both of you." Vernell's eyes narrowed suspiciously. "Is there something I ought to
know about Sheila?" he asked.

"God Almighty knows!" I said, jumping up
off the curb and whirling around to face Vernell.
"You Spiveys'll dog a girl from the grave! Hellfire!
No! I had no idea and I didn't have an affair with
your brother!"

Vernell smiled sadly. "It don't really matter
none now, Maggie. Jimmy's dead and you and I are

gonna be partners in the mobile home business. It's fate, Maggie. Pure T fate."

Not my fate! Not my future! I was so mad, I couldn't even begin to take it all in. Damn that Jimmy!

"Come on, Vernell!" I cried. "Get up!"

"Where're we going?" He had a foolish grin on his face, just the way he used to when he'd come home drunk and think he was going to get lucky.

"Vernell, I am taking you home."

"I knew it!" he whooped. "I knew you still wanted me!"

I stared at the pitiful wreck of a man in his scruffy polyester, with his stinky breath, and shook my head. What had I done to piss off the universe?

I tugged him up off the curb and headed for my car, only to face the panel truck blocking me in.

"Give me your keys," I demanded. When he didn't move, I stuck my hand in his pants pocket and pulled them out. Vernell giggled. "Shut up and get in that truck! I'm driving, so don't even think about getting behind that wheel. You're knee-walking, dog drunk!" Vernell giggled again.

"I always did love it when you were mad," he said, wrapping a big arm around my shoulder and resting his drunken head on top of mine.

I stood there for a moment, trapped by the weight of him and trying to urge him forward. From a distance, we must've looked like a happy couple. At least that's what I figured Marshall Weathers was thinking as he watched from his vantage point across the parking lot.

13

I slammed Vernell's truck into reverse, stripping half the gears and propelling Vernell across the slippery bench seat.

"Get off me!" I cried, pushing at him with my right hand and trying to keep a grip on the steering wheel with my left. Vernell giggled and rested his chin on my shoulder. I could feel his eyes boring into the side of my face and I almost gagged on his breath. Marshall Weathers was still watching. He was wearing shiny, aviator-style, dark glasses. Even from a distance, I could tell he was laughing.

"The hell with him," I muttered, "and get the hell off my shoulder!" I cried, this time pinching Vernell in the fleshy area under his chin.

"Ouch! Dog, you are feisty when your dander's up!"

I pulled out into traffic, easily done since most

of the cars on Battleground stopped when they saw me coming. Vernell reached out and switched on what I took to be the radio, but suddenly the air was filled with the sounds of a choir singing the "Hallelujah Chorus" from the *Messiah*.

I was trying to concentrate on the rush-hour traffic, while trying to figure out the truck's shifting pattern. It was all I could do to make wild swipes at the dashboard.

"Vernell, turn that off!" The other cars were pulling off the road, as if responding to an ambulance. Vernell picked that moment to fall asleep.

"Vernell! Vernell, listen to me! Don't you dare fall asleep!" No response. Instead the sounds of the choir grew steadily louder, and there was a grinding noise from the roof of the truck. It was then that I remembered that Vernell had the dish wired to rotate clockwise whenever the truck was moving.

I looked in my rearview mirror. One lone car followed, a brown Taurus sedan.

"Aw, man! What did I ever do to you?" I yelled. What was God doing, appearing to my ex-husband? Where was divine intervention when I needed it? Pink robes!

I made a sweeping right-hand turn onto Independence Avenue, and began the final descent toward Vernell's brick mansion. How was I going to explain myself to Jolene, the Dish Girl? Maybe she wouldn't be home. Maybe she was out shopping and I would be able to leave Vernell and his truck parked in the driveway. But I knew, even as I thought it, that fate was against me. Jolene would be home. It was just that sort of day.

The brown Taurus rolled to a stop underneath the tree where I sat at night to watch for Sheila. I pulled up into Vernell's driveway with only one casualty: the handcrafted, Victorian mailbox. I flattened it like a pancake, an action which brought young Jolene dashing to the door.

She was dressed all in white, from the headband pushing back her bleached-blonde hair to the tips of her little white tennis shoes. She stood in the doorway, her eyes slowly registering our arrival.

"Got a delivery for you, Jolene," I yelled, trying to make myself heard above the music that hadn't stopped when I'd turned off the engine.

Jolene's beady little eyes narrowed, and she puffed out her chest, as if thinking maybe her breasts would do the talking.

"I don't think they're gonna help you with this," I said, walking up the cobblestone path to the front door.

"What have you done to him?" she shrieked. "Is he dead?" Her little white tennis skirt fluttered against her perfectly tanned thighs.

"In a manner of speaking," I said. "He's dead drunk. He's dead to the world. But no, I guess that's not exactly what you were asking, is it?"

Around the cul-de-sac, the neighbors had begun to emerge, casting angry and curious glances in our direction.

"Turn off the music," she demanded, stomping her little white-shoed foot on the ground.

"Well, honey, what's his is yours. You turn it off."

She marched over to the truck, pulled the key from the ignition, fiddled with the interior switches, and finally gave up. The music had now switched to "Rock of Ages."

"So I hear you think Vernell should sue me?" I said, stepping up behind her and scaring her so badly, she jumped.

"Yes, I do," she answered coldly. "You used his brother's affections to your own advantage."

"Now ain't that the pot calling the kettle black," I answered.

From inside the truck, Vernell moaned in his sleep.

"Get off my property!" she said.

"When I'm done," I said. "First, we got some unfinished business."

Jolene took a tiny step backward and began to hyperventilate.

"I don't have any business with you," she said. She tossed her blonde mane in an attempt to dismiss me, but I invaded her personal space again.

"You have been low-rating me in front of my daughter," I said. "I don't like that."

"I have said nothing but the truth," she answered.

"Truth is," I said, snatching her up by her little white tennis sweater, "I didn't kill Jimmy Spivey, and you have no right to say I did." Behind me, I heard a car door slam and the sounds of footsteps moving quickly across the street and toward the driveway. I knew who that was. Frankly, the thought of adding assault charges to murder didn't worry me. I was too excited at the prospect of blackening Jolene's eyes.

"If you so much as hint that I am anything but a sterling vision of motherhood, I will personally return to this house and kill you!"

"That's enough." Marshall Weathers's strong hands gripped my arms, forcing me to unhand the now sobbing Jolene.

"Arrest her, Officer!" Jolene screamed.

I was going to spend my evening in jail. I could smell it coming.

"Well," Weathers said slowly, his face an inscrutable mask behind his glasses, "I reckon I could do that." I could feel the silver cuffs snapping tightly around my wrists. It was going to be a reality. I could smell the jail-cell dinner. "But, if I did," he said, "it might be more of a problem for you."

"How's that?" Jolene said, sticking her chest under Weathers's nose, and smiling like an ingenue.

"Well, if I have to call a car to the scene, and take a report, then I'll end up having to cite you for public nuisance. You know, violation of the city noise ordinance. Parking violations. All sorts of things."

Jolene did a slow burn. "So that's the way it is, huh? You're on her side! My brother-in-law not even cold in the ground and she's the one who killed him. You'd think you people would be more concerned with justice."

Weathers didn't budge. "Oh, no, ma'am. I'm just stating a fact. Things would get official and I wouldn't be able to stop them. Better you should just let me escort your unwelcomed visitor off the property and let you attend to controlling the noise problem. Besides," he said, smiling softly at me, "I have a few questions I need to ask Miss Reid."

The truck was now blaring "Bringing in the Sheaves." Vernell had started snoring almost as loud as the music.

"All right then!" Jolene cried. "Take her away! And keep her away from us. The funeral's tomorrow. We don't want the likes of a natural-born killer showing up at a holy burial."

I started to answer her, but Weathers let his hands tighten on my arms, steering me away from Jolene the Dish Girl and on down the cobblestoned drive.

"Don't say a word until I get you in the car and down the street," he said in a voice only I could hear. His mustache tickled my ear. "She could've had you locked up."

"What for?"

"Terroristic threats to start with. You've got a violent temper, Miss Reid."

We were almost to the car. "Don't even go there with me, Detective."

"Hey," he said, opening the passenger side door, "I'm not the one getting my tail in a sling."

I looked back at Vernell's castle, with his truck still blasting away and Jolene tugging at Vernell's deadweight, drunken body. *I could have it a lot worse*, I thought, *I could be her*. It was just like Mama always said: Don't go coveting your neighbor's husband, 'til you've walked a mile in his wife's shoes.

Detective Weathers pulled slowly away from the curb. He didn't say another word and I was not in the mood to insert my foot any farther into my mouth. It was occuring to me that my profile was a little too high when it came to the police. I'd have to find another way to elude Weathers while still getting the information I needed.

As if reading my mind, Weathers looked over at me. "So, who's little red wagon are you gonna go upsetting next?" he asked.

"I went to see my daughter," I said calmly. "When her father showed up, obviously inebriated, I drove him home. I did it as much for Sheila as for him. When Vernell gets off the wagon like this, it's an embarassment to the entire family, especially a vulnerable teenaged girl."

We were pulling into the strip shopping center, heading for the parking space next to my Beetle.

"That's what you want me to believe," he said.

"Actually, I don't give a dead rat's ass what you believe," I answered. "I know the truth."

Weathers turned to look at me, his arm stretched along the back of my seat, almost touching my shoulder. The Taurus now rested in its slot beside my little car. "Exactly," he said. "You know the truth. That's all I want from you, Maggie, the truth." He let his fingers slip down until they rested lightly on my shoulder. I froze as he gently caressed the side of my neck.

"I haven't lied to you yet," I lied, but my heart wasn't in it. What was he doing to me? I turned and reached for the door handle. If I stayed any longer, I'd be trapped telling one lie after another, or worse, falling under the spell he seemed to weave with no effort at all.

"Before you go," he said softly, the dangerous

tone back in his voice, "I have a couple of things for you to think about." He pulled his hand back, straightening up ever so slightly.

"And what would that be?" My heart was pounding again. I could feel him watching me, smell his cologne, hear the soft squeak of his leather jacket as he moved ever so slightly toward me. *Touch me again. Just one more little touch. . . .*

"Sheila didn't go to work Wednesday night for one," he said.

"Well, big deal. Everybody gets a night off now and then," I answered, suddenly feeling my heart leap to my throat. *No, no, no.*

"She told her stepmother she had to work, but she called her boss and said she was sick."

I didn't say anything. I couldn't.

"She told me she went shopping," he said slowly, "but I don't believe her. Would you know anything about that?"

"When were you persecuting my daughter? Why wasn't I there?" My voice jumped. I sounded guilty. I just knew I did.

"I talked to Sheila yesterday, in my office, with her father and stepmother present. I was interviewing her just like I did you. She is not a suspect."

I wanted to reach across the seat and tear into him. I wanted to beat him. All thought of romance had vanished. I wanted to hurt him for ever coming near my little girl. Instead I forced myself to stay still. I couldn't put Sheila in jeopardy by showing my fear.

"I'm late for work again," I said, my voice controlled. I reached for the door handle, then decided

I had enough reserve to play his game. "There was something else you wanted me to think about?" I hoped I sounded cool, as if Sheila's whereabouts at the time of the murder were inconsequential.

"Oh, yeah, I almost forgot." He leaned over toward me. "I thought we might talk about the night before Jimmy's wedding. I just thought you might like a chance to tell me your side of the story."

I jumped out of the car and slammed the door. Who'd talked this time? Who in their right mind would've told him about that little episode? The answer came as quickly as the question. Roxanne.

14

That night, the Golden Stallion was hopping. The all-male dance revue, the Young Bucks, were in town and strutting their stuff on the dance floor. It was a sight to behold. A tribe of young farm boys, their muscles pumped, their hair perfectly slicked back against work-tanned skin, wearing their jeans tight enough to cause concern about future progeny. It was all happening right in front of me, and I had all I could do to keep my mind focused on the job at hand.

Weathers knew much more about me than I knew about him. The Digger story was one thing. I figured Weathers brought that up just to show off how much he was capable of finding out. That story wasn't going to hurt me, not like the story of Jimmy's wedding rehearsal dinner. Now that could hurt me.

Jack sidled up while I sang "My Heart's on Fire, but Your Hands Are Still Cold." It was a rowdy little tune about a drunken cowboy who loses his love to another. I had the Young Bucks restless and the cowgirls breathless, just urging them on. If anyone in the place went home lonely tonight, they'd have only themselves to blame.

"Evelyn needed my car tonight," Jack said, between verses. "Can you give me a ride again?"

I looked over at him and nodded. Who in the world was this Evelyn, and why wasn't she coming to pick him up? She'd lose him to someone if she kept up this kind of behavior. Of course, if she was anything like Jack, they probably had some open type of arrangement. Hell, she probably lived with two or three guys in a commune somewhere.

I could never stand for that, I thought. *I'm a one-man woman.*

The song came to an end and Sparks gave the band the nod to go into their break tune.

"Folks, we'll be right back," he announced. "Gotta tend to a little business, if you know what I mean." He laughed, as did the crowd. All I had on my mind was some fresh air and a little solitude. Sometimes watching all those couples together out on the dance floor really got to me.

I pushed my way backstage, past the stage-hands and groupies waiting to transact business with the boys in the band. I stepped out onto the fire escape and walked over to my car. No one ever looked for me there, especially if I didn't crank the engine, and slid down in the seat where I wouldn't be noticed. I needed time to think.

* * *

Jimmy got married in August five years ago. At the time, we all figured we knew why. Had to be that Roxanne was pregnant. Jimmy had practically made a career out of avoiding marriage. But with Roxanne, he was announcing his engagement a mere four weeks after he'd met her. And the engagement wasn't even announced in the traditional manner.

At the time, me, Vernell, and Sheila were living out in Oak Ridge on what Vernell referred to as a "gentleman's farm." What it really was, was a brick three-bedroom ranch that sat on four acres. Vernell figured that because it took a riding lawn mower to cut the grass and because there was a detached garage in the shape of a barn, he could call it a farm.

It was pretty, though. The house sat up on a little rise, set back from the road. A porch spanned the front of the house, and in the summer we'd sit out there and watch the cars passing by and the corn growing in the fields across the street where the real farmer lived. We were sitting out there the afternoon Jimmy came to announce that he was gonna marry Roxanne.

His little red pickup swung into our dusty dirt driveway, spinning out as it rounded the corner and slinging gravel everywhere.

"Wonder what the hell bee's got up his butt," Vernell muttered, watching Jimmy push his truck up the hill. "Probably got trouble out to the lot again. You know, I'm getting sick of his lazy ass. Don't take a rocket scientist to run a business. If the boy can't handle it, he ought to get somebody in there who can. Hell, he could put in a manager and go play golf all day and make more money than he is running it himself."

I didn't say a word. It was the same-old same-old as far as I was concerned. The Spivey brothers fought about everything, constantly. And they were worse when one or both of them had been drinking.

"Hellfire," Vernell said, rising up out of his rocker. "And here it is about supper time. Darned if that boy don't smell you cookin' from across town. Jimmy!" he yelled out, stepping down off the porch. "You're tearing up my yard!"

His yard! Vernell figured his outdoor duties were discharged when he bought me a used John Deere riding mower.

Jimmy stepped down out of his truck, his Braves cap twisted around backward and a Bud Lite in his hand. We were headed for trouble, I thought. Maybe food would sober him up.

"Hey, Jimmy," I called. "Come on in. You're just in time for dinner."

"Cain't stay," he yelled, like maybe with me being ten feet away I couldn't hear him speak in a normal tone. "I just come to tell you something." He was looking straight at me, ignoring his brother completely.

"Now, Jimmy," I said, standing up and preparing not to take any of his nonsense, "I made your favorite, fried chicken."

He hesitated, then took a few steps toward the porch. "Greens or beans?" he asked.

"Beans with taters. Cornbread with cheese.

And for dessert, I made a banana cream pie. So come on." I wouldn't have let him leave anyhow. Any fool could see he was drunk.

Jimmy walked straight as an arrow to the porch steps and sank down on the top one. "Banana cream?" His eyes had unexpectedly filled with tears and the hand holding the beer began to shake. "Aw man, I sure am gonna miss your cooking."

I sank down beside him. Vernell was eyeing Jimmy as if he were a subspecies. In Vernell's world, even a drunk man ought not cry.

"Jimmy, now you know Vernell's just kidding when he gets on to you. He don't mean nothing by it when he teases you for coming to eat so often." Okay, so Jimmy ate with us more than he did his own mama. I didn't mind. "We like having you here, don't we, Vernell?" I gave Vernell a nasty look and he grunted in our direction, still eyeing Jimmy the way a hound eyes a skunk.

"Not no more," Jimmy cried balefully, "I'm getting married. Next Saturday."

This galvanized old Vernell into action. "No wonder you's all emotional!" he yelled. "You about to go and let loose of your freedom. Hellfire!" Vernell let out a loud rebel yell. "Who's the lucky jailer, I mean, woman?"

I stood up and pulled Jimmy with me. "We'll talk about it over supper," I said. "When's the last time you ate, Jimmy?"

"I don't know," he said, not sounding at all like a lucky bridegroom.

"Well, that's your problem, son. You need

something on your stomach. A man can't live by beer alone."

I led Jimmy into the kitchen, Vernell following, but still maintaining a healthy distance in case his brother were to start emoting again. They both sat at the table, content to let me run around the kitchen, setting out plates and silverware. The scent of fresh fried chicken and moist southern corn-bread danced across the roomy kitchen. It was my favorite time of day, the time when smells and sounds outweigh the reality of a home fraught with tension and too little love between partners.

I tried to stay busy and let Vernell and Jimmy do the talking, but I became aware that Jimmy was watching my every move, and pitching his voice so it would carry to me. I started to get a bad feeling about Jimmy's engagement, especially in light of the facts as they began to emerge.

"Her name's Roxanne," I heard Jimmy say. "She's a widow-lady. I met her out at Mama's Country Showplace." Great place to meet women, I thought, in a honky tonk made famous for the quality of its Saturday night bar fights.

"She used to skate derby for the Rockettes, but she blew out her knee. Got tripped up by a rival."

"How long have you known her, Jimmy?" I couldn't help asking.

"Four weeks. That was long enough for me. I know, you're thinking four weeks ain't much of a time to know no one, but I know all I need to know. She's it."

Vernell snickered and Jimmy just sat there. Any other time, Jimmy'd have been at his throat for insinuating. Jimmy didn't seem to care.

"Do you love her? Have you met her folks?" I couldn't help myself.

"Maggie," he sighed, "it's time. I can't wait forever, and it's time." The remark flew right over Vernell's head. Jimmy was getting married on account of desperation and loneliness. He was giving up on the notion of waiting for me to leave Vernell and marry him.

I did everything I could that night to bring my foolish brother-in-law to his senses, but with Vernell there, I couldn't speak directly. I tried all that week to hunt Jimmy down, because he was avoiding me. He knew I'd talk him out of marrying Roxanne, the twice-before married, ex–roller derby queen.

I didn't see Jimmy again until the night before the wedding. That's when all the trouble broke lose, and that's when I knew for certain that Roxanne and I would never have a sisterly relationship.

The rehearsal dinner, hastily arranged by Mrs. Spivey, was held at the Twilight Supper Club out off Route 29 on the way to Reidsville. It was held there for two reasons. It was the elder Spiveys' favorite place to spend Saturday night. And because they were regulars, it was the only place in town where they could secure affordable accomodations on such short notice.

The Twilight was a Greensboro institution. Set up shortly after World War II as a dance club to entertain the returning young Greensboro natives, it had not changed in the intervening forty-odd years. The house band that played all the big band favorites was still there, with most of the original members. The front door was padded with quilted leather and a big "T" adorn the door, traced out with large brass upholstery tacks.

Mrs. Spivey arranged the evening personally with Travis Dean, now an elderly man in his seventies. She rented a bus to pick us all up and had Flora's Bakery concoct a cake that she kept carefully concealed in a huge white box. She assured us that it was going to be an evening to remember.

The fact that Mrs. Spivey despised Roxanne on sight and principle made no difference in the evening's plan. Mrs. Spivey was just happy to be marrying Jimmy off. The way she seemed to figure it, a man in his early thirties, unmarried, was bound to be a reflection of his mother's shortcomings, and Mrs. Spivey was not a woman to have shortcomings. She had worked for Cone Mills for almost forty-three years, had risen to the rank of shift supervisor, and she did not take anything off anybody at any time. This included her sons and her weak-minded, passive little husband, Vernell Senior.

By the time the bus rumbled up our Oak Ridge driveway, forty minutes before the festivities were due to start at the Twilight, Mrs. Spivey had worked up a good head of steam. She was a large-boned woman with dyed auburn hair, rhinestone-rimmed, oversized glasses, and huge cubic zirconia rings which she flashed at every opportunity. Because she had arranged for a bartender and a bar to come along with the bus, she and every other

member of the wedding party were well on their
way to being intoxicated.

When Vernell stepped up into the bus and saw
that he was behind the others, he made a beeline for
the bartender. I stood up by the driver and took
stock of the situation.

The only person on the bus I could not
identify was the woman who turned out to be
Jimmy's intended, Roxanne. Roxanne five years
ago was nothing like Roxanne today. In fact, when
we saw her, Vernell and I each drew in a sharp
breath, for what turned out to be different reasons.
Vernell was impressed by Roxanne's cup size, while
I was struck by the similarities between the two of
us. Other than, of course, our physical measure-
ments.

Roxanne was short, like me, only shorter, and
she had bright red curly hair, the very same shade
as mine. I looked from her to Jimmy and saw him
smiling, a triumphant, what-do-you-think-of-that?
smirk. I just shook my head. Now I knew for certain that something had to be done.

By the time the reconverted school bus rolled
into the Twilight parking lot, there wasn't a sober
Spivey in the lot. Mrs. Spivey led the parade down
out of the bus and into the Twilight, her fake fur
coat flapping wildly behind her, the big white cake
box nearly obscuring her view of the pathway to
the front door.

Roxanne and Jimmy followed the elder Spiveys
down out of the bus. She clung to his arm, staring up
at him through the lace of her veil which she had
insisted upon wearing during the rehearsal, which

had, by the way, been held on the bus. The preacher Mrs. Spivey had lured into performing the ceremony held the door for the happy couple. He clung to it more for support than as a gesture of good manners. He, too, had fallen from the wagon of faith and into the quagmire of intoxication.

We made such a loud and unruly entrance into the supper club that even the Two-Tones, who were slap in the middle of "Begin the Beguine," were forced to quit playing. At a signal from Mr. Dean, the band broke into a rousing version of "Here Comes The Bride."

Jimmy and Roxanne processed in a slow, weaving pace down the middle of the dance floor, their bodies bathed in the eerie red light of the dining room. For a moment, the Spivey family looked almost normal. Happy, laughing, barely weaving with the alcohol, the Spiveys had decided to put on a good show for their Jimmy.

The evening progressed at a rapid pace, or else the Mai Tais I swilled were working to collapse time in upon itself. The happy couple was toasted. The steaks arrived. And soon, people began to wander away from the table, heading for the dance floor or back to the bar. Mama Spivey's head was drooping over her empty plate. Pa Spivey had taken the opportunity to sneak onto the dance floor with one of the waitresses, and Roxanne left to go powder her nose. Jimmy, momentarily unaware of my presence, relaxed.

He was eating his steak, his dark hair falling over the side of his face, his jaws working with the concentrated effort of chewing. For a moment he looked just like what he really was, a sad little boy.

"I want to talk to you," I said, "and I'm not taking no for an answer." I didn't have to speak loudly, I was only four seats away, but still the sound of my voice startled him. He looked up, blushed, swallowed, and paused with his fork halfway to his lips.

"Maggie, don't." He had a determined look on his face, as if keeping me from speaking would save him from thinking about what he was about to do with Roxanne.

"We have to talk, Jimmy. You're doing this for the wrong reasons." I leaned closer and spoke a little louder as the bandleader soloed on his tenor sax.

"You're killing me!" Jimmy said, his voice carrying suddenly, as the bandleader brought the song to a close. Jimmy flushed and stuck the uneaten forkful of food in his mouth.

Mrs. Spivey, who'd been half asleep, jerked to attention and whipped her head around to see the cause of Jimmy's distress. Her eyes narrowed when she spotted me.

"Maggie! Leave him be!" I realized then that Jimmy's unrequited love had not gone completely unnoticed. Jimmy was supremely embarrassed. He blushed even redder, pretended to choke, and looked down at his lap.

"Mrs. Spivey, he doesn't love her. That's my only beef with the whole deal."

Jimmy was carrying his coughing fit a little too far, bringing his hands up to his neck, jerking in his seat. Just like a Spivey to overact.

"It don't matter," Mrs. Spivey yelled. "He can't

go around the rest of his life mooning after his brother's wife!"

Jimmy slipped to the floor, sliding under the table. Even for a Spivey, this was a bit much. His face was a dusky red, and his eyes had rolled back in his head. I didn't waste any time at all. I ducked down under the table, crawling my way over to the disabled Jimmy.

Above me, I heard Ma Spivey screaming. "You two get up from under there!" I don't what she thought I was doing, but the reality was enough for me to handle.

"Jimmy! Can you hear me?" His face was a mottled reddish blue. I bent my head close to his mouth. Not a sound. That's about when Roxanne reappeared from the ladies' room.

"What the hell's going on here?"

I had my fingers halfway down Jimmy's throat. I didn't feel anything, so I sealed my lips over his and blew. Roxanne bent down and peered under the table.

"Jimmy! Oh my God!" She was gone, standing upright and screaming at Ma Spivey. "They're making out under the table! At my wedding rehearsal!"

This brought the band to a standstill and the wedding party on the run. I felt them stampeding, the floor trembling beneath me as I struggled with the dead-weight Jimmy.

"Help me get him out!" I yelled, but the others were too busy listening to Roxanne to hear me. I flipped Jimmy on his stomach, knelt behind him and tried to pull him up. I formed my hands into a knot by his diaphram and pulled as hard as I could.

Someone pushed me aside.

"Leave my wife alone!" Vernell yelled.

He grabbed Jimmy from my arms, attempting to haul him out from under the table, his arms wrapped around his brother's torso.

With a sudden jerk, Jimmy's body flew up. Vernell staggered backward under the weight of his brother, and a huge wad of steak went flying from Jimmy's mouth, past me and across the table into Mrs. Spivey's lap.

Jimmy gasped, his eyes fluttered, and he awoke just as Vernell's fist went flying toward his face.

Ma Spivey screamed "Stop!", but it was too late. Jimmy sank to the floor again and Vernell stared wide-eyed, from me to his mama.

"I heard it all!" Ma Spivey exclaimed. "Jimmy said she was killing him!"

Roxanne lunged toward me, but someone grabbed her, holding her back. Jimmy was coughing and writhing around on the floor, struggling to scramble to his feet.

"He was choking! Did y'all not see the hunk of steak?"

They ignored me, all yelling at once. Jimmy struggled to his feet, a dazed look on his face.

"What happened?" he asked.

The wedding party turned on him, all talking at once. It was a huge mess. Somehow, Jimmy pursuaded a reluctant and suspicious Roxanne to believe that he had choked and we were not kissing. With Jimmy's testimony, Ma Spivey and the others were forced to accept that I had not tried to kill my brother-in-law, but you could see in their eyes that some doubt remained. Especially with Ma Spivey and Roxanne.

I looked back on that night, five years ago, and I could see how Marshall Weathers had gotten the wrong impression of me again. Out in the country we used to say, "If it walks like a duck, talks like a duck, and smells like a duck, it's probably a duck." But I wasn't a murderer, no matter what I smelled like.

"Are you coming inside or are you gonna sleep in the car?" Jack had snuck up on me, at least it felt that way. In all probability, I'd been lost in my memories. He leaned against the front fender, waiting for me to move.

"Go on ahead," I said, stirring. "I'll be in in a minute."

"You all right?" he asked, concern mirrored in his eyes.

"Finer than frog hair split down the middle." I didn't meet his gaze for long.

He shrugged and turned away. That was something I liked about him. If I said I was fine, then he let me be fine, no matter what evidence there was to the contrary. When I stepped out of the car, he was disappearing inside the club without a backward glance.

I'd reached the stairs, almost to the back door, when I heard the *ping* and saw a tiny flash of light. It took the second shot for my brain to register that someone was shooting at me.

I think I screamed. I know I ran for the door,

grasping at the handle, ducking down, every nerve in my body painfully tingling with fear. I half fell in the back door, too scared to do more than run for the first person I saw. Cletus.

"Help me!" I yelled. My body was at war. Part of me was scared to death, the other part, numb with denial. *Don't be silly! No one shot at you!*

Cletus, for his part, responded like a bouncer, instantly and with a sense of authority, no rushing, just steady, solid presence. He stood next to me, muscles bulging, dressed all in black, his bald head gleaming in the club lights, a tiny earpiece and wire running down to a small box clipped to his waist. Cletus was on the job.

"What happened?" he asked, his eyes scanning behind me, running to the sides, looking for trouble. I pointed to the back door; by now the denial side of my body had won out. I was calm, even a little embarassed.

"Out there," I said. "I think somebody shot at me." The band, unaware of my situation, saw me and went into my intro. I had to get back on the stage. A new thought entered my mind and blew away the denial. "What if the shooter came into the club? What if he was already in the club?"

Cletus spoke into his walkie-talkie. Across the room, I saw two of the security staff begin to move, one toward the back door and one out the front. The guy working the front door picked up the phone.

"Clete, what if he's in here?" I asked.

"He didn't come in here with a gun," Cletus answered calmly.

"How do you know?"

Cletus looked at me. "I know," he said. "You're all right."

I was facing a dilemma: Did I trust Cletus to really know the club? In the six months I'd worked here, nothing had ever happened. But someone had just tried to shoot me.

The band was coming up on my spot. I either ran up those stairs now or missed another intro and faced Sparks after the set. I ran. After all, it was my job and I needed it. I'd just have to trust that Cletus could do his job. I grabbed the mike and walked out onto center stage.

He was too hot to handle.
He said, "Baby don't touch."
I said, "I live for the moment,
I ain't asking for much."
You've never had trouble,
you never had style.
Well son, you're fixing to tumble
'cause I'm totally wild.

The Young Bucks were back on the dance floor. The night was coming to its hormonal peak. This was the last set, the last chance for the unattached to hook up before the bartenders announced last call and the houselights went up. Alcohol was having its desired effect on the crowd. Anyone who wanted to dance was out on the floor, with or without a partner.

Jack wandered up. "Why're the cops back?" he asked.

I looked out past the dance floor. Two uniformed officers stood talking to Cletus. He'd called the cops.

"Someone shot at me out in the parking lot, right after you went inside."

I looked behind the two officers, expecting to see Weathers. If he was there, he hadn't come inside.

Jack grabbed my arm. Sugar Bear was playing the last few measures of the song. The dancers whirled around the floor, oblivious to everything but their carefully timed steps and twirls. Jack and I were standing in the eye of the evening's storm.

"He didn't . . . You're . . ." Jack was at a loss.

"He didn't hit me. I'm fine." I turned away from him and stepped back to the mike. I didn't want to think about it. I wanted to be inside the music. I wanted to be alone. I wanted to be the singer, not the victim.

15

Jack let me stay inside myself. We rode all the way home in silence. The police had come and taken their report. They weren't the same officers that I'd come to expect. They were young, and if they knew anything about me and Jimmy, they didn't say. They didn't seem surprised that someone had shot at me. In this part of town, on High Point Road, gunfire on a Saturday night was nothing new.

Cletus had escorted us to my car and made a big show of checking it out before I could drive off.

"We'll take good care of you, Maggie," he said, resting a big, beefy hand on my shoulder. "Probably somebody got liquored up and didn't watch where they were shooting." I nodded, but I didn't believe that for a second.

"Did the police find anything when they

looked around?" I stared across the lot, suddenly seeing bad guys behind every car and shadow.

Cletus shook his head. "No, only thing they found was a couple of thirty-eight casings. That's all."

Jack stayed silent, lost in his thoughts. That was just how I wanted it. He seemed to sense this and left me alone, even after we got back to his place. He wandered over to the woodstove and busied himself stoking it, then adjusting the vents. I walked around the open space, unable to relax. Those shots fired in the parking lot had something to do with Jimmy. I could feel it.

I heard the sound of a wine cork softly popping, then the sound of liquid hitting the back of a glass. I stood in front of the CD player, staring blankly at the equipment.

"Here," he said, appearing by my side with a glass of red wine.

"Thanks, but I don't drink red wine," I said. Red wine didn't do much for me. Too dry.

"Try it," he said.

I took the glass, like a good guest, and brought it to my lips. It wasn't bad. I liked the way it slid down my throat without burning. It reminded me of the berries on my grandma's place, just before we picked them for jam-making.

Jack punched a button on the CD player. Jesse Winchester began singing "Yankee Lady."

"You like this, don't you?" he asked. "I saw it was on here, so I figured you were listening."

I nodded and took another sip of wine. My stomach felt warm when the wine hit. My shoulders were beginning to loosen up. I went and stood by the tall window that went from the loft upstairs all the way to the floor downstairs. Outside, the moon glowed, almost full. Jesse Winchester sang about leaving Vermont.

Why couldn't I find a man like Jesse Winchester, I wondered. A strong rich voice, singing about loving women. I bet he didn't take potshots at women. I took another couple of sips of wine and let my body sway softly. I bet Jesse wouldn't spend all his time drunk, forgetting he had a family waiting at home for him.

Jack's red wine was probably one of the most delicious liquids ever invented, I thought, finding myself near the bottom of the glass. My face felt flushed, and I realized that I felt a little floaty. *Shouldn't be drinking wine on an empty stomach*, I thought, but that didn't stop me from holding out my glass when Jack came around with the bottle.

"It's good," I said.

"I like it right much," he said. I was humming along with Jesse. Jack put the bottle down on top of the CD player and turned to face me. Then he reached out for my wine glass, taking it from my hand and setting it down next to the wine bottle.

"Come here," he said softly. "Let's dance."

I didn't move.

"Come on, Maggie. It's the Tennessee waltz."

I stared at him. "I can't," I said finally.

"Sure you can." He laughed. "It's just a dance."

"No," I said, suddenly feeling like a panicked, tearful child. "I can't, Jack."

Jack dropped his arms to his side. "Why not?"

I took a deep breath and let the words fly out in a rush of air. "Because I can't dance."

There, I'd said it. I hated being asked to dance. It was worse than anyone knew, because with all my heart, I wanted to dance, but couldn't. A memory jumped back into my head, the same one that always came. Me and Darlene in dance class, dressed in pink leotards and tutus. Darlene gliding effortlessly across the floor, and me frozen, unable to tell right from left, the last to cross the floor, the baby elephant.

I wasn't going to cry. I bit the inside of my lip and started to reach for my wineglass. Jack grabbed my hand.

"Come here," he said again. This time he moved into me, sliding his arm around my waist. "You can do this."

He didn't know me. He didn't know how I felt.

"Maggie, relax. Close your eyes and breathe. Just let me hold you."

I hesitated, staring at him, trying to figure out what he really wanted. But he looked so genuine, I started to feel foolish for not humoring him. I did it. I let Jack play his New Age games. I'm sure he knew I didn't like it, but he didn't give up.

"Okay, let your head rest on my shoulder." He was swaying softly, taking me with him. Jesse sang softly about Bowling Green. The wine was a tranquilizer, moving me with him. Jack smelled like exotic spices and I inhaled deeply.

"Mag, you're doing it. That's it." I swayed against him. He slowly whirled me around, gently teaching my feet to move. Then the song ended and the next one was faster. I moved to push out of his arms.

"Maggie, stay. You can do this."

"No, I can't."

He handed me my wine glass. "Take another sip," he instructed. I took more than one.

"Hey, girl," he sang along with Jesse, and whisked my glass away. He was moving, his arms holding mine, forcing my body to move along with his. My feet were actually going! I laughed, delighted.

"That's it! See!"

Jesse was singing about letting go and I did. I was someone else. I was a dancer. Jack was humming, smiling, his eyes closed, totally involved in the music. We danced. I don't know for how long, maybe an hour, maybe more. Suddenly I became aware that the music had stopped and we were still moving, slowly.

Jack opened his eyes and smiled. "See? You're a dancer. I knew you were a dancer." He brought his hand up and softly pushed my hair away from my face. His face was inches from mine. My heart started to race and I realized that Harmonica Jack was about to kiss me, and that furthermore, I was going to let him!

His eyes softened and he smiled at me, his face coming closer to mine. I closed my eyes, still not believing that this was really happening. Jack's fingers cupped my chin. Just as I felt the whisper of his lips upon mine, someone beat on the loading bay door, making us both jump.

"What in the hell?" Jack jerked back, alarm replacing tenderness.

"What time is it?" I asked, looking at the clock in the kitchen. It was just after six A.M.

Jack had moved to the door, grabbing a wooden bat that stood beside the refrigerator.

"Do you think we should open it?" I asked, but I meant, *Are you nuts? Don't open that door!*

The banging started again and Jack hit the garage door button. The door hadn't moved six inches when I called out to Jack.

"Put the bat down. It's the law."

Weathers was wearing black snakeskin boots this time, with silver tips on the toes. Damn his hide!

He was smiling, dressed in black pants and a crisp white cotton shirt.

"Good morning, folks," he said, smiling like this was a social call. "Saw your lights on as I was on my way to work." His eyes glided past Jack, over to the window. The sonofabitch had been watching us!

"Detective Weathers," he said, extending his hand to Jack. "How're you doing?" He didn't wait for an answer. "I need to borrow Ms. Reid for a little while, if I may?"

I stepped up between the two men. "I'm really tired, Detective," I said, "perhaps it could wait."

Weathers's eyes glistened. He loved this.

"Well, this is kind of time-sensitive," he said. "I find it best to move on these things while they're fresh in folks' minds." He took a step back, looking toward his car. "Do you need a coat or anything? It's kind of cold out there."

"No, I don't need a coat," I fumed. *And you'd be the last one to know if I did,* I thought. "Let's get this over with."

I walked past the two men, toward Weathers's car.

"Maggie," Jack called. I turned around. "Here," he said, tossing me the remote door opener.

It was his way of letting me know he'd be there, waiting.

Weathers was already cranking the engine when I reached the car. He didn't look at me, just put the car into reverse and backed out of his parking space.

"So, is this the big downtown talk?" I asked. We were headed straight toward the police station and I knew what that meant. Weathers was fixing to spend hours asking me questions. But instead of turning onto Eugene, he drove straight past, heading away from the municipal plaza.

"So where are we going?"

"I just thought we'd ride a little bit," he said, but I could tell he had a destination in mind.

It was an early fall morning in Greensboro; ordinarily I might've enjoyed it, but when Weathers turned onto Mendenhall, I knew where we were going. Weathers was taking me to my house. For a moment, I didn't know what to say. If I told him I didn't want to go to my place, then he'd be all the more determined. I was sure of one thing, Weathers wanted me to be uncomfortable. It just seemed to be his main goal in life.

I could tell he was waiting for my reaction. I

could feel him watching me from the corner of his
eye, so I settled back and tried to pretend I was
enjoying the ride.

"What a pretty morning," I said. "Leaves are
just starting to turn."

He grinned a little to himself. "Uh-huh."

He turned down the little back alley that ran
behind my bungalow, made a sharp right, and
pulled up into the tiny backyard, just like I always
did. He cut the engine and turned to face me for the
first time.

"Wanna go inside?" he asked.

"Aw, I'm sorry," I said. "If I'd known you
wanted to come here, I'd have brought my keys." I
shrugged my shoulders. "But I don't have them
with me!"

Weathers pulled his keys out of the ignition
and smiled. "That's all right," he said, "I've got a
spare."

"A spare? How'd you get a key to my house?"

He pulled the door handle and started to leave,
the keys jingling in his hand.

"Wait!" I said, but he didn't. He was out of the
car, heading up my back steps before I could get
out of the car and go after him.

"Detective, stop!"

He turned around and looked at me, his eyebrow raised in a question mark, his head slightly
cocked.

"What's the matter?"

"I don't want to go in there!"

He turned away from the back door and the
smug, cocky look was gone. He walked to the edge

of the top step and sat down, patting a place next to him. I stayed where I was, at the foot of the steps, watching him the way you might eye a wild dog.

"Why don't you want to go in there, Maggie?" he asked.

"I don't know," I lied. A swirl of emotion surged up, encompassing me. It wasn't my home anymore. I knew that now. It wasn't safe. Jimmy's blood stained my grandmother's rug. How could I ever go back there?

"I just want to go back to Jack's and get some sleep. I've been up all night." The wine was wearing off, leaving me in a fog.

"Didn't look to me like you were thinking about sleeping a little while ago."

"Well, that'd be none of your business, now would it?" I snapped.

He shrugged and smiled slowly. I found myself staring into his blue eyes a little too long, long enough for him to notice.

"I'm just thinking you could do better," he said. He leaned back against the step, his elbows resting on the deck behind him.

"Oh, right," I snapped, "like you, I suppose?" I don't know how the words flew out of my mouth. I could feel my cheeks heating up, and I looked away.

Weathers grinned and raised his eyebrow again. He had me. He reached slowly into his shirt pocket, carefully pulling out what looked like a picture.

"I bet you could even do better than this," he said, handing the photo to me.

"Oh my God," I said, sinking down onto the

steps, the picture clutched in my hand. How was it my life kept chasing me like a bad dream?

There I was, in my black bikini, six years ago, out on Holden Beach. Jimmy had his arms wrapped around me from behind, a mischevious grin on his face. We might've been any couple, any-where. Only trouble was, we were just clowning around.

"Where'd you get this?" I asked, already knowing the answer. I kept it in the back of my underwear drawer, a reminder to me that there had been a time when I looked good in a bikini. It was my motivation to remember my diet. Now it looked like just another link between me and my murdered brother-in-law.

"You guys searched my underwear drawer?" I asked. "And now you walk around with the key to my house on your key ring?" I couldn't believe it. If it wasn't bad enough that someone had come into my house and killed Jimmy, now the cops could root through my underwear any time they liked.

"Well," he said slowly, "not exactly."

"Not exactly? What does that mean, not exactly?" I jumped up off the step and whirled around to face him. With him sitting on the top step, and me standing just in front of him on the ground, we were eye-to-eye.

"We searched everywhere on the initial search warrant, Maggie. That's our job. But we can't just come and go into your house without cause."

"Then why do you have a key to my house?"

"I don't."

"You don't?"

Weathers shrugged his shoulders. "Nope."

"So, you were lying. Why?"

"To see what you'd do," he said.

I looked down at my boots. They were the sharpest-toed boots I owned and at that particular moment, all I could envision was kicking Weathers right in his shiny white teeth.

"I know you're mad," he said. "Hell, I'd be mad, too."

I looked up at him and he knew I didn't believe a word he said. "You know," I said, scuffing the ground with the toe of my boot, "the funny thing is, I'm more disappointed than mad." His eyebrow was up again. He hadn't expected this. "You see," I said, "I thought you were different. Vernell, Jimmy, hell, even Harmonica Jack, they've all got an agenda. I expect them to lie to me. But I thought you were a cut above. When I looked out onto the dance floor that first time I saw you, I thought to myself, Now there's a man you can trust. You can look right into those blue eyes and see he don't lie."

I coughed out a short, sarcastic laugh and stared at him like he was maybe a bad accident.

"Just goes to show you," I said, "what bad picker genes'll do." I drew myself up as tall as I could, straightened my shoulders, and looked him right in the eyes.

He stared right back, and where any other man might've started in with a host of sorry one-liners, he said nothing. I spun around and headed for the car. I didn't look back, didn't try to guess if he was following me. I just opened the door and sat down in the passenger seat, staring out the side window.

He stayed where he was for a moment, then slowly unfolded his long lanky body and walked toward the car. He sat in his seat for a moment, before reaching up to put the keys in the ignition and start the engine. Then he turned to face me.

"You know, Maggie, in this business people lie to me all day long. You come to expect it. Killers don't play fair, so you've gotta do whatever it takes to get to the truth. That's what I do, Maggie. I've been doing it so long, I don't even think about it. I just put in what's needed for a given situation. This ain't about genetics, Maggie, it's about a man's life wasted. So yeah, I set you up. But I do it just as much in hopes that you're innocent as I do in case you're not." His eyes were searing into mine, the little muscle in his jaw twitching. "And do I think you can do better than that?" he said, gesturing to the picture I'd thrown down on the seat beside me. "I know you can."

He looked away then, throwing the Taurus into reverse and backing out into my alley. He picked up the microphone that lay between us and barked into it. Weathers was back on the job, and for some inexplicable reason, I felt as if I'd missed something important.

Weathers pulled the Taurus right up in front of Jack's loading dock, put it in park, and sat waiting for me to leave. Funny thing was, now I didn't want to go. I felt like I wanted him to understand something about me, but I just couldn't lay my hand on what it was.

"That picture," I said, my thoughts trailing to a stop.

"Yeah?" His hand rested on the wheel, but he was watching me.

"That was six years ago. We were just clowning around at the beach." Weathers didn't say a word. He waited. "The Spiveys rent this big house at Holden Beach every year. It was kinda fun, you know?"

He nodded ever so slightly.

"I didn't come from a family that did stuff like that. It was one of the things I liked best about the Spiveys." I was taking up air space and saying nothing. But it was almost as if I had to keep moving my mouth to get around to what I was thinking.

"Jimmy was a sweet boy, Detective. He meant well, but he couldn't help himself. He just lacked ambition. I don't know what he would've done with the love of a good woman, but Roxanne wasn't the one. I tried to be like a big sister to him. I guess he took it wrong. But you should know this: I never did anything to make Jimmy think I loved him. I never violated my vows to Vernell. Not with anyone. Not ever."

Weathers had turned a little in his seat and was giving me his full attention.

"And I was plenty lonely, Detective. So you go on and check me out. You root through my underwear drawer and dig up my past. You take it to mean whatever you want, but you won't find a murderer. I'm guilty of a lot of things. I've been foolish in love, and probably gullible in situations you'd see coming a mile off. But I don't intentionally set out to hurt people, Detective, even when they've hurt me."

I reached down and picked up the photo of me and Jimmy. He looked so young and happy. Who in the world had killed him? He'd loved me, in his own lost-boy way, and somehow, I'd let him down. Not just by not loving him the way he wanted me to love him, but by not listening, not hearing something that might've saved his life. And now maybe I was the only one with sense enough to find his murderer. Maybe I was the only one who really cared. Vernell was stuck inside a bottle and Roxanne only wanted Jimmy's money. I looked at the picture again for a moment, remembering the crash of the ocean behind us, and the smell of the salty air that hot August day. Then I stretched out my hand and offered the picture to Weathers.

"You keep this," I said. "I don't need it anymore."

Weathers reached out and took the picture, and his fingers brushed mine. Our eyes met and held, the shock of skin on skin dancing up my arm, flipping my stomach over like the drop of a rollercoaster. He leaned across the seat and cupped my chin with his fingers. Ever so slowly and gently, Marshall Weathers kissed me. I melted into him, feeling myself sinking deeper and deeper.

He pushed back, his face inches from mine, looking deep into my eyes.

"Like I said, Maggie, you can do better."

I pulled away and turned to fumble with the door handle. I had to get out of the car because I'd suddenly had a memory that Weathers couldn't know about and I couldn't explain.

"How will I know, Mama?" I'd asked one

summer day out on the porch, the two of us swinging on the wooden porch swing.

"Honey," she'd answered, "when the right man comes along, you'll know."

Suddenly the air inside the car was too close, and my head was spinning. I was too tired. My mind was playing tricks on me, and I was too tired.

"Good-bye, Detective," I said, my voice coming out in a husky whisper.

"I'll be in touch," he said.

I couldn't look at him. Suddenly, I was eleven, sitting on the porch swing with Mama, while part of me, the adult Maggie, was running just as fast as she could.

I ran up the steps to the loading dock and hit the remote button. Behind me, I heard the crunch of Weathers's tires pulling away and I sighed with relief. The garage door moved too slowly, and all I could think about was getting inside. I half expected to see Jack, but the downstairs was empty, another relief. I didn't need to deal with any more men at this particular moment.

I wandered over to the couch and sat down, pulling off my boots and searching for a quilt all in the same move. I wasn't going upstairs. I was going to pull myself into a little ball, right there on the sofa, and sleep and sleep and sleep, until all my crazy thoughts went away.

16

I woke up suddenly, startled and disoriented, but wide-awake. I had been dreaming about something, something important, something about Jimmy, but whatever it was vanished as I opened my eyes. In front of me on the coffee table sat Jack's white coffee carafe, a clean mug beside it. Jack had come and gone, it seemed, and this time he had not left a note.

I poured a cup of his strong French roast and proceeded to indulge in my one secret passion: the motivational infomercial. Aside from being held hostage by the Bonita Faye cosmetic lady once every few months, infomercials were my main personal indulgence. Especially this one guy. He was a tall man who sat out by his pool, behind his mansion, talking about how I, too, could become more successful than my wildest fantasies.

He was always on. If I flipped through the cable channels, he would be waiting for me, and I knew almost every word of his message by heart. He was a poor child, outcast by his peers because of his immense size. But he believed in himself. He called upon the power within, and rose through the ranks to finally parlay himself into a multi-million dollar corporation. His eyes shone as he stared out at his beleagured audience. "You can do this," he'd urge. Then he'd bring on a bunch of shiney-eyed women, who all told tales of personal despair turned to gold.

This morning as I listened, I realized that I had been focusing on the wrong path. I had allowed myself to be caught up in the reality of my accusers. I had veered from the course to my financial success. There was a whole side to this situation that I had ignored. Jimmy was dead, there was no going back and fixing that situation, but he had left me a gift. I had a responsibility to myself, Sheila, and Jimmy's unsuccessful memory. If what Vernell said was true, and I had no reason to doubt him, I owned forty-nine percent of a very successful mobile home business and it was time to step up to the plate and assume responsibility for its continued success.

It was after two o'clock in the afternoon. For most of the business world, things would be winding down, but not the mobile home sales business. They seemed to be almost always open, that is, if Vernell's hours while we were married had been any indication. "We stay open until the last customer leaves satisfied" was their motto.

I stretched and poured a second cup of coffee. I was about to go down to the intersection of Holden Road and I–85 and claim my inheritance. If I knew Vernell, he'd be thinking that I was going to be a silent partner. He was probably thinking he could buy me out for a quarter the value of the business. Maybe that was why he'd been acting so peculiar and friendly. Maybe he was thinking I was an easy mark. Well, that might've been true a few years back, before I bought the Curley-Que Beauty Salon, but not now. It was time to look at the books.

I raced upstairs and hopped into the shower, my mind going ninety miles an hour with ideas. Mr. Motivation said that you must always dress like the successful person you intend to be. That was going to be a problem, as I had only country-and-western success clothes here and I wasn't going back to my place to hunt up a suit.

"They'll just have to deal with me as I am," I muttered to the shower. "Success is success, no matter what the costume."

I tried to tame my hair, pulling it back tight against my head, but curls insisted upon escaping, ringing my face. I toned down my makeup, but that only made my freckles pop through, and I looked like a teenager.

"That's all right," I said to my green-eyed mirror image, "once they meet up with the 'personal power deep within me,' they'll know they've met their match and I'm the one in charge."

I ran downstairs and poured another cup of coffee to take with me as I hit the road. Caffeine was my friend this afternoon and I had a feeling I was going to need all the friends I could get.

I sang as I drove across town, a song idea popping into my head. "He was a one-horse town on my freeway to love." I thought for a moment, searching for the next line as I drove past the coliseum. "I blew right by him. What was I thinking of?"

It was a beautiful September afternoon in Greensboro. The rainy summer had turned the leaves bright with fall color. When I'd first moved to Greensboro with Vernell, many years ago, I'd been afraid to live in such a big city. Now it felt like a small town, full of parks and neighborhoods.

The VW rumbled along down High Point Road, turning left onto Holden Road. I was almost there. A little edge of excitement began to gnaw at my stomach, or maybe it was hunger, since I hadn't eaten since yesterday. "Cast a commanding shadow," I muttered to myself, remembering Mr. Motivation's mantra for success.

Vernell and Jimmy's Mobile Home Kingdom was wedged in with a half-dozen other mobile home lots, all situated alongside I–85. "Prime location, Maggie," Vernell had claimed once. "Prime in terms of your customer visability and prime in terms of easy-on, easy-off for delivery."

I hadn't paid it much mind at the time. I hadn't been interested and back then, the Holden Road exit of I–85 had been viewed as out in the country. I'd never dreamed that Greensboro could extend so far in such a few years. Vernell and Jimmy's pasturelike lot was now a tiny wedge in a sea of single and double-wide trailers, all waiting for the right person to come along and claim their housing prize. Jimmy and Vernell specialized in "Been turned down everywhere else? Credit a mess?" customers.

"Hey," Vernell used to say into the camera, "if you got a job, we'll get you a home." The Mobile Home Kingdom, simply the best in the business. I laughed to myself as I pulled up in the parking lot, but it was to cover all the emotions and memories that threatened to spoil my good mood.

Vernell started the mobile home business with Jimmy right after we married. I'd been out to the lot countless times in the early days, even helped out with the office work back then. Now it was a thriving business that would live on without Jimmy. Jimmy'd been so proud when Vernell turned the day-to-day operations over to him. He'd strutted around the lot, sticking his chest out, prouder than Mama's king rooster. Where'd it gotten him? The business wasn't growing at the rate it had in the early days. It had "leveled out," as Jimmy liked to say, but he and Vernell were always arguing about it.

"What do you expect with all the competition?" Jimmy used to ask, but it was never enough for his brother. Nothing was ever enough for Vernell when it came to business and money.

I pulled the car right up to the double-wide that Jimmy had converted into a model/business office. There were plenty of customers, even this late in the day. The office had a ridge of brightly colored plastic flags flapping across the top of the roof, and country music blared through the loud-speakers. For a moment I was intimidated. What was I about to step into?

I didn't have time to give it any more thought. Just like a used car lot, the sales force smelled fresh meat and two salesmen started for me at the same time, coming from opposite directions. The larger man won, waving off his competition with a mere flick of the cigarette in his left hand.

He continued toward me, his eyes locking onto my face, but subtly taking in my physical appearance in a way that only a professional sleazeball can. He was over six feet tall, looked like he worked out with steroids, and had gold chains dripping down his chest like a throwback to *Saturday Night Fever*. He looked to be in his mid-thirties, with dull brown hair and hard, dark eyes.

"Hey, pretty lady," he said, as he got closer. He said it like we'd been intimate friends for years. "I'm Tommy Purvis, and this here's my lot. I am just the man to put you in the home of your dreams."

"I don't think so," I said.

"Pardon me?" Clearly he wasn't used to being shot down.

I had come with good intentions, but this man was flying all over me. "My lot" indeed. I stiffened my shoulders and looked square into his wide brown eyes.

"I said, I don't think so. Number one, this isn't your lot. You work here, but you don't own it."

"Well, now," he sputtered. "Technically . . ."

"Technically, I think I'd come a sight closer to owning this lot."

"Yes," he said, "at the Mobile Home Kingdom, the customer is king. And a pretty little thing such as yourself doesn't need to worry in Tommy Purvis's hands."

"But I'm not a customer. I'm Vernell Spivey's ex-wife. So I need to see the manager, Mr. Purvis."

His face was running through some changes. When I'd been a customer, he'd wanted to please me, but now I was the big boss's ex. He wasn't sure he owed me anything.

"Now, if this is about alimony or something such as that, your ex don't exactly come around here too often and we—"

"Mr. Purvis, it does not matter what it is about. The fact is, I want to see the manager and I want to see him now. So, if you can't point me in his direction, I'll just go on inside and find him myself."

"I'll go get him," he said.

"Just tell me where his office is," I said. I didn't want Tommy Purvis to have the opportunity to warn him.

"His office is the last room on the left as you go inside," he said. "But he's kind of tied up right now, and it might not be such a good idea to interrupt him. Besides, I'm the assistant manager. I can probably take better care of you than old Don anyday." He gave me his best smile and half-winked. I couldn't believe Jimmy'd hired an idiot like this, but then again, the boy probably led the lot in sales.

Behind us, a beat-up, blue pickup truck came skidding into the lot, roaring toward us almost as if the driver were out of control. I jumped forward toward the office and Tommy Purvis spun around to see what was going on. The truck stopped a mere foot or two away from where Tommy stood. The driver was yelling through the windshield, apparently at Tommy.

I took advantage of the confusion and headed for the business office. Behind me, I heard the truck's door swing open and a barrage of swear words, all directed at Tommy, his mother, and his future sons. Apparently I wasn't the only one who'd taken a disliking to Mr. Purvis.

When I stepped inside the model home and the door swung shut behind me, I could no longer hear the raised voices outside. I had entered Jimmy and Vernell's idea of mobile home excellence. It was quite different from the four-hundred-square-foot plywood shack Vernell had first erected on this lot. This was luxury and I found myself distracted.

The carpet was thick, plush, sculptured pile, the kind that swallows up your feet and sucks all the extra noise out of the air. Canned Muzak played softly in the background and the fireplace in the corner was lit, even though the air-conditioning had to run full blast to compensate for the heat. Ahead of me was a pure white kitchen, the kind I'd always dreamed of having, but never actually attained. Until Vernell's recent midlife crisis, he'd lived like a poor man, squirreling his money away or plowing it back into the business.

For a moment, I was lured into the manufactured home dream. That is, until I took a good look at the walls and saw the thin ridges and tiny buckles that indicated inferior quality.

The dream was further shattered by the thick

overlay of cigarette smoke that clung to the furniture and filled the air. Customers sat in front of desks, their heads bending over papers that the salespeople laid before them. I guessed at the drill. "Now what can you afford to pay a month?"

My destination was the closed door to the room in the back. I slipped through the kitchen, passing a bedroom converted into an office. File cabinets ringed the walls and papers were scattered everywhere. A phone on the desk showed at least four lines lit up, all blinking.

I stepped up to the last door on the hallway and paused outside, listening through the thin walls for the sound of voices. I didn't have to listen long.

"Well, that'd be your own damn fault, now wouldn't it?" a deep male voice rumbled. Silence, then: "No, now don't get all upset. It just complicates things at this end." More silence. He was on the phone. "We'll work something out. I'll do what I need to do at this end before that actually happens." Another spell of silence, then: "Me too, honey." There was another pause, then: "Damn it! Stupid airhead!"

I was about to turn the door handle when I heard another sound. A female giggle and a tiny squeal. That's when I opened the door.

"Oh!" I said. "I'm sorry. I didn't know you were with someone."

It was quite a vision. A heavyset man with prominent hair plugs and a red face sat behind a huge desk. Perched on the edge of the desk, exposing most of her thighs and leaning her big-chested body forward, was a redhead. A young, embarrassed redhead. She jumped like I'd shot her, but he recovered quickly and smiled, pushing her off the desk at the same time.

"Run on, Miss Sexton, I'll be in shortly to review those figures."

I just bet he would, too.

"Don Evans. Can I help you?" he said, rising from his chair. He wore a Ralph Lauren polo shirt and expensive chinos.

I stepped forward and extended my hand. "Maggie Reid," I said, "and Jimmy Spivey just left me his share of the business."

His face moved seamlessly from an expression of sorrow to one of open helpfulness. "Ah." He sighed. "I had heard that Jimmy had made some unexpected changes in his will. I'm sure you were as surprised as"—he paused here for a moment, searching for the right words—"well, as anyone would be at hearing such news. And after such an untimely death." Evans shook his head sadly. "I'm gonna miss old Jimmy," he said.

I looked around the little room and realized that this was Jimmy's office. His nameplate was sitting on the edge of a bookshelf, and the space where it had been on the desk was rimmed with dust. Don Evans had wasted no time at all in moving in.

"Well, being as how Jimmy left his share in the business to me, I figure he'd want me to take care of it. I know how much it meant to him," I said.

Don Evans moved from behind the desk, a sad smile on his face. "Of course," he said. "What a wonderful attitude. You don't have to worry about this place on a day-to-day basis. Jimmy had it all set up. He barely had to do a thing except collect the money!" He chuckled. "I run the everyday business of the lot. I keep up with the salespeople, the business end of things, gettin' your trailers set out on the lots, all that petty stuff."

"Well, that's wonderful to hear," I said, putting on my best smile. "I just thought I'd come down, introduce myself, and find out a little more about how things are done. I'm sure my accountant can explain the financials of the business."

I didn't actually see Evans stiffen, but he did, ever so slightly, and his tone dropped a little. "Accountant?" he asked.

"Mr. Evans," I said, "I'll be frank with you. Over the past six years, I've heard Vernell and Jimmy argue, I don't know how many times, about the business. They each had their side to it, and it was clear to me that they each had a different opinion of how things ought to go. I figure I'm going to need to learn all I can about this place so I can hold my own with my ex."

Evans had a frozen smile on his face. "Well, of course," he said. "I'll be happy to show you everything. Miss Sexton can explain the books. She's been our bookkeeper for five years now."

"Oh, I'm not one for numbers," I said, walking up to the desk and running my finger through the dust outline of Jimmy's nameplate. "I'll just let Jerry do all that."

I hadn't planned on this. Driving up, I hadn't had any idea of where I was going to go with the Mobile Home Kingdom, but suddenly the idea of an audit crystalized. The more Evans seemed to blow me off, the firmer I was in my resolve. Crazy Jerry Sizemore would be just the ticket for this case.

I met Crazy Jerry when I bought the Curley-Que. My lawyer recomended him, and I soon found out why: Jerry was the best in the business, never mind that he was completely crazy.

Jerry had roared up to the Curley-Que that first time on a Harley-Davidson motorcycle, a big one, chopped with a front end that extended further than the legal limit, I was sure. He wore a fringed suede jacket and a coonskin cap. His salt-and-pepper gray hair hung down to the middle of his back, and he had a ruby stud in his right ear. I hadn't wanted to hire him, but my attorney made me keep him.

He was a wild man, a Vietnam veteran who drank Wild Turkey and rode with bikers, but he was also brilliant. Jerry would get to the bottom of anything going on in the Mobile Home Kingdom, I felt sure.

"I'll have my accountant give you a call," I said. Evans was too wise to fight it, but the wheels were turning behind his eyes.

I stepped a little closer to Don Evans. "I can't stay too long today," I said. "But I thought it best that I stop by as soon as possible and introduce myself. I'm sure we'll work well together."

He didn't know what to say and I was sure he'd be on the phone to Vernell before my car was off the lot, but that was fine, too. On my way out, I popped in on Miss Sexton. She was staring intently at her computer screen, hoping I'd go away. I stood there for a second, watching her work. Another redhead, I thought. Poor old Jimmy.

"Miss Sexton," I said, stepping right up to her desk, "I'm Maggie Reid." She looked up, a flat, disinterested look on her face. "Jimmy left me his share of the business, so we'll be working together from now on." I let the words hang in the air for a moment, watching as they slowly filtered down through Miss Sexton's brain.

"My accountant will be coming by to look at the books. I'd appreciate all the help you can give him," I said. "Later on, after he's through, maybe we can get together and talk a little bit about the office."

"Yes, ma'am," she said. "We're all gonna miss Jimmy." A little tear welled up and spilled over her eyelid. Unless I missed my guess, she really meant it.

I left her there, dabbing gently at her eyes, and made my way out of the office. I'd had enough for my first vist. I'd know more after I sent Jerry in to nose around. I stepped out into the fresh air of the late fall afternoon and stood, surveying the vast lot of mobile homes. The blue pickup and angry driver had gone, but Tommy Purvis was entertaining another visitor.

He leaned against a late-model Thunderbird, his heavy butt jutting out into the late afternoon sunshine. From the way he had his torso half stuck into the driver's side, I figured it must've been a female admirer. I could've slid right past him, hopped into my car, and made a clean getaway, if not for the fact that Tommy's rear end and his girlfriend's Thunderbird were blocking my exit.

"Hey, Purvis," I called.

Tommy swung around, a displeased look on his face.

"Can you ask your girlfriend to move her car?" I asked.

The Thunderbird lurched forward suddenly, almost carrying Tommy with it. It didn't stop, careening with a rooster-tail of gravel as it left the lot. Tommy stared after the car in shock, but I knew why his female admirer had left so suddenly. It just wouldn't have done for a grieving widow like Roxanne to be caught flirting by her ex-sister-in-law.

17

I knew Jerry Lee Sizemore wouldn't disappoint me. His machine had been on when I'd called, but Jerry rarely answered the phone. "I don't like gettin' that personal with folks," he'd say. I knew otherwise. Jerry didn't answer the phone for two reasons: Half the time he was drunk, the rest of the time he was entertaining guests, usually women.

My lawyer explained it to me when she'd given me his name and number to call.

"Jerry Lee Sizemore doesn't have to work another day in his life. Back before he went to 'Nam, Jerry Lee was a geek, a financial genius, but a geek none the less. He invested in computers. Put that together with his partial disability payments, and Jerry could live out his days in modest comfort. Trouble is, Jerry runs to excess." She sighed, but there was a slight, knowing smile creeping across her face. It was the smile of a woman who's been there and liked what she found.

"Poor Jerry." She sighed again. "He's a genius. He'll take a look at the Curley-Que, and if it's right, no one'll know better than him. If he would only lay off the Wild Turkey and give up the hot tub . . ." She shook herself back to the present and handed me his card. "Have a good time," she said. "He's partial to redheads."

I'd called him that day. I was desperate to make the Curley-Que work. I was newly divorced and scared to death about my future. This just had to work.

His machine had come on after one ring.

"Tell me who you are," it barked. "Tell me what you want. And don't try and bullshit me with ideas. Just tell me the facts."

I was so thrown off by his message, I hung up. Then I rehearsed my message and called back. Jerry Lee Sizemore didn't surface for two whole days. Days that I spent anxiously waiting by the phone.

He called at two in the morning. I was sound asleep, but he sounded as if it were the peak of the day. He didn't apologize, just took down what information I had and hung up. Three days later, he turned up at my cottage.

I heard him long before I saw him. He rode his Harley without baffles, didn't care that it was against the law, and apparently didn't obey the helmet laws, either. I was outside planting pansies when he pulled up. He looked like any other biker with the exception of his fringed suede coat and his coonskin cap. I knew he wasn't anyone I knew or was likely to know, so I ignored him. When he strode up my little walkway and planted himself in front of me, I finally looked up. Jerry Lee Sizemore was one frighening individual.

"You Maggie?" he asked.

"Maybe."

"Well, you either are or you aren't," he said. "Wouldn't you be the one to know?"

I didn't say anything. I was staring at the bottoms of his tattered jeans and his black scuffed boots, hoping he'd go away.

"Here," he said, thrusting a manilla envelope into my hands. "The salon's a keeper if you want it. You want me to explain it to you?"

That's when I realized who he was and practically fell all over myself inviting him inside.

"You got anything to drink?" he asked once we were in my tiny dining room. He was tall, but then every man over five-feet-nine is tall when you're barely five-feet-two.

"Coke, tea, water?" I offered.

He gave me an impatient look. "Hell. I mean liquor."

"I've got the bottle of tequila from my honeymoon," I said, "but it's old and there's a worm in it."

Jimmy Lee Sizemore's eyes lit up. "That'll do nicely," he said. "Bring out two glasses."

"I don't drink that stuff," I said.

"You want to hear about this place or not?" he asked.

"What's one got to do with the other?"

Jerry pulled out a dining-room chair, swung it

around backward, and straddled it. He smelled faintly of chlorine and suede, and the ends of his long silvery hair were damp. Jerry Lee was not one hundred percent sober. And from the wrinkles around his fingertips, he had just pulled himself out of the hot tub to make his delivery.

"I don't drink alone," he said. "Counselor at the VA told me one time, if you drink alone you're an alcoholic. So get two glasses."

I stood there looking at him for about a second, then realized that he held the key to my new business, and got two glasses. At first I sipped the tequila while he swigged. Then, as the day leaned into late afternoon and I realized I was about to own something big for the first time in my life, I too swigged.

Jerry Lee Sizemore grew on me. Maybe it was the liquor. Maybe it was his pale gray eyes and that hurt dog look he got every now and then. Maybe it was the way he explained the details of my very first business venture, never belittling me, talking to me as if I actually knew what I was doing. Whatever it was, he had his effect, and soon I found myself sighing, just like my lawyer.

He never made a pass at me. Instead, he invited me out to his place the following afternoon, to sit in his hot tub, which now seemed to be the most ideal vision of ecstasy. I walked him to the door, or rather, he let me lean against him while he walked, absolutely straight, to the door. I stood and watched him carefully put on his coonskin cap, attaching an elastic strip under his chin to keep the relic in place while he rode. I could hardly wait for that next afternoon.

Fortunately, by morning, I had sobered up. I made polite apologies to his machine and escaped back into the pool of women that got away from Jerry Lee Sizemore.

That's why I was half surprised when Jerry Lee Sizemore didn't disappoint me by ignoring my call. I don't know how he knew where to find me, but he did, bursting into the Golden Stallion as I finished up the second set of the evening.

"So, you decided to join the living," he said, his voice filling up every molecule of space around us. "'Bout time. You were a prissy little thing a few years back." He eyed me up and down, those gray eyes taking in my purple suede miniskirt and traveling on down to my cowgirl boots. "Hey," he said, suddenly concerned, "you haven't gone and screwed up that hair salon, have you?"

"Jerry Lee, I am not working here because I'm a bad business woman. The salon is fine."

"Well, good then. It's about time you got your hands outta old ladies' hair and into something juicy!"

I ignored that and told him about my inheritance. He liked his facts crisp and sharp, with no *I thinks* or guesses involved. He didn't write anything down, didn't even appear to be listening all that well. He was winking at waitresses and obviously ogling the cute young things who waltzed seductively by. But I knew he was tracking every detail of what I said. Jerry Lee could do many things at one time.

"Give me a couple of days," he said finally. "This one's liable to be a bit complicated. Mobile home business'll run all kinds of scams on you."

"Like what?" I asked.

"Aw, you know, two sets of books, kickbacks from your set-up guys, your wholesalers. All kinds of crap."

Somehow I couldn't see Jimmy doing that. In the first place, I didn't think he was that ambitious. In the second, he wasn't that smart. He'd have had enough trouble with one set of books, let alone two. And Jimmy may've been many things, but he wasn't a cheat, especially to his own brother.

"I'm just saying it's complicated, that's all," Jerry said.

He looked up at the stage, at the boys in the band, and the roadies running around switching mikes and stringing an extra cable or two.

"You got yourself quite a little gig here, don't you?" He was smiling like he approved.

"I like it," I answered.

"Glad to see you loosening up," he said, turning back to me. "Used to look like a scared bunny rabbit. Now you're looking like a woman."

I didn't know what to say, so I said nothing.

"I'll get up with you in a few days. Maybe this time you'll come out to my place."

"I don't think so, Jerry. Hot tubs aren't my thing." I looked him square in the eye and he laughed.

"Nah, didn't think so," he said. "But it was worth a try."

With that, Jerry Lee Sizemore was gone, striding out of the Golden Stallion, his long silver hair shining under the spots, his suede coat as smelly as ever and his coonskin cap sticking out of his coat pocket like fresh roadkill.

"Who was that guy?" Jack asked, walking up as soon as Jerry vanished.

"My accountant," I answered, watching the effect.

Jack looked after Jerry and smiled. "Cool," he said. He slapped his harmonica against his thigh. "Cool, cool, cool." He was starting to zone off. I could see it happening, the faraway stare, the vacant smile. Jack was thinking about someone or something else.

"Hey, you're coming back to my place tonight, aren't you?" he said, reining himself back in.

"Why? You need a ride? Does Evelyn still have your car?"

The mythical, elusive Evelyn. Why didn't she ever come watch Jack play? All the other guys in the band had girlfriends who hung around at a table, their eyes always on their men, watching out for competition. Why didn't Evelyn come and join in?

Jack was smiling, that same goofy, out-to-lunch smile he'd had on a moment ago. "No," he said, "she gave it back. I just wanted to make sure you'd be there."

"Oh, wait," I said, suddenly aware that I might be cramping his style, "if you and Evelyn want some time alone, I can stay away."

Jack laughed, as if I'd said something funny. "Don't worry about us. Evelyn doesn't want any more time alone with me than she gets. It'd cramp her style." He slapped his harmonica a few more times and started to wander away. "I'll just meet up with you back at the ranch."

I watched him walk away, remembering the way last night had ended for the two of us. The picture of us standing in front of his window, dancing, then not dancing, as the sun began to brighten the new day. What was I going to do about him? Somehow, that almost-kiss seemed to have happened in another lifetime, a lifetime that no longer fit with the way I felt tonight. Jack wasn't the man I wanted. The man I wanted wanted me, but he wanted me for murder.

My stomach flipped as I remembered the feel of Detective Weathers's fingers against my skin and the taste of his lips. Did he really think I could've killed somebody?

"Maggie!" I looked up and found one of the doormen gesturing impatiently. "I been calling you and calling you! You've got a phone call."

My first thought, as always, was of Sheila. She was the only one in my life who would call me here, and then only if something was wrong. I quickened my pace, half running toward the phone.

"Sheila?"

There was silence on the phone and then music, scratchy and thin, sounding as if it came from a long distance away.

"Thank heaven, for little girls. . . ." Maurice Chevalier's voice, gay and lilting, sang through the receiver.

"Who is this?"

"For little girls grow older every day." Then silence. Then a raspy whisper. "Where's *your* little girl, Maggie?"

18

I screamed, but no sound escaped my throat. The scream stuck, with the unshed tears of terror in my chest, squeezing the breath from my body. The phone line had gone dead, the connection severed. Somewhere someone had just threatened my daughter.

I didn't say anything. I couldn't. Instead I made jabbing motions at the keypad, trying to dial Vernell's number and failing to remember it.

"Damn it!" I cried. Cletus, who'd wandered up to help collect the cover charge and check IDs, stopped what he was doing, alerted by my tone.

"What's the matter, Maggie?" he asked, but I couldn't stop to answer. I had to go. I had to get to Sheila.

I pushed past him, running now, from the Golden Stallion entrance to the back. I know I shoved someone out of my way, when I heard a surprised, angry cry echoing behind me. I heard footsteps following me, but I didn't stop until I reached the dressing room and had grabbed my purse and keys.

"Maggie, stop!" It was Jack, his face concerned. He grabbed my arm and held me. "Take a breath."

"Let go of me," I screamed, wrenching my arm away. "He's going to hurt Sheila!"

I was running again, with Jack right behind me. "Who? Maggie, stop! What is it? Wait!"

But I was gone, the mother in me taking over. I had to get to Sheila. My voice was screaming her name over and over in my head. It throbbed, pulsing with my heartbeats, stronger and louder. I had to find my little girl. I slammed the car into gear, tearing out onto High Point Road, screaming at the cars that got in my way.

It was after midnight on a Thursday night, a school night. Sheila should be at Vernell's, in bed, sleeping. I drove, talking to myself, careening down Holden Road, cutting across Greensboro in search of my baby. I issued instructions, like "Don't hit that car!" I screamed at other drivers, and finally I prayed. "Don't let my baby get hurt. Be with Sheila! Protect her!" The tears came then, filling my eyes. But I couldn't cry, not now.

I made it across town in five minutes, flying down Vernell's darkened cul-de-sac and screeching to a halt in front of his garage doors.

Sheila's black Mustang sat in the driveway. That wasn't good enough, not by a long shot. I raced from the car to the front door, pounding on it, ringing the doorbell and trying the handle.

"Open this door!" I cried. "Vernell!"

But it was Sheila herself who answered. She was dressed for bed in her long white T-shirt, her face scrubbed pink, and an expectant look on her face. She was not at all frightened or cautious, as she should have been. She never should have opened the door.

I flew into her, pushing her backward into Vernell's expansive foyer, slamming the door behind us.

"Oh, my God, Sheila!" I cried, sinking down with her onto one of the steps that led to the second floor of Vernell's house.

"Are you all right?" I asked. I pulled her to me, holding her as tightly as I possibly could. My breath came in ragged gasps and dry sobs that I couldn't control.

Sheila was scared now.

"Mama, what's wrong?"

Above us, lights flared on, doors opened, and footsteps started down the hall.

"What in the hell is she doing here?" Jolene asked. She stood at the top of the steps in a filmy white negligee.

Vernell came staggering out behind her, fighting to become conscious. His thick black hair stood up on one side of his head, and lay flat on the other.

"Hey, Maggie," he said, a bleary smile jumping across his face before he realized Jolene was right by his side.

I sat, rocking Sheila back and forth in my arms,

just as I had when she was a baby.

"Mama!" Sheila protested, struggling to get free.

I looked up at Vernell, ignoring Jolene. "I got a call at the club tonight," I said. "Made me think Sheila was in danger. A man threatened her."

"What?" I had Vernell's complete attention now. "What do you mean? What'd they say? Who was it?" The questions flew out of Vernell. Instantly, he was awake and angry.

"He played a little bit of this old song about little girls and then asked if I knew where Sheila was."

Jolene's shrill laugh cut off Vernell's next question.

"That's it?" she asked from her position at the top of the stairs. "Someone calls up and asks if you know where Sheila is and you freak out? Why, that's the most ridiculous thing I ever heard!"

Vernell looked from her to me, uncertain for a moment. Sheila stiffened in my arms.

"A man said that?" she asked. "You're sure?"

I grabbed her even tighter. "I'm sorry, sweetie," I said, "but yes. That's why I came over here the way I did."

Vernell was down the stairs, an angry scowl on his face. "Ain't nobody gonna hurt my little girl." His thick black eyebrows furrowed together, and his face was a dull reddish brown. "Sonofabitch! Did you call the police?"

I started to answer, but Jolene interrupted. "Now, don't you people think you're getting a little carried away?" Vernell looked up at her, clearly irritated. "I mean, babe," she cooed, "the man only asked if Maggie knew where Sheila was. Why, the way I take it, he was making more of a statement about a mother who stays out till all hours cavorting in a honky-tonk than he was talking about Sheila."

She moved a little closer to the edge of the top step, adjusting her posture to feature her most prominent assets, and smiled seductively. "And look what it's done," she said. "Got you and me out of our warm snuggly bed, and woke little Sheila up. Woke her up out of her own safe bed, I might add." She scowled at me. "All on account of her mother's overreaction." Vernell was starting to look confused.

"I wasn't sleeping," Sheila huffed. "And if my mama wants to come see about me, it don't matter when it is!"

Jolene ignored her. "What would make you think Vernell couldn't take care of his only daughter?" she called down to me. "She's safe here, not like in that ratty old neighborhood where you live, in a house that don't even lock good!" Vernell started to break in, but Jolene rushed ahead. "You gave her up, Maggie! Her own mother! Now look at you! Out till all hours, and now you're acting concerned. Why you—"

"Shut your mouth, Jolene!" Vernell suddenly yelled. It was the old Vernell that I remembered from the good days. Sober and taking up for his family, only in this case, Jolene was the outsider. "I won't have nobody talking to Sheila's mama that way, do you hear me?"

Jolene was shocked, her face going pale with

the impact of tumbling down from Vernell's pedestal. The honeymoon was over.

He turned to me and Sheila. "You all right, baby?" he asked her tenderly.

"Yeah, Daddy, I'm fine." But she wasn't fine. Her body trembled against mine and her fingers were icicles.

"Kiss your mama, then, and run on up to bed. It's late."

Sheila pried herself out of my arms, kissed me on the cheek, and then clung to my neck for a long moment before she let go.

"I want to see you tomorrow," I said firmly, trying to make her look at me, but failing.

"I don't know," she muttered. "I have to work."

Vernell stepped in. "Girl, what's wrong with you? This here's your mama. That comes first."

He looked at me. "Don't worry. I'm gonna drive her to school personally tomorrow, and you can pick her up, if it suits." Sheila started to protest, but broke off at the stern look of warning from her father. She turned and walked up the stairs, past Jolene, to her room. I'd waited sixteen years for this kind of support.

"Thanks, Vernell," I said.

He shrugged and scratched at his belly, forgetting, I suppose, that this wasn't exactly appropriate behavior to display in front of an ex-wife, especially when the current wife was hovering like an avenging angel.

"I don't know what the hell's going on," he said with a sigh. "This week has about run me to the end of what all a man can endure, what with Jimmy gone." He looked very sad, and I reached out to touch his arm.

"I'm so sorry, Vernell," I whispered.

"Vernell!" Jolene had had enough.

"I'll keep a close watch," he said, as he walked me to the door. "She's my baby, too, you know."

"I know, Vernell."

He opened the door and watched as I walked over to my car. "Take care of yourself, Maggie."

I looked back. Jolene was drifting down the staircase like a descending spider. Vernell was the one who needed to watch his back, I thought.

I started the car and backed carefully out of the driveway, past the flattened mailbox, out into the cul-de-sac. Vernell had closed the front door and by now was facing an angry Dish Girl. I let the VW slide across the street, under the cover of the drooping pin oak, and watched.

The downstairs lights went out. Eventually only one room stayed lit, Sheila's. She was sitting up there, worrying, I just knew.

"Don't worry, baby," I whispered into the darkness. "Mama's right here."

I sat under the big tree branch and watched for I don't know how long. The sound of Maurice Chevalier's voice echoed in my head, replaced by Jolene's accusatory voice: "What kind of a mother are you?"

Maybe the warning had been directed at me. Maybe someone knew about Jimmy being dead in my house, and me being a singer and having a daughter. I'd heard about people getting anonymous phone calls after they'd been in the paper or on TV. Maybe that Jolene was right. But there'd been that phone call at the Curley-Que, too. I pondered on that awhile. Was she right? Was I a bad mother? What kind of right did I have to go off and pursue my own dream?

Sheila's light finally winked out a little after two A.M. I sat there a few more minutes and then drove off toward Jack's. There was no sense in going back to the club. The boys would all be heading home by now. The night was drawing to a close.

I putted slowly across town, lost in a fog of indecision and confusion. I pulled into Jack's parking lot, slid into a space near the loading dock and walked toward the door, all without consciously taking in my surroundings. Only the harmonica music drifting slowly across the lot intruded into my awareness. Jack was sitting on the concrete loading pad, waiting for me, a Rolling Rock in one hand and a C Sharp harmonica in the other.

"You scared the shit out of me," he said. He didn't look scared, though, he looked just as he always did, calm and peaceful. "I've been sitting out here, waiting."

It was only when I stepped up onto the dock and sank down beside him that I noticed his hands were shaking ever so slightly.

"Jack, I'm sorry," I said. He turned to me, his eyes filled with concern and some other emotion that I couldn't read. "I had to go see about Sheila. I couldn't have stayed and explained."

"Is she all right?" he asked.

"I don't know. I think maybe, for now, she is." Jack sighed and took a swig of his beer. "Vernell's fine little wife thinks the man on the phone was trying to point out what a bad mother I am."

"Well, that's just horseshit!" Jack said. He reached over and put his arm around my shoulders, pulling me close to him. It was cold outside and Jack's body was warm.

"I don't know what to think. All I know is, it scared me to death."

"Scared me, too," he said. "You've gotta start taking better care of yourself. Watch what you're doing. Fix the damn lock over at your place and let the police help you. This is getting serious, Maggie. I tried to explain it to Sparks, but I gotta tell you, Maggie, he was a little pissed."

That was all I needed. "I'll call him tomorrow."

"Well," Jack sighed, "better let him cool down a bit first. Just show up on time tomorrow night and talk to him."

"What did he say, Jack?" I asked, suddenly more afraid.

"He said he'd had enough of you running in and out. Said he had a band to think of and that if you couldn't be reliable, he'd have to let you go."

"Great! Just fine!" I said.

"Try not to let him get to you," he said. "His bark is worse than his bite." He squeezed me tight, then stood up. "Let's go inside. It's freezing out here."

It wasn't until we got inside and into the light that I realized something else. Jack had been crying. He tried to hide it with a thin, watery smile, but his eyes were swollen and red. In my lifetime I will admit that I had not seen many men cry. It was unusual and a little frightening. But then, Jack was unusual, a man who was comfortable with his feelings. Still, I couldn't help walking up to him and touching him tenatively.

"Jack? What's wrong? Have you been crying?"

He turned and smiled softly, but his lips trembled. "I'm fine," he said.

"Did I scare you that badly?" I asked.

He laughed a little and shook his head. "No, don't worry about it. It doesn't have a thing to do with you. Except"—his voice faltered for a moment—"except just don't let anything happen to you, all right? I couldn't stand to lose anyone else right now."

"Is it Evelyn?" I asked.

"Yeah, but let's not talk about it right now, all right, Maggie?" He reached out and stroked my hair gently, as if I were much younger than him, and not the other way around. "Let's just go upstairs and go to sleep." He stressed the word *sleep*, as if I should understand that he, too, realized the moment we had shared was past.

I let him take my hand, and we walked up the stairs to his bedroom. This time, when I slipped in between the sheets, it no longer occurred to me to worry about his nakedness. Instead I rolled over to face his back, reached out my hand, and let it rest on his shoulder. Later, when he thought I was asleep, I heard a quiet sob escape his lips and felt him tremble.

I lay there wondering what to do, my hand still

resting on his shoulder. In all of my life, I had never seen a man hurt this way, not over a woman, not over anything that I could recall. Even when my brother Larry's wife left him, he hadn't cried. I'd found him out behind the old barn, chopping wood in the middle of January, working so hard that even bare-chested in thirty-degree weather, he was sweating. But I never saw him cry.

Eventually, I heard the soft sound of even breathing and realized that Jack had drifted off to sleep. I lay awake for a long time, thinking about the men in my life, and wondering if one of them had been the voice on the phone, if maybe someone I knew had killed Jimmy and now wanted to see me dead. But why? What had I done to make someone so angry they'd threaten my daughter and try and frame me for murder?

19

I awakened alone and with a plan. Jack was gone and the carafe of coffee was waiting for me on the kitchen counter. I sat on the sofa, drinking and rooting through my purse and wallet. I had been surprised to see Marshall Weathers's card floating around in my bag a few days ago. I hadn't remembered him giving it to me, but now when I needed it, it was nowhere to be found.

"Come on, Weathers, I know you're in here," I muttered. I pulled out my wallet and started taking every picture, credit card, and paper out of the worn leather slots. It had to be there somewhere. Only after I emptied every last item out of my purse did I find the beige business card, wedged under a piece of leather at the bottom.

I sat for a few moments, studying the card and debating: Call or don't call? "Just don't think about it," I whispered to myself. "Just pick up the phone and do it." My fingers were cold and I realized that I was shaking on the inside. "What are you afraid of? He'll listen to you. He'll take you seriously." But maybe he wouldn't. Maybe he'd blow me off like he had when someone shot at me. Maybe he'd think I was making it all up to throw the suspicion off of myself.

I jumped up off the sofa and ran across the room to the phone, picked it up, and dialed before I could stop myself. He answered on the first ring.

"Marshall Weathers," he said, his voice deep and businesslike.

I hung up.

A few moments later the phone rang, echoing through the cavernous room. I jumped and stared at it. I started to reach for it, and changed my mind. I couldn't do it. What if it was him? "You're being ridiculous," I said aloud. The phone continued to ring but I walked away. Calling Weathers was a bad idea.

"I'm making a big deal out of nothing, probably," I said to the empty room. "I'll get my locks fixed. I'll just go over and pick Sheila up after school. Between me and Vernell, we can watch her. If somebody lays a hand on my baby, me and Vernell'll kill him."

That was the right decision. If I left it up to the police, they might not watch her like I could. They might figure I wasn't telling them the truth, and my little girl would be caught in the middle. That is, if Sheila were even in danger. Chances were, it was just a Nosy Parker with too much time on his hands, looking to scare someone.

I ran upstairs, took a quick shower, and threw on a pair of jeans and a purple sweatshirt. Eventually, despite what I'd told Weathers, I was going to have to go back into my house, even if it was only to pick up more of my belongings. I wedged on a pair of tan suede, low-top cowgirl boots and ran down the stairs. Weathers was leaning against my car when I stepped out into the bright fall afternoon.

"Ever hear tell of Caller ID?" he said.

"So, when I hung up you got my number?"

"It ain't rocket science," he said.

I jammed my hands in the back pockets of my jeans and stood on the dock staring at him. It was just as well that we were both wearing sunglasses. I couldn't see those powerful blue eyes and he couldn't look through mine and see what I was feeling. He stood there, his arms folded, smiling. I figured he was feeling right proud of himself.

"So, what'd you want to talk to me about?" he asked.

"It wasn't anything much," I said. I took my time walking down the steps and over toward him. "If it'd been worth bothering you about, I'd have stayed on the line. As it was, I simply changed my mind. So you ran over here for nothing, and I hate it for you."

The smile never left his face but that little muscle began to jump in his jaw. He looked at his watch, then back at me.

"It's past lunchtime," he said. "You eat yet?"

My stomach growled. "No." I was close

enough to touch him if I'd wanted to. For an instant the idea crossed my mind. What would it be like to touch him? He stood there, still smiling, waiting and not saying a word. It was up to me, somehow I just knew it.

"You want to go grab a bite?" I said. I didn't look at him when I spoke. It wasn't that obvious; I let my eyes wander to a spot just below his collarbone. The man made me nervous, or else I'd had too much coffee.

"Sure," he said, like a teacher who's been waiting on a student to come up with an obvious answer. "That'd be fine. Where you got in mind?"

Weathers was never going to be a man to use two words when one would do. I tried to think of where to go, and could only remember the last place we'd been, the only place we'd ever been together. "Yum-Yums'll do, I reckon."

He nodded, the decision made. He didn't even ask if I wanted to drive. He simply headed for his car, unlocked the door, and waited.

"I don't feel like driving anyway," I muttered to myself. "Use his gas."

He was talking on his cell phone as we drove off, a series of grunts and "uh-huhs" that gave me almost no indication of whether the call was business or personal. He cut across town, heading for lunch, his driving as clean and spare as his conversation. I was a shameless eavesdropper. I stared out the window, tried to act disinterested, and listened as hard as I could.

"Yeah, uh-huh, well, I know that." He leaned his head to the left, balancing the cell phone while he turned down the radio. "I know that, too," he said, but this time he seemed a little impatient. "Here's what you do," he said. "You tell her I said no. She'll understand that." He listened for a moment, grunted something I couldn't make out, and hung up.

For a moment he seemed to have forgotten that I was even in the car. He had pulled into Yum-Yums, and now sat with the car in park, his arms folded across the steering wheel, staring at the brick wall in front of him.

"Trouble at work?" I asked after a minute, in which we sat stone silent in his car.

He didn't jump perceptibly, but he came back from wherever he'd been and looked across at me.

"Come on, let's get us a hot dog," he said. He didn't answer the question.

"Must've been personal," I murmured to myself, not that there was any logic involved in that deduction. Just call it woman's intuition. I wondered who the "she" was that he'd said would understand "no."

I wondered about it the whole way up to the counter. I placed my order, almost without having to think, and went back to speculating about Weathers. I knew what I was doing. I was putting off the inevitable. I was going to have to talk about Sheila. I could feel it building up in me like a storm. My mother's intuition told me that the voice on the other end of the phone had meant to scare me, and also to threaten my daughter.

If Weathers knew what I was doing, he didn't comment. He seemed lost in his own thoughts. We took our hot dogs and walked to a booth across the room, under a chart showing a World War II aircraft carrier. He carefully unwrapped his hot dog, grabbed a couple of napkins out of the dispenser and handed me one. Then he focused on eating.

We sat for a couple of minutes in complete silence, until I couldn't stand it any longer. There was no one in the booths nearby, no other conversation to listen in on, and no distractions to keep me from talking.

"So, how'd you come to be at the Golden Stallion the night I auditioned?" I asked. A harmless question.

"Is that what you called me to ask?" He quit eating and sat perfectly still, waiting.

I felt myself turn red. "No, I'm just making polite conversation, that's all." He still didn't say anything. "I mean, you haven't been in since that night, that I'm aware of. I just wondered."

"Keep careful track of the Golden Stallion patrons, do you?"

I gave up. Shook my head in disgust and took a sip of my soda, only to have it misfire and go up my nose. I choked and coughed, my eyes watering with the effort to regain control of my windpipe. He laughed. Laughed so hard, I finally had to join in, and we laughed until I realized I was losing control and on the verge of tears.

"Okay," he said, suddenly reaching across the table, his fingers stretching to cover mine, "why did you call?"

"Someone threatened my daughter. I know you may not believe that, that's why I hung up. I just didn't know who else to call and I had to talk to someone."

He straightened up, his fingers edging back into his lap. It was business now.

"What do you mean?" he asked.

I looked back at him, right into his eyes. He was really listening, and so I told him about the phone call. My voice shook, my hands trembled, and I felt cold, even though the steam from hundreds of hot dogs filled the tiny restaurant. I was so afraid.

He leaned back against the booth, his head cocked slightly to the left, listening as I went through the details of the phone call. He didn't laugh at me or make light of the threat. He just nodded, as if he was all too familiar with threatening phone calls.

"So, do you think this is something I should take seriously, or was it a crank call?"

"I don't know," he said. "Could be either. I don't think you oughta go getting totally paranoid, but I don't think you can just dismiss it, either." He smiled slightly. "You tick anybody off lately?"

I almost came up off of my seat. "Of course I ticked someone off, Weathers," I said. "Someone's so ticked at me that they're trying to make me out to be a murderer! And if that fails, they're gonna flat out kill me! I know that's not exactly what you want to hear, but it's God's honest truth." I didn't give him the opportunity to deny it.

"The whole Spivey clan must be angry with me. The grieving widow is especially angry, on account of Jimmy left his share of the business to me. Vernell can't be too pleased, although he sure is putting on a good show of it. He thought he was rid of me. Now I'm his business partner and maybe, he thinks, his brother's killer. So, I'd say, in answer to your question, yeah, I got a whole slew of people ticked off at me." I leaned back against the booth, breathless.

"All right," he said. "Let's set the record straight, again. I am only interested in finding out who killed Jimmy Spivey. I have no personal vendetta against you. I am working just as hard to find the innocent parties in this investigation as I am to find the guilty ones. You need to quit looking at me as if I'm your enemy, Maggie. We'll get a lot further if you start trusting me."

I wanted to. Oh, how I wanted to trust this man. "Well, it just seems as if I'm the only person you're investigating."

"We've covered that, Maggie. I'm not 'investigating' you. I'm asking questions."

A crowd of teenagers came through the door, out of school and hungry, laughing and talking as if they hadn't a care in the world. For a moment, Weathers allowed himself to be distracted, but then he was right back at it.

"How's Vernell get along with Sheila?" he asked.

"Fine. Why?"

"Well, you said the voice on the phone was male. You mentioned Vernell was probably plenty angry at you. I'm just asking questions, Maggie."

"Oh, Vernell's harmless," I said. "He wasn't a nice husband. He treated me like a dog, but he's a good daddy. He wouldn't harm a hair on Sheila's head."

"Maybe not, but you're the one brought his name up."

So I had, but I was only trying to make a point. Vernell wouldn't harm a fly, would he?

"Have you talked to Vernell?" I asked.

"Sure." Nothing more. The professional mask was back in place.

"Where was he when Jimmy died? Could he have done it?"

Weathers studied me for a moment, making up his mind. "Vernell says he was on his way back into town from Stokesdale. We haven't been able to confirm or deny that yet."

Vernell didn't have an alibi. But that didn't mean a thing. I flashed on Vernell in the Golden Stallion, the night after Jimmy's death, drunk and decked out in his blue polyester leisure suit. Sure was a funny way to show grief for the loss of your only brother.

"But Vernell would never hurt Sheila," I said.

"Nobody's hurt Sheila," he answered.

"It's gotta be somebody else."

"Probably is," he said. His face was closed and I couldn't read him.

"Well, we've got to make sure she's safe," I said. "Shouldn't you have somebody watch her?"

Weathers shook his head. "That's TV, Maggie. We don't have enough manpower to put an officer on everybody who receives a threatening phone call. I don't know any police department that does. Unless someone actually tries to hurt Sheila, our hands are tied. But," he said, before I could start in, "that doesn't mean that I'm not taking this seriously."

"Then what are you going to do about it?"

"We, Maggie," he said. "What are *we* going to do about it. You've got to talk to Sheila, get her to be cautious. Then you've got to try and help me figure out who would want to scare you. Because that's what I think this is, an attempt to frighten you. We just need to know why."

There was something about Marshall Weathers that made me believe what he was saying. Not just believe him, but feel comforted and reassured by his words. He knew we could figure this all out. He seemed so sure of himself. He didn't seem upset or even very worried. It was as if he dealt with this kind of thing every day, and of course, he did. This wasn't the worst thing he'd ever heard of, but he wasn't dismissing it, either. He was making me feel like I had some control over what happened. The voice on the phone had been trying to scare me. In reality, no one had hurt Sheila, and I could help make sure that no one did.

"Okay," I said. "Fair enough. I'll talk to Sheila and I'll keep talking to you."

Weathers nodded, satisfied.

"I still don't think Vernell has anything to do with this," I said. "He's my ex, and by rights I could hate him, but he's harmless."

Weathers shrugged. "You may be right," he said, "but I don't take nothing for granted when it comes to ex-spouses. There's always an axe to grind somewhere, no matter how deep it's buried."

I looked over at Weathers, noting the tiny twitch back in his jaw. It didn't take a rocket scientist to figure that I had just gotten a glimpse of the man who lived behind the professional exterior.

I opened my mouth to ask the next question, to find out a little bit more about this man and his past, but he saw it coming.

"Gotta get back," he said, sliding out of the booth and heading for the trash can. "I got work to do, and you've got a daughter to look after."

I couldn't argue with that. I followed him out into the parking lot, the afternoon sun hitting me squarely in the eyes. He was on the cell phone once again when I climbed into the passenger seat. For a minute I wondered if he was really talking to anyone at all. Maybe hugging the phone was his way of avoiding questions from me. Still, I listened.

"Hey!" he said, his voice a bit rougher than it was when he spoke to me. "Listen, I been thinkin' and I got a different way to go on this here." He was watching the road, but for an instant he glanced over at me. "I want you to draw something up and get her to come in and sign it. I'm tired of fooling around."

He looked almost sad, his eyes dark blue wells. Couldn't be a professional call, I thought. There was nothing in his tone to give away sadness, but I had an urge to touch his knee, a sure sign that my womanly intuition was on alert and sending signals. Just like me to hone in on another wounded dog. Probably them bad picker genes leading me down one more dead-end road.

"Yeah, huh." He grunted. "I know it." He listened, making the turn onto Elm Street and preparing to pull back into Jack's parking lot. He sighed, a frown creasing his forehead.

"I ain't much for Monday morning quarter-backing," he said. "Let's just get on with it and see what you people can get accomplished." Then, an afterthought: "And keep it simple, y'hear? She started the whole mess, but that don't mean we gotta make it sting worse." He slammed the phone shut and threw it down on the seat between us.

"Lawyers," I sighed, shaking my head and taking a stab in the dark.

"Ain't that the truth," he said, before he could catch himself.

"Listen now," he said, turning to me, "you get up with Sheila, make sure she's all right. I'll be in touch."

I hopped out of the car and turned back to say good-bye. "Maybe you can tell me all about your divorce next time," I was going to say, leave *him* with the smart aleck comment this time. But he was already back on the phone, barking at someone. He lifted his hand up, a dismissive wave good-bye, and was gone.

I was left standing in the parking lot once again, my mouth hanging open and looking like a big dummy. Back when I was growing up, whenever Mama witnessed someone who had a particular talent for leaving others speechless and getting their own way, she'd stand back and admire the whole act for a few moments. Then she'd turn to us young'uns and say, "Now there goes a prize violin."

Weathers had played me like a fiddle all right, but the band was just tuning up and Maggie Reid was gonna have the last word.

20

I could hear the choir tuning up and the organ wailing as I stood outside the Ledbetter Creek Methodist Church, waiting on Bonnie. Churches made me nervous, ever since Daddy fell out drunk one time in our home church and the pastor thought God had struck him dead and tried to revive him in the sacred baptismal pool. After that, I decided to leave organized religion to them what do it best.

I was half hiding underneath the shade of a pin oak, tugging at my blue skirt and wishing it was a tad longer. It's one thing to be a Reba McIntyre look-alike on stage, but it is quite another to carry it to church. I had on a high-necked white shirt and prissy white shoes. Not a rhinestone in sight. And I must've passed, 'cause Bonnie almost walked right past me.

"Hey," I called softly.

Bonnie was taking one last drag on her cigarette and shooing three of the six children off toward Sunday School. She stopped, startled, and guiltily pitched her smoke in the bushes.

"Lord, honey, you liked to scared me to death! I thought you was one of the bazaar ladies." She took a deep breath and gave me a thorough once-over. "Dang, Maggie, you must want this'un bad to dress like that!" Not that Bonnie was the picture of conservatism. She was just used to looking like someone's mother.

"I got good news for you, though. I forgot, we're having a pinto bean supper after church today!"

"How's that good news? I don't like pinto beans and the last thing I want to do is—" Bonnie cut me off with a wave of her hand.

"His mother will be working the line, you idiot! We'll sit at her table!" Bonnie turned and started up the stairs to the sanctuary.

"Praise God," I whispered and followed her.

The church was relatively small and very old. Thick windowsills and whitewashed walls. Pretty stained-glass windows depicted the saints and Jesus, all having a time of it being Christians. Bonnie slipped into a pew halfway up the red carpeted aisle, tugging me in beside her. All the church members were old, or at least that's how it seemed to me. They smiled and waved to each other, but when the opening hymn began and the congregation stood, they became seriously devout.

Bonnie nudged me as I fumbled with my hymnal. "See her?" she whispered. "The lady two rows up, just in front of you, with the gray curly hair."

I looked. Bonnie's description fit just about every woman in the place, but I knew Marshall Weathers's mother instantly. When she turned to watch the choir approach our eyes met briefly. Electric blue lie detectors. She wasn't tiny, like some of the others, but taller and grandmotherly. The kind of woman who wears an apron around the house and forgets to take it off 'cause she's always in the kitchen. She looked tanned and happy, and I imagined her out in the garden picking beans for supper.

Bonnie raised an eyebrow at me, then winked. She was loving this. Intrigue came simple to a woman with six children.

I don't remember the pastor's sermon. He was a small, bland little fellow with cherry red cheeks and a look of surprised innocence about him. His voice came out in a hushed monotone that the ladies, Mrs. Weathers included, all seemed to strain to hear. I was too busy watching her and wondering about the mother of my detective to listen to the service.

When the choir started the last hymn, Bonnie gave me another nudge. "We gotta get straight on down to the fellowship hall if we want to sit with Flo and them. As soon as the preacher gives the benediction and people start to file out, you follow me."

The "Amen" had barely left the preacher's lips when Bonnie charged the aisle like a water buffalo. She cut past the ladies who waited to shake hands with the minister, plowed through little groups of chatters, and led me straight outside into the noon-time sunshine and across the little churchyard to a low white building.

Bonnie didn't stop her single-minded pursuit until we were sitting at a table along the far left-hand side of the narrow fellowship hall, happily ensconced among five gray-haired women.

"Sit here," she'd said, placing me next to the one empty chair at the table, facing a blank wall with a colorful picture of Jesus at the Last Supper. "That's her chair there. You wait, as soon as the line gets started, she'll come around!"

But when Flo Weathers did appear, I found myself suddenly shy. What was I gonna do now?

"Well, hey there, ladies!" she cried, setting her plate of pinto beans, cornbread, and coleslaw down with a gentle thunk. "Bonnie," she said, looking at me, "who's your friend?" And before Bonnie could swallow her tea and answer, Flo took matters into her own hands. "Anybody ever tell you you look like Reba McIntyre?" she asked. "I got a son who just worships that woman!"

The others laughed, apparently well familiar with Flo's patter.

"I'm Flo Weathers. Welcome to Ledbetter Creek Methodist." Bonnie had choked on her iced tea and was trying to catch her breath. "Bonnie's usually better mannered than this, must be livin' around all them young'uns got her flustered. What's wrong with you, Bonnie?" Bonnie had turned red and was coughing fit to beat the band. When it came right down to it, Bonnie didn't have the temperament for subterfuge.

"I'm Maggie Reid," I said, smiling right back at her, but trying not to look too closely into those clear blue eyes.

"Flo, Maggie works with me down to the Curley-Que, but she's going into a new . . . Ow!" Bonnie grabbed her leg and howled, unable to tell Flo I was a singer on account of me kicking her under the table. "Oh," Bonnie said, catching my eye.

"Hairdresser, huh? You single?"

The ladies laughed again, a comfortable here-we-go-again laugh that signaled familiarity.

"Listen, Maggie," Flo said, leaning closer to me. "Don't pay them a bit of mind. I'm just a mother looking out for her handsome, smart, and newly single son."

I raised my eyebrows and smiled politely. "Well, yes, ma'am, I am single," I answered.

"Hmmm," Flo said, breaking a piece of cornbread, but not making any moves to eat it.

"Tell me about your son," I said, doing my best not to catch Bonnie's eye or look anything but neutral. Bonnie was choking so badly now, she had to leave the table.

"Oh, he's a doll!" one of the blue-haired ladies said. The others murmured their agreement. "And so polite," another said. "A real lady killer," the third one said.

That stopped the crew in their tracks and they all looked across at the little birdlike lady with the blue-and-pink straw hat. She turned scarlet.

"Well, what I mean is, he's a gentleman, of course, but a real charmer!"

Flo looked back at the line where the servers

were doling out plates of beans and saw something she didn't like. She hopped up and was gone before anyone could say another word.

"I'm sure he's a nice boy," I said, smiling, "but if he's newly single, he's probably not anxious to meet anyone new."

A slight cloud passed over the group, then a plump lady with a bright purple dress spoke up.

"What happened to little Marshall was a pitiful shame!"

"I'm sorry," I said, picking at my pinto beans. "Did his wife die?"

"Oh Lord, no, and sometimes we think it might've been better if she had." The purple dress looked back where Flo was dumping beans into a large pot, then back to me. "His wife left him for another man!"

"No!" I said, seeing Bonnie approach the table, her face now a modest pink.

"Yes!" they all cried in unison.

"And him working like he does, solving all those horrible murder cases!" The purple dress was upset. "She just run out. Left everything but her clothes and took off with one of his best friends. He ain't been quite right since. Flo's just worried sick! He don't go out much. He don't come to church. He don't hardly even associate with his friends anymore, either. I guess he just don't trust nobody and I can't say as I blame him."

"Well, it's been over a year," the bird lady said. "He needs him a new horse is what he needs. Swing back up in the saddle!"

"Martha!" the others gasped.

"Oh, don't act like such a bunch of prissies!" she snorted. "I changed that boy's diapers. I watched him raise hell all through school. He just needs a good woman, that's all. Trouble with him is, he don't know it! Thinks we're all the same, faithless hussies! Thinks work's all there is to life." The ladies sighed collectively. Martha was a loose cannon.

Flo was walking back toward the table, and everyone but Martha set about shoveling beans into their mouths.

"Ain't that right, Flo?" Martha said.

"What's that?" She was smiling, settling back into her seat and reaching for her tea.

"Don't Marshall need him a new woman?"

Flo looked over at me and laughed. "Yes, Lord! But don't go scaring Miss Maggie! She'll think we're desperate to marry him off."

"Well, aren't we? Who's the one wanting after grandkids?"

Flo sighed and looked at me. "You know how it is, a mama just hates to see her baby hurtin', no matter how old they get or how tough they act."

"I know just what you mean," I said. "I got a baby of my own."

Flo smiled. "You know, you just might like my boy, and I know he'd like you."

"Oh, well, maybe I'll meet him sometime," I said casually.

"Oh, you most certainly will. He's due to be here any minute. He wouldn't miss one of our pinto bean lunches. Brings all those boys he works with, too!"

Bonnie choked and started coughing wildly.

My heart started pounding and the only thing I could think of was escaping. I looked over at Bonnie, trying to catch her eye.

"Honey," I said loudly, rising out of my seat and moving over to hers. "Let me help you!"

I snatched Bonnie up out of her chair, grabbed my purse and hers, and looked back at my luncheon companions. "Well be right back! These spells just come on her so sudden, and the only thing for it is fresh air."

I started Bonnie toward the front doorway of the fellowship hall only to see a group of men approaching. I recognized one as a detective and quickly spun Bonnie on her heel and made for the rest room at the back of the long room.

"Quick!" I said. "Get in there before he sees us!"

We headed almost at a dead run for the bathroom, with me praying for escape and Bonnie barking like a dog. I ducked into the pink-tiled room and took stock of our situation.

"What're we gonna do now?" Bonnie gasped.

I looked around the room, taking in the three stalls, the two sinks and the one window.

"Bonnie," I said, "tough times call for thick skin. We gotta get out of here."

"But he'll see us! You don't want that, do you? You want him to know you've been querying his own mama? That's liable to make him mad."

I walked over to the frosted glass window and pushed it open, staring out at the cemetery that lay behind the church.

"Bonnie," I said, "you first."

"I can't do that!" she shrieked. "What about

the kids?" She was right. She couldn't go off and leave her kids.

"All right, " I said, trying to sound calmer than I felt. "You go back in there and quietly round up the young'uns and leave. If anyone asks where I am, just act like you don't know." But I knew she'd be lost the second he looked at her. Bonnie was not a professional liar. "Just try to slip out without Flo seeing you. Can you do that?"

Bonnie looked nervous, and she fumbled with the clasp of her purse, like maybe she was going for a cigarette.

"All right," she said finally. "I'll do it."

"Good! And Bon, could you do one more thing?"

"What? I don't think I can take much more pressure!"

"It's simple," I said, slipping off my shoes. "Just give me a boost out the window."

With Bonnie's help I squeezed up onto the windowsill, over the ledge, and out, landing with a thud on the ground outside. Bonnie's frizzy blond head popped over the edge, looking down.

"You all right?" she asked.

I stood up, brushing fresh grass clippings off the back of my skirt and slipping my shoes on. "I'm fine. All right, get to it, or they'll really be looking for you! I'm gonna make a run for it."

Bonnie giggled. "Maggie, I've gotta say this is a side to your personality I've never seen before."

"Well, I can't let him get the upper hand," I said. "He knows way more about me than I know about him."

"I think there's more to it than that," she said softly.

I didn't answer her. Instead I walked quickly to my car, watching my back for signs of the ever-present Weathers. Finally, I had something to go on, some little tidbit to give me an edge. Only trouble was, I felt sorry for him and felt not at all like taking the upper hand.

"Well, you just harden your heart, girl," I said out loud. "He's got them all fooled. He's not broken-hearted, and he's not feeling the least bit sorry for you."

I thought about the way he'd kissed me, the memory of that kiss filling my body with long-buried anticipation. No, he wasn't feeling sorry for me. He was pure danger, ready to use any trick in his bag to reel me in.

21

The Irving Park Country Day School looks like a Norman Rockwell painting, with red brick buildings, thick white Grecian columns, and green sodded lawns. Even the students seem to have stepped off the canvas, with one lonely exception. Sheila was sitting in the middle of the front lawn, her long straight hair falling across her shoulders and hiding her face. Her shoulders were slumped miserably over her crossed legs. She was all alone.

She hadn't seen me pull up. I took advantage of that, and sat watching my belligerent baby. Life in Daddy's world wasn't turning out to be the piece of cake she'd been hoping for. Girls walked past her in little groups of twos and threes, all chatting amongst themselves, never saying a word to Sheila. I had my hand on the door handle, ready to run up to her, when he arrived.

Keith, the miserable slob, pulled up in a brand new red 4Runner. At first, I didn't want to believe it was him. I just knew he couldn't afford a snazzy vehicle like that. But there was no mistaking Keith. He pulled up in the circular drive, clearly in violation of the sign that said BUSES ONLY, and jumped out of the driver's seat.

"Sheila!"

At the sound of her name, Sheila's head jerked up like a marionette's, and her sullen frown was replaced by a broad smile. Clearly she'd forgotten that I was supposed to be picking her up, not this baboon.

I stepped out of my car and started walking toward the happy couple. What did she see in him? This was not going to be a pretty confrontation. Sheila wasn't going to be happy to be hauled off by her mama. I tried to put myself in her place, to remember what it was like to be sixteen and in love for the very first time.

His name had been Tony, and my mama hadn't liked him worth a flip. A flat-topped greaser, Mama had seen right through his smooth line of talk.

"Honey, that boy's nothing but bad road and foolish decisions," she'd said. But I didn't listen. That's the thing about adolescent hormones and bad-picker genes, you can't hear the voice of reason when you're walking down the road of desperate love. It'd been desperate love with Tony. He was gonna be my ticket out of the reality of my daddy's drinking. Trouble was, Tony was just like Pa, only mean to boot.

I saw that same desperate look in Sheila's eyes.

Keith was her key to salvation. It wouldn't matter so much that Vernell had gone back to drinking full-time or that her Uncle Jimmy was dead, or that the girls at Irving Park looked right past her when she entered the room. Keith was gonna fix all that.

"Hey, sweetie," I said, breezing right up between them. "You must've forgotten that I was picking you up." I didn't give Sheila a chance to answer. "Keith," I said, turning to him, and trying not to stare at the fluorescent pink dog collar around his neck. "I hate for you to have ridden all this way for nothing."

Sheila started to protest. "Mama!" Her mouth puckered up into a pout, ready to do battle. But Keith interrupted.

"Sheila!" His voice cracked like a whip, and I found myself staring at him. It was the tone of an angry parent. "That's your mom you're being disrespectful to." Then his face softened and he turned to her. "Sweetie, we've got all the time in the world. You don't hardly get to see your mama. You girls go on and shop or whatever. I'll be around."

Sheila melted, but my insides froze up. It was like listening to Tony in the old days. He had her wrapped around his little finger. Telling her what to do and giving us permission to leave him. Why the nerve of that sleaze! *You girls go on and shop . . .*

Sheila got all mushy-faced and melted into his arms. He kissed her, then pushed her gently away. "Go on. I got band practice anyway." Then he looked at me. There was no mistaking the fact that he was angry. He smiled, but his dark brown eyes were smoldering.

"Y'all have a nice time," he said. Then he reached in his pocket and pulled out a small wad of money. "Here, sweetie," he said, turning back to Sheila. "You might see something you want." He peeled off a couple of bills and stuffed them into Sheila's hand. They were twenties. He wanted me to know it, too. It was like he was marking his territory.

"Gotta run," I said, trying to keep my voice light. "'Bye, Keith." I walked away, willing myself not to run back and slap the boy. If Sheila even thought I didn't like Keith, she'd love him all the harder, and that was one thought I couldn't stomach. No, best to let time take its toll and hope she came to her senses.

Sheila sailed over to the VW, adrift on a cloud of adolescent love. She waited until we were on our way down the drive before she roused herself enough to speak.

"Isn't he just awesome?" she asked.

"Uh-huh," I muttered. Just awesome. "How's he come to have so much money?" I asked.

I could feel Sheila's eyes boring into the side of my head. I'd said the wrong thing, as usual, with her.

"Well, not from dope dealing, if that's what you're thinking!"

"I wasn't thinking anything," I said, keeping my voice cool and even. "I just wondered. I don't know a lot about him." Except that I knew he'd been arrested for dope dealing once; that much I'd learned from one of my neighbors.

"Mama!" Sheila sighed in exasperation. "I told

you before, he's got a regular job. You just don't like him because he loves me and you don't think he's good enough for your only daughter. It's text-book classic, Mama. You've got empty-nest syndrome, and you're probably pre-menopausal."

"What!" I ran into the parking lane of Bryan Boulevard, swerving back up onto the pavement, but not without spewing gravel.

"Oh, Mama. Really. I'm almost seventeen. We can talk about these things. Miss Dominick, my psychology teacher, says it's quite normal at your age for you to be clinging to your children and try-ing to recapture your youth. That's why you're doing this stupid country band stuff."

It was a reflex. My hand shot out and I swiped the top of her head.

"Ow, Mama! That hurt!"

She thought I was playing. She did not realize how close she was to extinction.

"How old is little Miss Dominick?" I asked.

"She's young. That's why we all like her," Sheila said. "She knows what's happening. Not like some old, dried-up prune."

"Well," I said, "let me just tell you a thing or two." I was losing it, I knew, but man, it felt good. "I am thirty-four years old, Sheila, and I am hardly in danger of losing my mind, my body, or my hor-mones. I do not have empty-nest syndrome or any other syndrome, as you call it. I do, instead, have a life and I have a right to that life, no matter how much you disapprove. Maybe you should go back to little Miss Dominick and talk to her about daughters who have a hard time letting their mothers have lives!"

Sheila eyed me like I was a mistaken kinder-gartener. "I don't have trouble with you leading an appropriate life, Mama," she said coolly. "But wearing miniskirts and jumping around on stage at your age is embarrassing. And I have my own life. Keith and I are very serious, Mama."

Those last few words struck fear into my very soul. "What do you mean, very serious, Sheila?" Oh Lord, did we need to see a doctor about birth control? That creep!

"He wants me to marry him, Mama."

"You aren't old enough, Sheila."

"You married Daddy when you were eigh-teen!"

"That was different." I regretted the words as soon as they'd left my lips.

"Why?"

"Because I didn't have what you have, Sheila. I didn't have college money sitting in the bank, or a chance to make more of myself. I needed your daddy, at least, that's what I thought. But it wasn't true. I didn't need him." I was failing at this, I knew.

"Well, I need Keith and I don't care what any-body says!"

"Well, you'd better think long and hard about ruining your life before it can even begin!"

"Is that what you did when you married Daddy?"

The conversation was disintegrating. We were almost to Vernell and Jolene's driveway and the more I spoke, the further down my throat my foot went. I stopped the car in the driveway next to

Jolene's huge white Cadillac and turned to face Sheila.

"Yes and no," I said. Sheila's eyes widened and she looked as if she was about to cry.

"I loved your daddy, Sheila, or at least I thought I did, but I married him for all the wrong reasons."

Sheila gasped. "You were pregnant with me!"

"No, hon, honest to Pete, that happened on our honeymoon. No, I married your daddy because your grandpa was drunk most of the time and I wanted to get away." An understanding reached Sheila's eyes. Lately Vernell was the same way, drunk more than he was sober.

"But I didn't give myself credit, Sheila. I didn't know that I could survive on my own. I didn't think I had any options and I thought I was in love. It was stupid, honey. We didn't know ourselves or each other well enough to commit for the rest of our lives."

"But you loved each other," Sheila said.

"Sure, but love don't always make a marriage, honey. You got to be ready for marriage. You got to know yourself as well as your partner. All's I'm saying is take your time. Don't jump into something out of desperation."

Sheila heard me, but the wall was coming back up. "Well, I do know myself. I am mature for my age and I love Keith."

"Good, then," I said. "If you two have a strong love, then it will last no matter what. It'll last until you go to college and then some. After all, a lifelong love doesn't go away just because someone gets an education."

Sheila rolled her eyes.

"Do you want me to take you to the doctor?" I said finally.

"God, no, Mama!" I breathed a sigh of relief, but too quickly. "Jolene'll take me to her doctor. It's less embarassing!"

As if on cue, Jolene stuck her head out the front door. "Phone," she yelled out to Sheila.

"I gotta go, Mama," Sheila said, already halfway out the door.

"Sheila, wait, I'm not finished with this conversation."

"I know, I know," she said impatiently, "but really, Mama, I gotta go. I won't rush into anything," she said, a concession to my worry. "But you gotta understand something, Mama. You and Daddy won't always be around. I can depend on Keith. He'll take care of me."

She was gone then, running up the cobblestone drive and into Vernell's brick palace. What had happened to my baby? Only two years ago, we'd talked about everything under the sun. She hadn't let the thought enter her head that I could ever leave her. What had happened to change her? Where had my little girl gone?

Jolene stretched out her arm and handed Sheila the phone. Sheila took it and ran inside without a backward glance, but Jolene made a point of smirking triumphantly at me. She could make my daughter come running anytime she wanted to. Sheila lived with her now and I was out in the cold.

Maybe it had been a mistake to let Sheila go live with her father. But what choice had I had?

Sheila had made up her mind; there was nothing I could've done. I drove off feeling empty and afraid for my baby and like the worst mother in the world. Where was the control in my life? Why did I feel like I was on a runaway train without brakes?

I drove, my car wandering across town on autopilot. The late afternoon traffic was beginning to build, but I hardly noticed. I was in a funk that had no end, a deep bottomless pit of self-pity that seemed to swallow me whole. The only thing that brought me back into the present was the awareness that I had just pulled into my backyard, the very last place on earth I'd wanted to visit.

I sat there behind the wheel, staring at the back door that led into my bedroom. Who the hell cared, I thought. What was the big, superstitious deal about not going into my own home? So Jimmy had died on my living room rug. I couldn't just run away forever. After all, wasn't that what I always did, run away? If I'd gone to court and tried to fight to keep Sheila, maybe the judge would've forced her to stay.

"Maggie, you are being ridiculous!" I said into the cool, late afternoon air. "Sheila is doing what all teenaged girls do to their mothers, she's trying to make her life your fault. Now, get a grip and get on with it!"

I grabbed the keys from the ignition, hopped out of the car, and slammed the door behind me. Now was as good a time as any to face the demon of Jimmy's death. The band wasn't playing tonight. There wasn't even a rehearsal scheduled. What better time?

"You are a chicken girl, afraid of her own

shadow. If you continue to act like the world is biting you in the ass, you'll always be at the mercy of everybody else." I was talking aloud to the neighborhood, climbing the steps to my back door, and sticking my key in the lock before I could change my mind. "We're going to go inside and clean this mess up. Then we're going to settle back in." I don't know who I thought the "we" was, but it felt good to pretend I was part of it.

I stepped inside, turned on the lights, and made myself walk straight through to the front of the house. I turned on the living room light and stared down at the floor, willing myself to look at Jimmy's bloodstain on my grandma's rug. It was still there. I don't know why that fact surprised me a little. I guessed it was my denial, still trying to trick me into the belief that this had all been a nightmare.

I pushed aside the furniture and rolled the rug up into a long thin tube. Dragging it through the house was more difficult than I'd anticipated. The old rug was heavy and seemed to resist my need to move it. But finally I dragged it out the back door, down the steps and over to the trash can. There I left it, not really sure that I was going to drag it to the curb on trash day, but relieved to have it out of the house.

"There!" I said to the empty yard and the heavy rug. "There."

I walked back up the stairs and into the kitchen, filling a pail with hot water and Pine-Sol. Mama always said Pine-Sol and a good airing would run the troubles right out of a house. I was going to give it my best shot.

I scrubbed for an hour before I got to the bedroom and saw the red light flashing on the answering machine. It was a good excuse to take a break. I hit the button and waited while the machine rewound. It was an ancient thing, a leftover from Vernell. He'd wanted to be available twenty-four hours a day to his "people," as he called them. I'd always figured if they wanted you bad enough, they'd call back. Still I found myself using the thing, just in case Sheila needed me. Just in case.

There was a series of four hang-ups and then a familiar voice, gruff and slightly inebriated.

"Like shooting ducks in a barrel, Maggie," Jerry Sizemore's voice grated. "I got some information you oughta have. I'll be at my place until I hear from you, so grab you a swimsuit and come on over here." He rattled off a set of instructions that would take me to the southeast part of Guilford County, apparently down every little side road in the county. Then there was a pause and he chuckled. "If you're thinking I'm gonna tell you this over the phone, you're wrong. And if you're thinking of forgetting to bring your suit, I'll make you sit in the tub naked. What I got on your inheritance is worth it, Maggie." I heard the clink of glass on glass and I knew he'd been pouring another shot of tequila. "Hell, girl, I ain't all that dangerous," he said. "I just like the sight of a pretty girl sitting in my hot tub while I'm discussin' business." The phone line went dead. The little man in the machine dated the call three hours ago. Damn, that Sizemore worked quick.

I put down my sponge and stared at the

answering machine. I was going to have to go to him, I knew that. There was no use in trying to call him. Jerry Lee Sizemore meant what he said. I stood up and carried the dirty pail of water to the back door, opened it, and sloshed the water across my deck. Jerry Lee Sizemore was going to make a pass at me, but he was also going to tell me something important.

"No free lunches," I said to the backyard before turning around and heading inside. Jerry Lee Sizemore would be best handled with a strict, businesslike approach.

The bungalow smelled of pine. With evening's arrival, the lamps had begun to fill the rooms of the house with a warm, buttery glow. The hardwood floors gleamed and for a moment, it was as if nothing had ever happened in my home. For an instant, I was comfortable and safe, glad to be back. But then the little prickles of fear edged their way back into my awareness.

"Ah! Don't do that!" I cautioned myself. "Keep moving!"

I replayed Jerry's message, writing down the directions to his house. Then I grabbed my keys and my swimsuit and walked out the door, leaving every light in the house on. No more staying with Jack. No more running away. I was coming home tonight, this time for good.

22

It was totally dark when I reached Jerry Lee Sizemore's house, but there was no mistaking it. A huge Vietnam veterans' MIA flag hung attached to a big post on one side of his driveway, and the American flag hung on the other side. The property was posted with NO TRESPASSING signs, barbed wire ran along the top of the chain-link fence, and the entrance gate, which was standing open, had a huge wrought iron S welded into the centerpiece. As I drove slowly past the entrance, I noticed yet another sign, smaller than the others, mounted on one side of the gate. "This property protected by Smith and Wesson."

As I moved into the long, pitch-dark driveway, lights flickered on, lighting my way down the rutted, red-clay drive. Jerry'd rigged motion lights on every pine tree that edged the drive. His big, log-cabin style house seemed to suddenly jump out in front of me, bathed in still more lights, with a circular drive and a flagpole that was mounted dead center in front of the house.

I pulled my car up to the front steps and cut the engine, afraid to open the car door and actually get out of my vehicle. A compound like this had to have a guard dog. With my luck, Jerry wouldn't get to me before the guard dog did.

After several minutes I realized the dog wasn't coming and neither was anyone else. I opened the car door and listened. In the distance I could hear music, Cream, from the '70s. The song was "White Room." No dog came to eat me, so I got out of the car and headed up the wide steps to the front door.

YOU MADE IT THIS FAR, a sign said, SO COME ON THROUGH THE HOUSE TO THE BACK. WE'RE PROBABLY IN THE HOT TUB.

My anxiety vanished. He and his friends were all partying in the back. He wasn't lying in wait to seduce me. I just had an overactive imagination, the same problem I'd had all my life.

I grabbed the large brass handle and pushed open the heavy wooden door. Jerry's house was as welcoming on the inside as it was forboding on the outside. Southwestern in theme, Jerry's living room was filled with overstuffed chairs and sofas in a brick red Indian blanket print. A book lay open, with a pair of reading glasses resting on the pages, beside a recliner. An empty shot glass stood next to the book.

I walked on, toward the sliding glass door that overlooked a massive deck. The music was louder now but still I could hear the swooshing sound of the hot tub. Tiki torches burned in holders along the deck railing. Huge potted fig trees and ferns lined the deck, making it a private nightime enclave. Now I knew why Jerry liked to conduct his business from the hot tub; his deck was an oasis.

I stepped out onto the deck, gently closing the sliding glass door behind me. At the far end was the hot tub, or at least I assumed so from the sound of water. It was hidden completely by plants and flowers.

"Jerry?" I called.

No answer.

"Hey, I hope you're semidecent." I was walking slowly across the deck, an uneasy feeling beginning to gnaw at my stomach. Maybe he'd passed out. "Hey, Jer, it's me, Maggie. . . ." I stepped to the edge of the fake forest. There was no sound, only the music and the gurgling of the hot tub. The night sky above me was black and starless.

I took a deep breath and forced myself to slip through the screen of plants. Jerry Lee Sizemore lay on his back, his body swirling slowly in the twelve-person hot tub, an ugly red stain blossoming across his chest.

23

When he answered the phone, I held it tighter against my ear, willing him through the receiver and into my head, willing him to lend me some of his strength.

"Help me," I said, my voice barely rising above a whisper. "Oh my God, help me."

"Maggie?" Marshall Weathers knew my voice. "Where are you?"

I was crying now, choking and gasping, feeling every edge of control I had disintegrating.

"I'm scared," I cried.

"I know you are, Maggie, and I want to help you. Tell me where you are and I'll be right there."

I told him exactly where I was. I stumbled over the words, sobs leaking out at every pause, but I told him and knew he would come to me.

"Maggie," he said, "I'm going to put you on

the phone with Bobby, here. He's going to stay with you while I start driving. Talk to Bobby, Maggie." He was on his way without even asking what was wrong.

A younger male voice replaced Marshall's, but still I clung to the phone, standing in Jerry's living room, my back to the deck and Jerry's body.

"Maggie?" the young man said. "Maggie, I want you to try and tell me what happened so I'll know what backup to send with Detective Weathers."

He wanted me to help Marshall. I could do that. My heart was pounding in my chest, I thought I was going to throw up, but I could do this one more thing.

"He's, he's, he's . . ." I hiccuped, "dead. My . . . Jerry Lee Sizemore, he's, he's . . ."

"Dead," Bobby said calmly. "Okay. Okay, Maggie. Are you sure?"

"Yes," I said, my voice rising an octave. "I'm sure! He's been shot!"

"Okay, Maggie, stay with me here a second." There was the sound of hushed voices as Bobby issued instructions to someone.

"When will he be here?" I asked, unable to keep myself from exploding with fear.

"Ten minutes, Maggie. Hang in there. I'm sending some other officers. They'll be there sooner because they're closer."

But they weren't. It was Marshall Weathers who arrived first, flying down Jerry Lee's driveway, his blue light still flashing.

He didn't seem to move quickly, but he was on

the porch and at my side in what seemed like an instant. It seemed natural to go to him, to let him take me into his arms, if only for a moment.

"You're sure he's dead?" he asked, moving past me, toward the interior of Jerry's house.

"Yes."

Behind us sirens wailed, lights flashed along the driveway. It seemed as if the entire police force was arriving, filling Jerry Lee Sizemore's expansive front yard with vehicles and uniformed officers.

Marshall stopped the first pair at the foot of the steps. "Go around back," he said. "We got one that's probably dead in the hot tub. Might oughta look and make sure there's no more. Let's make a fifty-foot area in front of the house, then go as far back as you can."

Another unmarked sedan came flying down the driveway, stopping inches from the patrol units. I recognized the man who hopped out of the car, moving quickly toward us. It was Marshall's young partner, Billy Evans.

Marshall waited until Billy reached the top of the steps, then he turned to me. "Stay here with Detective Evans, Maggie. I've gotta go take a look." Two EMTs walked up, bags in hand, questioning looks on their faces. Weathers nodded them in, and the three disappeared inside Jerry's house. Every nerve fiber I had stood on edge, waiting. I realized I was clenching my teeth and knotting my hands so tightly that my nails cut into my palms. I didn't feel safe when he wasn't in my sight.

When he returned there was a strange look on his face. He walked up to where I stood with Billy

Evans and then pulled him aside. Whatever he had to say, he didn't want me to hear. Billy looked down at Marshall's right hand, staring at a small metal piece laying in his palm—a shell casing. Then they both looked back at me. I knew, without anyone saying a word, that it was another .38-caliber bullet that had killed Jerry Lee Sizemore.

"Oh God." The words escaped from my lips before I could stop them. It was happening all over again. Weathers glanced back at me and then back at his colleague. "Why don't you finish up here," he said. "I'll take Ms. Reid back and get a statement."

My thoughts were racing, one after the other, too fast for me to track, bits and pieces that were gone like storm clouds before a front. *Black widow spider.* That's what Weathers was thinking. *And everywhere that Maggie went her gun was sure to follow. . . .*

"Come on," Marshall said, "we'll take my car. Someone'll follow with yours."

I let him lead me, not caring about my car. All I could see was Jerry's bloated body, floating before me, the ugly red stain on his chest a stark contrast against the lush tangle of plants, his sightless eyes staring up at an empty sky.

"It was a thirty-eight-caliber gun that killed him, wasn't it? You think I killed him, don't you?" I said. We were not even out of Jerry's driveway. "You're thinking it's the same caliber gun, that it had to be mine."

We were at the end of the driveway and he stopped to look at me. "So now you read minds?"

"Well, it's what I'd be thinking."

"That's you."

"All right," I said, "what are you thinking?"

Weathers turned out onto the road and started toward town. "Don't much matter what I'm thinking."

Marshall Weathers was the most frustrating human being I had ever encountered. He always bounced the ball back into my court, never answered a question, especially if it had anything to do with himself. I looked over at him as he drove. His face was a mask, not an unkind mask, but closed.

"It's all about control with you, isn't it?" I asked.

"I don't follow," he answered. But I knew he did. His mustache twitched.

"You've always got to be in control."

"Well, sure." He said it as if I'd said, "The sky is blue."

"Have you ever not been in control of a situation?"

"Maybe at the start of something," he said. He was uncomfortable with the turn in the conversation. His shoulders tightened and he stared straight ahead, not looking at me.

"Maggie, sit there for a while and think back on everything that happened from the time you got to Sizemore's until the time I got there." He didn't want any more personal questions. "Close your eyes and play it like a movie. When we get back to the office, I want you to tell me everything you can remember."

I didn't want to do it. I didn't want to see Jerry,

over and over, floating in his hot tub. I wanted Weathers to do that. I wanted him to take over and fix everything. But that was just the problem. No one else was going to fix it for me. All of my adult life, I'd had to face this same realization, time and time again. I always fixed everything.

At first, I'd been mad about it. There was no Prince Charming and I wasn't Snow White or Cinderella. Then, somewhere along the line, I got to feeling proud. I was Maggie Reid, and I could take care of myself. Still, when things got a bit much, like now, I found myself wishing for a knight in shining armor. Weathers was merely pointing me back to reality. He'd come when I'd needed him, but I was going to have to pull the killer out of the hat to save myself. Doggone it!

I closed my eyes and willed my mind back to Jerry Lee's phone message, then to his house. The gate had been open. Why? Was it always that way? He was expecting me, in a general way, but he had no idea when I'd show up. Had he expected someone else? What had he found out about the mobile home lot? The reality of Jerry's death was dawning on me. I'd asked him to look into Jimmy's lot. He'd found something, and now he was dead.

I gasped softly and my eyes flew open. Weathers was pulling into the underground garage of the police department. He reached a hand over and touched my arm lightly.

"Stay with it, if you can," he said. "Don't try and make sense of what you remember, just go for the details, the little things that might not seem to matter."

"You don't understand," I said. "He's dead because of me. I sent him to audit the Mobile Home Kingdom and he found something."

Weathers didn't react. "Let's go on up," he said. He opened the car door and stepped out into the gloomy underground parking lot. It was deserted except for the two of us, but we were not alone. From every corner, covering every angle, cameras watched and reported back to their monitors. The place was probably wired for sound, too.

Weathers walked quickly to the door, punched in a series of numbers, waited for a dull click, then pulled the heavy metal door open. He held it, ushering me through with a motion of his hand. He didn't want to talk here. We would talk where he said and when he said, and that was probably for good reason. I walked by his side, struggling to match his quick, long-legged stride, my mind rushing in all directions.

We rode the elevator in silence. He stood so close that had I moved merely an inch, I would've been touching his arm. I remembered how it had felt when he held me for that one quick moment after he'd arrived at Jerry Sizemore's. *Stop it! How can you think about that now?* I yelled silently. But I couldn't *not* think about it. The attraction that had simmered before threatened to boil over and consume me.

I brought my hands together and pinched the flesh in between my left thumb and forefinger, hard.

"What'd you do that for?" Weathers had been watching.

"To get my attention," I answered.

He raised an eyebrow and shrugged his shoulders. Now he could add *dingbat* or *crazed* to the list of adjectives I was sure he carried in his head to describe me.

"Guess that's a woman thing, huh?"

I glared at him. "Like men don't do anything to keep their minds on a task?"

"Don't usually need to," he said.

I thought of Vernell, reciting mobile home statistics to himself while we made love. Weathers was right. Men were the exact opposite of women.

"So what were you thinking that took your mind off Mr. Sizemore?" he asked.

The elevator jerked to a stop, pushing me against his arm. "Nothing," I said, jumping toward the door.

As the elevator door slowly pulled apart, I could've sworn I heard a slight chuckle from Marshall Weathers. I didn't look back. I walked ahead of him, down the long hallway to the CID offices. It was going to be another long night.

24

It was long past midnight. Plastic cups littered the table between us. The room smelled of stale cigarette smoke, burned coffee, and Marshall●Weathers's cologne. I'd had about all I could take of repeating the details of how I came to discover Jerry Lee Sizemore's body. I wanted out.

"I've told you everything I can remember," I said finally. It was not the first time I had made that statement, but I had hopes it would be the last.

Marshall Weathers was just as tired. His eyes were bloodshot. He stared into the bottom of his coffee cup, as if hoping it would offer him more than bitter dregs and caffeine.

"You're right." He sighed and pushed the coffee cup away. "Let's call it a night."

He pushed back against his chair, brought his arms up, and laced his fingers behind his neck. For a moment he closed his eyes and I watched him. His face was pale beneath his tanned skin. The lines around his eyes had deepened.

"All right," he said, bringing the chair legs down on the ground and startling me. "I'll take you home, or wherever it is you're staying." The little sarcastic tone was back in his voice. It bothered him that I stayed with Jack. He probably figured we were having a torrid affair. The idea tickled me and I tried not to smile, but couldn't help it. He really didn't like that.

"What about my car?" I asked.

"Give me your keys. I'll see that it gets delivered."

"All right. Let's go." I stood up and grabbed my purse. He moved slower than I did, with more deliberation. He moved, I thought, like a panther, always looking for his next opportunity, always thinking three steps ahead.

Neither of us spoke again until we were seated in his car with the engine running.

"Where to?" he asked. "The warehouse district?" He put the car into reverse and started to leave the garage, assuming.

I let him assume. He pulled out onto Washington Street, heading for Jack's on Elm, and I let him drive almost to Elm before I spoke.

"My place."

"How's that?" Weathers reached over and cut the radio down, as if he hadn't heard me.

"I'm back at my place," I said.

"Huh." A little sound that spoke volumes. *About time*, it said. "Well good . . . shouldn't have been with that hippie harmonica player in the first place," it said.

He made a left on Elm and cut over to Friendly, clearly pleased to be heading away from Jack's.

He waited until we were rolling up in my back-yard to speak again. "I don't want you to be para-noid," he said, "but you need to be cautious until we catch this guy."

It was the first true indication I had that he believed I wasn't a killer.

"Whoever killed your brother-in-law, and now your accountant, doesn't know that you're in the dark. He could be thinking that Sizemore got to you with his information."

I hadn't put all of that together yet, at least not consciously. But I was scared to death suddenly, so I knew in my heart he was right.

"All I'm saying is, don't take any unneccesary risks. Don't go out alone at night. Have someone walk you to your car after work. Don't go down to the mobile home lot anymore. The usual precau-tions." He threw that last one in almost as an after-thought, but I knew it was his main point. He'd said the words more slowly: "Don't go down to the mobile home lot."

"You take care of yourself and let me go to work on this."

I was about to say something sarcastic, but found I couldn't say anything. I was too scared to say a word. I looked up at my back deck, the light shining over my back door, every light in the house on, and realized I was terrified to go inside. What had seemed like such a perfect idea earlier in the evening now seemed foolhardy.

Weathers read me and cut the car's engine. "How about I come in and check around with you? Just put your mind at ease before I go?"

I didn't have to answer. He was out of the car, his hand reaching around to his side and unbuttoning his holster. By the time I reached him, he was standing on the deck, his gun drawn and waiting for me to unlock the door.

I must've stared at the gun, because he smiled slightly. "Don't worry," he said, "if someone's in there, I'll just shoot 'em."

I tried to smile back, but the sight of that big black gun rattled me. "You do that," I answered, but I heard the tiny quaver in my voice.

He went in first. He was a large presence in my little bungalow. His footsteps echoed as he moved across the hardwood floors. I closed the door behind us and followed him from room to room. He made a big show of looking in the closets, moving the clothes aside and peering behind everything. He looked under my bed. He looked behind the shower curtain. Nothing.

"Well, you're clear," he said, putting the gun away and moving toward the back door.

"Would you like a cup of coffee?" I asked. This time the squeaky tension in my voice was evident to both of us. I tried to laugh it off, but that only made me sound hysterical.

"I'm kinda coffee'd out," he said. "You'll be fine, Maggie. You got my card and my pager number. If anything happens, if you get worried, you call nine-one-one. If you need me, they'll reach me at home. But you call them first so they can get a car out here."

"Oh, I'll be fine," I said.

"Did you fix that lock on the front door?" he asked, his face suddenly concerned.

"Not exactly, but I have a chain latch I use when I'm here, so I'd know if someone was trying to break in."

He didn't look so certain now, and I was feeling even more anxious. He walked back into the living room, over to the door, where he lifted the chain and held it in his hand.

"Why don't you see to getting the lock switched out and repaired tomorrow morning?"

"I'll get on it," I said. I was seriously doubting my decision to leave Jack's and return home. But I had to do it sometime and if someone wanted to get to me, Jack's was just as easily broken into as my house.

"Go on home now," I said. "I'm fine. Really."

"I know you are," he said. "Just take normal precautions." The closer he moved to my back door, the slower he seemed to walk.

"Thanks for checking around for me," I said. "Go home and get some rest." I yawned loudly and stretched. "That's what I'll be doing," I lied. "I'll be getting a good night's rest."

We were inches apart at my back door. Mama used to say it was a sure thing that if you were feeling a certain way about a person, then they were probably feeling that same way toward you. Well, I knew how I felt. I felt like kissing Marshall Weathers again.

I looked up at him and saw him watching me.

Mama was right, all right. But he didn't do it. Instead he reached out and touched my arm. My heart started pounding and my mouth went dry.

"Enjoy church, did you?" he asked. I could feel my face turning scarlet. "Mama always likes to welcome a new face. She was right taken with you." I was speechless. "Of course, visitors don't usually leave by the bathroom window. That's a first for us."

"I was just . . ."

He let me hang there for a second, enjoying my discomfort. "Wondering?" he said finally.

"No, taking care of myself. If my life is on the line, then I want to know everything I can about the people around me. You're supposed to be in charge of clearing Jimmy's murder. How do I know I can trust you?"

The muscle in his jaw twitched, but he forced a smile. He wasn't liking this one little bit. "Well, I hope Mama was helpful."

"I didn't know you were divorced," I lied. No sense in beating around the bush. "Like me."

"Not exactly," he said.

"Not exactly like you or not exactly divorced?"

Weathers leaned against the back door and looked at me. "Both, I guess. Won't be final until she signs the papers."

"When Vernell left me for the damn Dish Girl, I nearly lost my mind. I went to bed for days and ate myself silly. But I had to go on. Guess that's why I'm singing now."

"You think?" he asked.

"Yeah. I mean, I guess it turned out to be for

the best, although it stung at the time. Isn't that how you felt?"

I knew better. I believed his mom and her friends, and the pain that briefly crossed his face confirmed it. He hadn't quite figured out how to wrap his mind around the fact that his best friend and his wife had both betrayed him.

"Yeah, I guess." He sighed. "You go on. She's happy and I'm glad for it." He was a bad liar.

"Makes it hard to trust someone ever again, doesn't it?" I said softly.

He looked at me for a long moment, looked right through my heart and into my soul, and then found he could do it no longer. "Aw, I guess looking back I could have seen it coming. I was working long hours. She needed more than I could give. I learned from it."

He looked down at me again, but not into my eyes. Instead he seemed to search my entire face, as if wanting to say something, but holding back, not willing to trust himself or me.

I took one tiny step closer, still waiting for him to meet my eyes. When he did, finally, he pulled me into his arms and kissed me. We stayed like that, in each other's arms, for only a few minutes, and then he pulled back.

"I need to go," he said, and in a brief instant was gone.

I closed the back door, turned the dead bolt, and leaned against it. Then, when I thought he wouldn't see, I peeked through the little cut-out windowpane at the top of the door. He was sitting in his car, staring up at the house.

"All right," I said, turning away from the door. "Let's show him we're serious. We can take care of ourselves." My voice echoed through the empty house.

I forced myself to march back into the living room. An antique sideboard sat against one wall. If I pushed it in front of the door and loaded it with books, no one could come through the front door. I grabbed at it and tried to pull, but it wouldn't budge. I pushed and it moved slowly, its heavy wooden legs groaning and leaving deep gouges in the floor. I didn't care. I pushed as hard as I could until at last it rested across the front door.

I rewarded myself by walking through the house to the back and peeping out my back window. He was gone.

"I'm fine," I said loudly. That's when I began hearing things.

At first it was a thud on my front porch. Then something hit the side of the house. I froze, listening. I hit the light switch by the back door and plunged the bedroom into total darkness. I didn't want anyone to see me moving around, a silhouette against the shades, a moving target. My skin was crawling. Someone was out there. I knew someone was out there, watching, waiting.

I moved across the room and picked up the cordless phone on my bedstand. I clicked it on and listened to the reassuring dial tone. I peeked through the curtains. Still nothing. It was all my imagination.

"You're being ridiculous," I said. "You need sleep." I fumbled through my dresser drawers, hunting for the blue-and-white-striped flannel pajamas that I'd inherited from my brother Larry one Christmas. Every year Mama gave him new pajamas and every year he tossed them to me when she wasn't looking. Larry was too manly to wear pajamas.

I started to undress, but stopped, listening, my heart pounding in my throat. The bedroom was too exposed, too open to prying eyes peering in through little chinks in the curtains. I went into the bathroom, but left the door open, just in case. I took the phone with me, too. As quickly as I could, I undressed and put on the pajamas, carefully rolling up the too-long sleeves and leg cuffs.

I darted from the bathroom, through the brightly lit kitchen and back into my darkened bedroom. I couldn't make myself turn out the lights in the rest of the house. They could stay on all night. I listened, my ears straining to catch every sound. A car door swung shut outside and I jumped. Was it next door? Down the street?

I grabbed the remote and switched on country music videos. Clint Black wandered across the screen, staring at me with his soulful black eyes, crooning his heart out. I fixed on him for all of two seconds and then had to hit the MUTE button. What if someone was outside and I couldn't hear them coming? I checked the phone again. I jumped out of bed and peered through the back door window. The yard glowed in the light from the back door.

The phone rang. I jerked it from its stand.

"Hello?"

Nothing, then a click.

The hairs stood up on my arms and the fingers that still clutched the phone began to tingle and sweat. "It was a wrong number," I muttered dully. The phone rang again and without thinking, I answered.

"Hello?"

"What are you doing there?" Jack demanded.

"Did you just call me?"

"No, and don't dodge the question. Why are you there?" I sank down on the edge of my bed, my knees too weak to hold me.

"Jack, it was time. I couldn't keep staying with you. Sooner or later, I had to come home. I'm fine." As I talked, I wandered out into the kitchen and grabbed the knife holder that sat out on the counter, clutching it with one arm and walking back into the bedroom. It looked good on my bed-side table.

"I don't like you being there by yourself," he said.

"Hey, I don't particularly love it either, but like I said, it's home and I needed to come back. Besides," I said, working to keep the panic out of my voice, "think of Evelyn. It couldn't look good for you to have another woman staying at your place."

"What makes you think I told her?" he said, laughing.

"Well, I guess in your shoes, I would figure the less said the better. But see, Jack, that's what I mean." I looked at the bedside clock. It was almost four in the morning. "Jack, what are you doing calling me at this hour anyway?"

"I just got in," he said. "I was worried." There was a slight pause. "Hey, you don't sound too sleepy. I mean, it doesn't sound like I woke you up."

"Guess that's why we're night owls," I said. Out of the corner of my eye, I thought I saw something move outside.

"Yeah, hard to go to bed early on your night off. It'd only screw up the schedule." I was wandering over to the window and lifting a slat in the blinds while he talked. The backyard seemed empty, but who knew?

"Well, if you're sure this is what you want, I'll let you get back to whatever you were doing." Jack sounded a little lonely. "I'm gonna miss having you around. Kinda got used to another body in the bed."

"Thanks, Jack. I really appreciate all you did."

"You got a place in my bed anytime." He laughed. "Take it easy."

I sat on the edge of the bed, holding the dead phone, listening to the dial tone humming out into the still room.

"It's four in the morning," I said aloud. "People don't break into houses at four in the morning. Too close to dawn." I stretched and stood. Might as well turn out some of the lights. I walked back through the house one more time, turning out all but one light in each room. In the living room, I hit the overhead light, forgetting I'd unplugged the lamp when I moved the table against the door. The room was completely dark.

Outside a streetlight glittered off the parked cars, and I stared through the front window curtains. The street looked deserted. No cars moved. My college student neighbors had finally called it a night. In another hour or two, it would begin all over again. People would walk out of their houses and start off for work or class, and no one would think twice about the night behind them.

I started to drop the curtain and stopped. Someone was outside. A shadow had passed around the side of the house. I was certain this time. I dropped the curtain and listened in the darkness. Something banged up against the trash cans I kept in the narrow pathway between my house and my neighbor's. A dog started to bark, and then another, until there was a chorus of howls and bays. The neighborhood alarm system had gone off.

I jumped off the couch and ran back for the bedroom. The phone. I had to get to the phone and call 911 before he got inside or cut the wires. I tripped coming into the bedroom, hitting the leg of my bedside table. As I reached to steady myself, the tiny table toppled, sending the lamp, the phone, and the knife holder crashing to the floor.

The lamp crashed and broke. The phone skidded across the floor, into a dark corner, and the knives flipped out of their holder, dropping in all directions.

"Damn it!" I said, trying to find the phone and coming up empty-handed.

My fingers closed on the heavy butcher knife just as a shadow crossed the back deck. He was out there, moving toward the back door.

I jumped up, the butcher knife clutched in my hand, and began to walk softly toward the door.

The door handle started to move, ever so slightly, just as I reached it. I made myself stand just to the side of the door. I could flip the light switch and find the phone, but if I did, wouldn't I be an easier target?

I stretched up on my tiptoes and leaned quickly toward the window at the top of the door. Maybe it was a dog, or my imagination. But it wasn't. A man was bending over my outside doorknob. As I peered down at him, he suddenly jerked upright and I screamed.

Marshall Weathers stood eye to eye with me, glaring in through the back window.

25

I twisted the dead-bolt handle and jerked the door open. Weathers was still glaring, his eyes bloodshot and his face grim.

"What in the hell are you doing, trying to break into my house?" I demanded.

"Breaking into your house? I'm not breaking into your house! What are you doing slamming lamps around and making all kinds of noise at four o'clock in the morning?"

We stood there, staring each other down, neither one of us budging. Then slowly he began to smile.

"What the hell are you smiling at?" I said. "I asked you a serious question."

He laughed. "You always sleep in them over-sized britches?" he asked.

I looked down. In my rush to get to the phone,

my pajama cuffs had come undone and my sleeves were now hanging six inches below my fingertips. I must've looked ridiculous.

I pulled myself up as tall as I could and tried to look dignified. "Well, what are you doing, lurking around my house?" I asked.

"I couldn't sleep. I got to thinking about you in here, with nothing but a chain on your door, and I felt like I might as well drive over and check you out."

"So what were you doing picking my lock?"

He gave me a disgusted look, a this-ain't-TV look. "I was checking your door when I heard all hell breaking loose in here. You're lucky I didn't shoot the lock off!"

I looked down then, and saw the gun in his hand.

"God! Put that thing away! You could've shot me!" I couldn't stop staring at the huge gun.

"Maggie, I am a professional. I wouldn't have shot you!"

It was cold outside, even for a late September dawn and the air smelled of rain. I started to shiver, wrapping my arms around myself to ward off the breeze that had started to blow, bringing with it the first raindrops.

"Well, this is ridiculous," I said. "At least come inside." I turned around, without waiting to see if he followed, and immediately tripped over a knife.

"Ow, damn!" I swore.

Weathers reached over and flicked on the light switch by the door.

"You always keep your knives in the bed-room?" he asked, studying the disarray before him.

"No," I muttered, bending down to study my big toe. "I do not. Now look what you did," I said. "My toe's bleeding."

"What *I* did?"

"Well, if you hadn't decided to slink around my bedroom, I would never have tripped over the bedside table. And if I had never tripped over the table, then the knife holder wouldn't have fallen, now would it?" I stood upright and scowled at him.

"You are nuts," he said. "And you'd better go get a Band-Aid for that toe before you stain the floor."

He didn't look at me. Instead he bent down and started picking up the knives that were scattered everywhere. I thought I saw his shoulders shaking and that made me even more irritated. He was laughing at me.

"Fine, then. Maybe you can find the phone while you're at it," I said, and stalked off to the bathroom.

My toe was starting to throb, and it took almost five minutes to find gauze and tape and stop the bleeding. Outside the tiny bathroom, I could hear Weathers moving around, pushing furniture back and forth and attempting to put my room back together. As I finished playing doctor with my toe, I became aware that there was no longer any sound at all coming from my room.

"You about done?" he called.

"Yeah," I answered, putting the bandages back up on the medicine cabinet shelf.

"Come here a sec."

I walked out of the bathroom and into the bedroom, a huge lumpy bandage swaddling my big toe.

"Well, it's the best I could do," I said, walking into my room.

Weathers was sitting on the edge of the bed, a white handkerchief in his lap. When I wandered up to him, he carefully folded back the edges of the square of cloth.

"This yours?" he asked.

My .38-caliber Beretta lay cradled in his lap.

"Where did you get that?" I breathed.

He was watching me closely, gauging my reaction. "It was under a bag, underneath your bed." He was waiting for me to answer him.

"Well, I didn't put it there!"

"Maggie, I got probable cause right now, right here in my lap. Do you realize what that means?" He didn't wait for my answer. "It means, by all rights, I could arrest you right now and book you for murder."

If he was waiting for a confession, it wasn't coming. I stared right back into his eyes, my face a stony mask of anger and confusion.

"The only reason we're not heading back downtown is that I can't prove, at this particular moment, that the two murder victims were shot with *this* thirty-eight-caliber pistol. But you know what?" His face was suffused with anger. "It won't take me long to find out. I'm gonna take this gun back to the office and send it to the crime lab, with a request to do a rush job on it, because there are two murder victims and the count is probably gonna climb!"

"You can't think that I put that there!" I said. "I wouldn't hide a murder weapon under my own bed!"

"Maggie, you were here most of the late afternoon and evening. You were only gone from your house for about five hours. There's no sign of forced entry." His voice trailed off as he left me to make the conclusion.

"Get out of my house," I said. I kept my voice low and even, but there was no mistaking how angry I was. "I thought I could trust you. I even went so far as to believe that you were on my side, but that was all an act, wasn't it? You come in here, go through my things, and all the time I'm thinking you're here to help me. I don't know how that thing came to be in my house. Your people tore this place apart after Jimmy died. They know it wasn't here. And now, suddenly, it's here." I stared at him coldly. "How do I know you didn't plant that?"

He stood up slowly, the twitching muscle in his jaw the only indication that he was angry. "I'm gonna pretend you didn't say that," he said softly.

I walked over to the back door, flung it open, and looked back at him. "And I'm gonna pretend I don't know you," I said.

He walked past me, out into the cold, rainy dawn, my pistol carefully wrapped in his handkerchief. I slammed the door behind him and shot the bolt home. I didn't need him. I didn't need anybody. I was going to find Jimmy's and Jerry's killer all by myself and Weathers would be plenty sorry when I did.

26

As the sky began to brighten slightly, I fell asleep. But not before I'd lain awake cursing Marshall Weathers and wondering who in the world would want to frame me for two murders. I awoke at ten in the morning, with only four hours of sleep, because an alarm was ringing in my head. I swatted at the clock before realizing that it was the phone. I lay there, waiting for the answering machine to get it, but it had been disconnected in last night's frenzy.

"What now?" I barked into the receiver.

Silence.

"I have had it with you," I said loudly. "If you want a piece of me, stand up like a man and say so!" I started to hang up, but stopped as someone began speaking.

"Is this Maggie Reid?" the woman asked.

"Don't mess with me," I warned. "I am not in the mood. And who exactly is this?" My heart was racing, but not because I was afraid. Now I was angry.

"Bertie Sexton, from the Mobile Home Kingdom." I sat straight up in bed. "I'm sorry to bother you, ma'am, but I think we should talk."

"Talk?"

Bertie Sexton was crying or had a very bad cold. She was snuffling and clearing her throat, with little catches of breath that sounded like stifled sobs.

"Did you hear about that guy?" she said softly. "Mr. Sizemore? The one you had come out and do the audit?"

"Where are you?" I asked.

"I'm at home," she said. Her voice broke and I knew she was crying. "They sent me home on account of I was too tore up to work. The police were out to the lot and they were all over us. I couldn't take it anymore." The girl was openly crying now.

"Look," I said, "get ahold of yourself, honey. You know where the Bisquitville is on West Market?" I got a sniffly sound that I took for an affirmative. "Meet me there in thirty minutes." I hung up before she could start crying harder. Mama always said that action was better than a bucket full of tears, and in Bertie Sexton's case that had to be true.

I flew out of bed, dressed, and crossed my fingers that the police had returned my car. They had, but they'd left it in a NO PARKING BETWEEN 6 AND

9 A.M. zone, then they'd ticketed it! Weathers's doing, no doubt. I didn't have time to stop and speculate. Bisquitville made strong, hot coffee and I needed plenty to get my brain going.

It was late in the day for Bisquitville's early regulars when I pulled into the parking lot. The phone company trucks were gone. The construction worker pickups were now replaced with Volvo station wagons and passenger vans, a sure sign that the second shift, preschool-mom regulars, were clustered around the tables and booths, comparing notes and complaining.

Bertie Sexton had beat me to a back booth in the crowded, smoky restaurant. She saw me as I walked through the side door, but looked away. Her eyes were black mascara-rimmed circles and her pale face looked ghostly in the harsh daylight that poured through the many windows.

I ignored her while I grabbed a large coffee and a bacon bisquit, and made my way over to her booth. She waited until I was seated across from her to look up.

"Thank you for coming," she said, in her baby soft voice. "I didn't know who else to talk to, what with Mr. Spivey being dead and Don, er, Mr. Evans, turning out to be not at all the man I thought he was. I figured with you being a woman and just coming into the business, well, there might be a chance to right some wrongdoings." There was an angry flash in her dark brown eyes, the flash of a woman scorned. I was fixin' to get the good stuff from Bertie Sexton and nothing suited better.

"Well now, honey," I said, reaching across the

table to cover her hand with my own, "you just take a deep breath and tell me all about it. You know, I had a feeling things were not quite right when I was in the other day. If they're not treating you right . . ." I let my voice trail off and tried my best to look sympathetic. As in, just tell old Aunt Maggie all about it.

That was all it took. Bertie scanned the little restaurant for interlopers, decided it was safe, and began to talk.

"When I came to work for Mr. Spivey, five years ago, the business was still growing. Mr. Vernell had gone off to tend to his other business and Jimmy needed someone to help out in the worst way." Her eyes widened a little and I knew then that Bertie had fallen hook, line, and sinker for Jimmy's fast talking.

"I tried to tell him there were problems, that some people weren't doing right by him or the customers, but I couldn't get him to listen. As long as he could run off when he wanted, the money kept coming in, and everybody liked him, Jimmy was fine. He didn't care what Tommy or Don did."

This was the good stuff. "You know," I said, leaning in closer, "Jimmy was a fine man." Bertie's eyes welled up with tears. "The very thought of someone trying to take advantage of him just makes my blood boil!"

Bertie's eyes flashed again. "He didn't have a wicked or disloyal bone in his body!" she said. "There he was, loyal to that terrible woman, and her sneaking around here like a yard dog, sniffing up after Tommy Purvis. They weren't even trying to keep it a secret, if you ask me."

"You mean Roxanne and little Tommy Purvis?" I acted like this was the biggest surprise in the world.

"Oh yeah, honey," she said. "All the time! The second Jimmy'd take off to play golf, in'd come Roxanne, like the queen of the world. She and Tommy'd sit out in her car for hours. Her just a-smiling and him acting like she was the hottest thing around. And you know, he didn't mean a bit of it. It was insurance, pure and simple."

"Insurance?" Bertie was going faster than I could track.

"Oh, sure," she sighed, "Tommy was taking kickbacks from the set-up guys." I must've looked confused. "You know, the guys that put the homes on the lots and secure them to the piers and all. If Jimmy'd found out, he would've just killed Tommy. But he knew Roxanne wouldn't let Jimmy fire him. Wouldn't suit her needs. And," she said, her voice dropping to a whisper, "I'm sure old Tommy was cutting Roxanne in for a goodly amount."

"Roxanne was taking money from her own husband's business?"

Bertie nodded sadly. "She and every other living creature knew Jimmy didn't love her. He tried, but he couldn't hide it. He was in love with someone else, if you ask me. I just never knew who it was." Bertie looked even sadder. "You think I like my hair this color?" she asked suddenly. "Jimmy used to say how much he loved curly red hair so I—" She broke off, staring at me. "Hey!"

I didn't know what to do. I kept my face neutral and played stupid.

"It was you!"

"Bertie, I was married to Jimmy's brother! I would no more . . ."

Bertie shook her head. "That don't mean much, as envious as Jimmy was of his brother."

"I never," I said.

"Oh, I'm not saying you did," she said. "But it sure explains a whole lot. Unrequited love." She sighed wistfully. "I was turned down for Jimmy's unrequited love. Just like in the movies."

I let her trail off into the romanticized version of her past, and then brought her back with a snap.

"And Don done him wrong, too?"

Bertie's eyes flashed and I knew we were closing in for the kill. "You better watch out for him, sugar," she said, "'cause he sure isn't worried a thing about you!" Bertie's cheeks were flushed and her ears were turning as red as her dyed hair.

"What do you mean, he isn't worried about me? He ought to be worried. If Jerry Lee Sizemore found out he's been doing wrong . . ." Again, I let my voice trail off and Bertie chimed right in.

"Oh, it didn't take Mr. Sizemore finding out," she said. "I knew for a long time what Donald Evans was up to. I even told Jimmy about it, not three days before he died. I just didn't care anymore."

The hairs stood up on my arms and I felt chill bumps run across the back of my neck. "What did you tell Jimmy?"

"About how Donald Evans was lining his

pockets with money from Ashdale Manufacturers while Jimmy lost out! Had to be close to three hundred thousand a year that Jimmy never saw."

"How could Jimmy not know?"

"'Cause Don wasn't here three months before he'd won Jimmy over and convinced him he could run the day-to-day of the lot. Then he cuts a deal with Ashdale to rep only their homes, and put them on Ashdale's lots, and use Ashdale's finance company. Jimmy would never have done business like that."

So why hadn't she told Jimmy sooner if she cared so much for him? I looked across the table at her, a long hard look, and realized what must have happened. Bertie wasn't just unattractive, she was homely. Underneath her thick layer of makeup, her skin was deeply pockmarked. One eye wandered ever so slightly to the outside of her face. And a padded Wonderbra was probably all that stood between her and the outside world. Don Evans hadn't wanted Bertie Sexton, either.

She saw the look on my face and her own face hardened with bitter anger. "He's got him a high-dollar girlfriend," she said. "Rolls around town in a white Caddy. Picks up her cell phone and says 'jump,' and old Donald comes running."

Poor Bertie. "Well, you two sure seemed cozy when I stopped by," I said.

Bertie pushed her thick red hair out of her eyes and attempted to fix both eyes on me. "Do you think I'm a fool?" she asked. "If he knew I'd found out about him and Ashdale and then told Jimmy, he'd kill me." She saw the shocked look on my face and rushed in. "Well, maybe not kill me, but you shoulda seen Jimmy's face after he went in and had it out with him!"

Bertie made a big show of looking at her watch, and then back at me.

"I can't stay," she said, "I've got things to tend to. I came to you only because I cared so much for Jimmy." I didn't believe that for one sweet second. "I was going to just leave. After that sweet Mr. Sizemore offered me a job, I thought I'd just walk away and not need the Mobile Home Kingdom. Everything's different now. And nobody pays like the Spivey brothers, least not until that cute Jerry came along." She sighed again, as if resigned to her lot in life. "But that don't matter now. What matters," she said, the angry glint back in her eye, "is that somebody needs to look out for me and the Kingdom. I know how Jimmy felt about his brother, and I hear he's bad to drink. He can't be counted on. No, the way I see it, I figure that somebody oughta be you."

She stood up, grabbed her purse, and stood staring down at me. Clearly I was the last hope in a long line of failed heroes. I watched her walk off, a frumpy wanna-be sex kitten. Now what? I wondered.

The moms were leaving Bisquitville, rushing off to run their errands in the two hours left before they returned to preschool to pick up their little darlings. I watched them, pairing up in twos and threes, and for a moment I felt envious. I wanted those years back. I wanted to rush off to the grocery store, then take my little girl home for a nap. I wanted to be me, before it all unraveled, before I knew what a louse Vernell was.

But who was I kidding? Something inside me knew that Vernell was no-good husband material before we even married. And no matter how many times I could magically transport Sheila back to toddlerhood, she still had to grow up into a rageful adolescent and leave me behind. A few years from now, who knew? Maybe she'd marry and have a daughter of her own. Maybe then she'd decide to be close again.

I shook myself and stood up. It wouldn't do to stay in one place too long. Not with the police and a killer on my tail.

27

Mama had a saying for times of trouble: Good intentions in a crisis are like feathers on a pig, they get in the way and probably do more harm than good. I was sure Detective Marshall Weathers had good intentions, but I knew the Spivey family from the inside out, and therefore I was the best candidate to sort out the whole mess.

If you want something done, do it yourself. Save yourself a whole lot of trouble and pig feathers. I could continue to sit by and wring my hands, or I could take the bull by the horns and steer the course of fate. It seemed only logical to direct my little Beetle over to the Mobile Home Kingdom. Furthermore, if I was responsible for Jerry Lee Sizemore's death, then I had a duty to his remaining kin and to his memory.

I pulled my little car up into the lot and parked right in front of the model trailer. This time no one came rushing up to greet me. No prowling salesmen, cigarettes dangling from their lips. No slick finance managers. There were a few cars and pickup trucks in the lot, but no sign of their owners.

I stepped out into the sunshine and squinted to read the sign on the door of the model. It was a cardboard clock, the little red hands pointing to two P.M., and a red-lettered sign that said "Gone to lunch." I ran up the steps and tried the door handle, but it didn't budge. I looked around the lot. Columns of single-wides and double-wides stood like rowhouses, some with their storm doors hanging open, some leaning back at an angle, as if not securely fastened to their temporary piers.

It was like a ghost town. The trailers were so closely packed that they cast one long gray shadow the length of the lot. Behind them, the cars whistled past on I–85. Out on Holden Road, it was lunchtime. Traffic moved along at a fast clip, carrying hungry workers to the nearby Mexican restaurants and fast food joints. The lot was eerily silent.

"Good a time as any to look around," I said out loud. "Not like I'd be trespassing."

I started off down the walkway, my cowgirl boots crunching into the fine gray gravel. The first three mobile homes I tried were locked, but the fourth was wide-open, the product of a forgetful or careless salesperson. I stepped inside the double-wide, reaching for a light switch before realizing that, of course, display homes weren't fully set up with electricity and running water.

Sun streamed in through the back windows, making it bright enough to see without lighting up the poor construction. It looked like a dream home. Fully furnished down to fake food on plates in the eat-in breakfast nook, children's toys in one of the bedrooms, and plants in planters by the back door.

"Oh, this is nice," I said aloud. "This is really nice." I walked down the long hallway to the master bedroom, touching the wallpaper, letting my feet sink into the thick, pile carpeting, and thinking that maybe Vernell and Jimmy had really been on the cutting edge of what was now a booming business. I stepped into the master bedroom and glanced up at the skylights in the vaulted ceiling.

The four-poster bed was piled with pillows and quilts. For one uncontrollable second I found myself thinking of Marshall Weathers.

"Stop that!" I said loudly. "Hum," I said. The old Mama trick for bad thoughts. Humming will keep him out of your head. "I'm Falling in Love with You" came unbidden to my lips, and I hummed away at full volume. But it didn't seem to do the trick. For when I stepped into the master bath and saw the oversized jacuzzi tub, my wicked thoughts were back. I hummed louder and stepped into the walk-in closet.

I still heard a faint whistle behind me, but there wasn't time to react. Something collided with the back of my skull and the humming stopped. I remember falling forward into the darkened closet, but little else.

* * *

"Mama? Mama, answer me!" It was Sheila's voice, trembling with anxiety, begging me to answer her, and yet I couldn't quite rise up out of the mist that surrounded me.

"What should we do?" she cried. "Should we call nine-one-one?"

A deeper, adolescent male voice answered. "I don't think we oughta jump to that," Keith was saying. "Remember, she and the cops don't gee-haw too good right now."

"But what if she's dying?" Sheila cried.

I must've moaned. I thought I was speaking. I thought I'd said, "Keith is right for once. Don't call the police." But Sheila and Keith didn't act as if they heard me.

"Listen," he said. "I think she's coming around. Maybe we can get her to a doctor."

I blinked my eyes and saw only blue sky. The brightness made my head pound.

"Mama?" Sheila's face loomed into view. The blurriness of her features began to fade as the world swam into focus. I was lying on the bed in the mobile home's master bedroom, staring up at the skylights.

I tried to sit up, but Sheila pushed me back against the pillows. "You'd better not move," she said.

"What in the world is going on?" I said, my voice coming out in a hoarse whisper. "What happened?"

"You tell us, Mama. Keith was checking to make sure the trailers were all locked up so he could take off for lunch and when he saw the door wide-open, he decided to check around. That's when we found you."

Keith stepped out from behind Sheila. He looked worried and I noticed his hand placed protectively on Sheila's thin shoulder.

"Honest, Mrs. Reid, I thought for a minute you was dead! There you were, facedown on the closet floor, still and cold. I didn't even know if you were breathing! Sheila liked to have died when we realized it was you."

"You shoulda seen Keith, Mama," Sheila beamed proudly. "He had CPR training in vo-tech school." I looked up at pimply, skinheaded Keith and shuddered. The thought of those chapped lips wrapped over my own and blowing stale breath into my lungs made me cringe.

"Surely I was breathing?" I asked, once again attempting to push myself up off the pillows.

"Oh, yes, ma'am," Keith said. "That's how come I knew you wasn't dead or nothing. I used to get knocked out all the time skateboarding."

That explained a lot, I thought. My head was pounding. "Sheila, why aren't you in school?" I demanded. "And what are you two doing here?"

Sheila favored me with her most adult expression. "Mama, it's a teacher workday. Keith let me use his truck while my car's in the shop. I was just coming back to take him to lunch."

"Back where?" I still couldn't pull myself together.

"Mama! Keith works here! I told you he had a regular job. He's the clean-up man." I looked at Keith, all decked out in a dirty blue jumpsuit, his name embroidered in red on the pocket. "He cleans out the trailers and helps set them up when they come in."

Keith tightened his grip on Sheila's shoulder. "Sheila's uncle gave me the job a couple of months ago," he said. "I'm working my way up."

Everyone's entitled to their fantasies, I thought. Working his way up, indeed! I really tried to sit upright this time, and finally suceeded, although my head hurt like crazy and my entire body felt detatched and unresponsive.

"Mama," Sheila said, her face rigid with worry, "what happened?"

"Honey, I have no idea. One minute I was looking around, the next, I'm here with you two."

"Mrs. Reid," Keith said, "it just isn't safe to go roaming around in these trailers, not without a salesperson or something. This isn't the first time someone's gotten into one of our trailers, looking for stuff to take or a place to stay for a little while. We're right by the highway, you know."

Well, duh, I should've been more careful. Of course. But what good was that piece of advice gonna do me now? I'd come to the Mobile Home Kingdom looking to find something the police could've overlooked. Instead, someone had found me, and I didn't for a second subscribe to the theory that a vagrant had bopped me on the head.

"Mama, do you want me to take you to the doctor?" Sheila stepped forward to help me down off the bed.

"No, honey, I'm fine. Really." When I stumbled in my attempt to stand, she and Keith rushed forward, one on either side of me.

"Sheila, you'd better take your mama home and stay with her for awhile. I'll come pick you up after work." Keith was taking charge and Sheila jumped to do as he said. They led me, like an old woman, to my car. Sheila carefully lowered me into the passenger seat before she turned to kiss Keith good-bye. It was a long kiss, full of promise.

"Don't worry about a thing," he said softly to her. "Your mama'll be fine. I'll be along to carry you out to supper later." She floated over to the driver's side, slid behind the wheel, and held out her hand expectantly for my keys.

It was a first. Sheila driving my car with me as the passenger. I didn't know what scared me more, the idea of riding with her down busy Holden Road, or facing the thought that someone at the mobile home lot had seen me arrive and had wanted to hurt me.

I closed my eyes and tried not to open them as Sheila drove. I knew that if I so much as peeked out at our progress, I would begin shrieking instructions. It would end in disaster or death, and, if Sheila really was a bad driver, I didn't want to see the end coming. No, I would take the coward's way out. I would squeeze my eyes shut and pray for the best.

Fortunately, I chose to open my eyes as we were mere carlengths from home.

"Look out!" I cried, ducking down below the window. "Don't stop! Keep going!"

This, of course, scared the fool out of Sheila, who reacted by applying the brakes and skidding to a dead stop right in front of the house. By that time I was almost on the floor of the front passenger side, my head pounding unbearably, and my eyes once again tightly shut.

"Drive!" I barked.

"Mama!" Sheila squealed.

"That man knocking on the front door is a cop! Get out of here!"

"Cool!" Sheila said. "It's a getaway!" She peeled rubber and skidded down the street, popping the car into second gear as she accelerated and pushed my ancient relic into cardiac arrest.

"Sheila! What'd you do that for?" We might as well have stopped, rolled down the window and screamed, "You can't catch me!" I knew without looking behind us that Marshall Weathers was on our tail.

I straightened back up in my seat and glimpsed in the rearview mirror. There he was, as certain as nightfall, as constant as daylight.

"Honey, just pull over," I said.

"No, Mama, I can lose him! Watch this!" Before I could open my mouth to stop her, Sheila accelerated, pulled up on the hand brake, fishtailed, and cut the corner onto a little side road that I knew was a dead end.

"Sheila! Stop! Right now!"

Marshall Weathers turned on the blue lights and stepped on the accelerator. He zoomed up behind us, and I could almost make out that little angry twitch in his jaw.

"Mama, I can do this!" Sheila wailed. "I'll save you! They'll never take us alive!"

Was she out of her damn mind? "Sheila, look out!" We were about to run up on the dead end. Sheila swerved, hit the curb, bounced up on the sidewalk and came, finally, to a halt. I reached over and pulled the keys from the ignition.

As Marshall Weathers walked purposefully up to my side of the car, his jaw definitely working, I rolled down the window and said loudly, "And that concludes today's lesson on driving with a stick shift."

Weathers leaned down and looked in the window. He didn't say a word, and if I had to guess, he was working to control his temper. Finally, he spoke.

"Ladies," he said.

"Afternoon, Detective," I said. "I believe you know my daughter, Sheila. What can we do for you?"

Sheila, taking her cue from me, smiled broadly and leaned forward to bat her eyes at the cute detective. "Cool, huh?" she said. "Mama's teaching me to drive a stick."

Weathers swallowed hard. "Perhaps you ladies might do best to practice in a less populated area," he said. Then he looked at me. He hadn't forgotten last night. His eyes were hard and unforgiving. "I want to talk to you," he said.

"Take a number," I answered.

"Now," he said, his voice dropping to an almost-whisper.

"Later," I said, "can't you see I'm in the middle of something?" My head was singing. It hurt so badly and when I looked hard at Weathers, his face suddenly split into doubles.

"When, exactly?" he said.

"Come by around seven," I answered. "Before I leave for work."

"If you try and run out on me, I'll come down to that dance hall where you work and haul you out like a common criminal."

"And if you do," I answered, pitching my voice as low as his, "my attorney will run your ass up a flagpole."

He whirled around and was gone, leaving me and Sheila slumped back against our seats, breathing hard.

"Well, how about that." She sighed. "We're finally equals."

"What in the world do you mean by that?" I asked.

"Well, like, we're both in trouble! It's not just me. We're hanging together."

"It is a sorry day, Sheila, when you think cool is being in trouble with the law."

Sheila looked hurt. "Well, I was only trying to help, Mama. I know you did what you did for a reason. I haven't stopped believing in you. I just wish you'd tell me the whole story. Did he molest you?"

I turned to look at my daughter. She had a pained and fearful look on her face. Her eyes brimmed with tears that spilled over and ran down her cheeks.

"Sheila, what are you talking about? Did who molest me?"

"Uncle Jimmy, Mama."

"Uncle Jimmy?"

Sheila nodded slowly, stretched her hand out, and let it rest on my leg. "Mama, I think I got it all figured out. That's why he left that money to you and me, 'cause I'm his love child and Daddy's not my daddy." Sheila was about to bust a gut crying. "He must've forced you, Mama. That's why you killed him, huh?"

That's when Sheila really let go. Her pitiful sobbing filled the car. My poor, sweet, baby girl had been laboring all this time under the delusion that I had killed her favorite uncle. What in the world would make her think a thing like that?

I got out of the car, walked around to the driver's side, and opened the door.

"Scootch across, honey," I said. "I'll drive us home."

Sheila was coughing and blowing and crying up a storm that I knew would eventually make her sick if I couldn't calm her down. The last time I remembered her crying like this, Vernell had packed his bags and walked out the door for the last time. There had been nothing I could say to stop the hurt that time. This was different. Sheila was confused and wrong, and as soon as I got her home, I was going to explain the entire situation.

I drove around the block slowly, in part because I didn't know where Weathers really was and in part because I was still seeing double. I managed to maneuver the Beetle into the backyard and drag my sobbing daughter up the stairs and into my bedroom. We both collapsed onto my bed and I set about the task of correcting my daughter's vision of her mother as a murderer.

I propped myself up on one elbow, reached across to the bedside table, grabbed a box of tissues, and shoved it into Sheila's hands.

"Sheila, I did not murder your Uncle Jimmy, let's just start with that and go on from there. I can assure you that you are your father's child." Sheila was sniveling, but she was not flat-out sobbing anymore. I had her attention.

"Your Uncle Jimmy always carried on like he loved me, but honey, he was really just putting on. Jimmy just loved everything his brother had." Sheila blew her nose loudly. "Over the years, me and Jimmy developed a friendship, a good friendship, but that was all."

I was sitting up on the bed now and so was Sheila. She'd pulled herself up, Indian-style, and was eyeing me through puffy, red eyes. I don't think she believed me, not totally. What was with her?

"All right," I sighed, "your turn. What made you think I killed Uncle Jimmy?"

Sheila didn't say a word. She adopted that sullen, teenaged-girl scowl that I was so familiar with, and stared down at her lap.

"Sheila, you're holding onto something," I said. "It's been eating at you ever since Jimmy died. You might as well tell me, because it's going to come out some way or another."

Sheila thought for a moment and then exploded. "Of course it's going to come out, Mama! That's what I'm afraid of! If the police find out, they'll arrest you!"

"Honey, the rate we're going, they're gonna

arrest me anyway. You'd best tell me, so I can deal with whatever it is."

Sheila looked terrified and I was starting to worry. At least I had the advantage of knowing for certain I hadn't killed my brother-in-law.

Sheila tossed her hair back out of her eyes and stared at me. She was ready to talk and I could tell from the set of her obstinate chin that I wasn't going to like what I heard.

"Nobody likes Keith. Not you. Not Daddy. Not even Jolene. But that don't matter none, because what we have is the real thing." She glared at me defiantly, but I didn't say a thing. It was her opening policy statement. Every teenager had one. It was best just to let it ride.

"We could never be alone together. Not at his place and certainly not at Daddy's. Jolene was always there, always watching me. So we didn't have anywhere to go."

It was beginning to suddenly fall into place. Her ring on the bathroom sink. Keith looking around the house, pretending he was looking for intruders.

"So you came here when I was gone. You still had your key. It was close to his house. It was perfect." I was angry, but more than that, I was sad. This wasn't how it was supposed to turn out.

"We're going to be married, Mama. It's just a matter of time. It's not like we weren't serious, or like I didn't love him. Anyway," she said, rushing on, "that's not what this is about. Not really." What in the world else could it be about? Sheila's face had grown very pale again and she was staring down at the tissue in her lap, tearing it into little shreds.

"I heard Uncle Jimmy die," she whispered. "That's how come I knew it was you."

I grabbed her hands and shook her. "What do you mean?" I asked.

"I got here before Keith that day and I was in my room when I heard the front door. I figured it was Keith, on account of how he knew to where to hit the door to make it open. Anyway, I just stayed where I was. It was fixing to get dark and I was lighting some candles in my room." Her voice trailed off and I could just envision my little girl preparing her boudoir for her skin-headed lover. "It was going to be our first time, you know, to go all the way."

"What happened?"

"When Keith didn't come right in, I started to walk out of my room. That's when I heard Uncle Jimmy's voice. I flipped out and started blowing out the candles. I didn't want him to find me there. He would've told you and you would've killed . . ." Her voice trailed off for a moment. "Anyway. Uncle Jimmy said, 'What are you doing here? I thought you'd be gone by now.' And then I heard a gunshot and Jimmy cried out." She stared up at me, her eyes big, dark pools of terror as she remembered.

"I hid under my bed for I don't know how long. After the gunshot, I heard the front door close, but I didn't know for sure if I was alone or what. I was scared, Mama. Scared of you!"

"Oh, sweetie," I cried.

"Then I heard Keith. I heard him whack on the

front door and come in. He said something like 'Oh my God!' And I knew then that Jimmy was shot. I ran out of my room and there Keith was, bending over Jimmy, this really bizarre look on his face. He said, 'He's dead, Sheila. What's going on?'" Sheila looked at me for a second, then back down at her hands. "He thought maybe I did it, but I told him no. He just looked at me and he knew. He said 'Your mama did this, huh?' So, see, even Keith guessed."

I was breathing through my mouth, trying to stay calm and focused. My thoughts were racing across my brain like thunderclouds, too fast to catch.

"Why didn't you call the police?" I asked.

Sheila gave me a look. "Mama! The cops would've thought one of us did it!" Sheila looked back at her hands, holding them out a little ways from her lap and staring at them. "I touched him, Mama. I had to make sure he was dead, even though Keith told me he was. I had blood on my hands, and some got on my jeans."

I reached over and took her hands in mine. They were freezing. "It's all right now, honey. Just keep telling me what happened."

"Keith told me to go on home. He said we should both get out and not tell anybody anything." Tears were dripping down off the end of Sheila's chin. "So, I did. It was dark, and I was so paranoid, I thought everyone was after me, that everybody knew what was going on. I kept ducking behind trees and stuff on my way to my car, because I thought every car that passed me was the cops, or you or Daddy or Jolene."

"Oh, honey, you must've been terrified!" My almost seventeen-year-old daughter, struggling with her uncle's murder, all alone.

"I got home and, for once, no one was there. I got to my room and got cleaned up before I heard Daddy pull in. He was drinking and looking for Jolene to fix him dinner. He didn't even notice anything was wrong." Just like the Vernell of late, oblivious to everything, even his own daughter. "Jolene came in an hour later, so loaded down with shopping bags she couldn't walk. She and Daddy got into it over her not having dinner on the table and it being almost eight-thirty." Sheila was clearly reliving that night, her face wrinkled with disgust. "She called him a drunk and he called her a slut. I just left. They never even knew I'd been in the room."

"Sheila," I said, "listen to me. I don't know who Jimmy was talking to, but it wasn't me. I didn't shoot your uncle. Now, we're going to have to do the right thing, and clean up this mess."

Sheila looked up at me, her eyes dark with suspicion. "What?" she asked.

"I want you to tell the police everything you just told me. They need to know."

"But Mama!" she wailed. "I can't! They won't believe us!"

"Sheila, it's going to look worse if they find out some other way, and believe me, eventually the police find out everything." I thought back to the look on Marshall Weathers's face last night as he held my gun up, waiting for me to come up with an explanation. He'd find this out, too. We'd have to tell him.

I looked at my watch. In two hours, he'd be at my front door, wanting to talk, wanting answers. My head was demanding my attention, pounding and throbbing. I looked over at Sheila and saw she didn't look much better. We had to pull it together before Marshall Weathers arrived.

"Sweetie," I said, "my head's killing me and you don't look so hot yourself. Why don't you go into your room and try and rest for a little while. I'm going to take something for my headache before Detective Weathers gets here. There's no sense in us calling him about this right now. It can wait a couple of hours."

To my surprise, she didn't fight me. She walked to her room like a zombie and lay across her old bed sideways. When I looked in ten minutes later, she was sleeping. I stumbled back to my room and fell across my bed. My head was banging against my skull, but that didn't stop me from closing my eyes. It had all been too much, and within moments I felt myself drifting off. It was a relief not to be conscious, not to think or remember.

28

Even in my sleep there was no escaping the long arm of the law. I dreamed that Sheila and I were running through a maze of fire-orange azaleas, with Marshall Weathers right behind us. Every now and then he'd yell out, "Wake up and smell the coffee, Maggie! Wake up before it's too late!"

"Go away!" I cried. "Leave me alone!" But he just kept on coming, closer and closer. I could smell him. I could hear his breath, panting behind me. Finally, I could feel him, shaking me and calling my name.

"Maggie! Maggie! Wake up!"

I opened my eyes. The lights in the house were all on, and Marshall Weathers was sitting by my side, shaking my shoulder and calling my name. I smelled coffee and realized this was not a nightmare, it was my worst possible reality.

"What are you doing here?" I sat up too quickly and my brain slammed against my skull. "Ouch!" I grabbed my head and rocked slowly forward. I felt sick.

"Maggie, what is wrong with you? I knocked on the doors, both of them, for five minutes at least. Then, when I saw your car, I knew you had to be here. Maggie, you didn't even have the chain on the front door. I just popped the door and walked right in."

Marshall Weathers looked concerned. He was frowning and looking at me like I was a strange form of lab specimen.

"Maggie, I couldn't wake you up. Did you take something?"

So now he thought I was a drug addict. How much lower was I going to go in his opinion?

"No, unless you count aspirin," I said. "I forgot. I went out to the Mobile Home Kingdom around lunchtime and—"

He didn't let me finish. "Didn't I tell you not to go there?" he fumed.

I just stared at him. "You want me to tell you, or do you want to lecture me?"

He just shrugged. "I made some coffee. I didn't know what was wrong with you. I thought maybe you'd overdosed or something. You kept moaning and telling me to go away. I figured coffee might be better than calling nine-one-one."

"Coffee beats nine-one-one any day of the week." I looked past him, trying to see out into the hallway. "Why didn't Sheila let you in?"

"Sheila's not here, Maggie. There's no one here but you and me."

"Oh, God!" I jumped up and ran past him. Sheila's room was empty. She was gone.

He stood right behind me, his hand on my shoulder. "So, you want to let me know what's going on?" he asked.

Well, did I? Did I want him scrambling all over Greensboro, looking for my daughter? And what if he found her and I wasn't there? Could Sheila tell him the truth without making herself look like a teenage serial killer? Somehow, given Sheila's tendency to play the drama queen, I doubted it.

"Nothing's going on," I said. "I lay down to take a nap and thought Sheila was going to wake me up in time to get ready for work before you got here, that's all." I led him back into the kitchen, looked at the clock on top of the stove and caught my breath. If I didn't leave within fifteen minutes, I'd be late and Sparks would fire me.

"You're not going to like this," I said, setting my coffee mug down carefully on the counter, "but I'm fixing to be late for work. I know I said I'd talk to you but—"

He cut me off. "Oh, you're gonna talk to me, all right. You're gonna start talking now and finish when I say we're through."

I tried to stare him down, but my heart wasn't in it. I was late for a job I loved too much to lose and worried sick about my baby. Weathers was the low man on my totem pole tonight.

"All right." I sighed. "Here's the deal. Let me get changed and I'll talk to you until I have to walk out the door."

"No, this here's the deal," he said. "You change. I'll drive you to work, and if you've answered all my questions, I'll let you go inside. If not, I'll just head the car on downtown and take you along with me."

"Then how'll I get home?" I said.

"You've got friends." The sarcastic glint was back in his eye. "And if you don't, then I reckon I'll just have to swing back by and get you."

That was just what he wanted. He wanted me in a little cage where he controlled my movements and saw everything I did. He didn't trust me, which was fine, because I didn't trust him either.

"All right. I guess we'll play it your way." I brushed past him and headed for the walk-in closet. Fine. Let him have his way about the small stuff. It didn't matter. What mattered was keeping him away from Sheila until I'd had time to find her, civilize her, and drag her sorry tail down to the police station. I could handle Weathers. Sheila wouldn't last two minutes with his rapid-fire questioning. Heaven knew what she'd end up telling the man, and heaven only knew what he'd end up making her believe.

I grabbed a black sequined number and stalked off to my room. He was right behind me.

"If you don't mind," I said, putting my hand on my hip and looking down my nose at him.

He grinned. "No, Maggie, I don't mind at all."

"I'd like a little privacy!"

"And I'm too old to fool twice. No way you're going out that back door again."

It was a standoff, and he wasn't budging. He

stood there, all six feet of long, cool cowboy, his arms folded over his chest and a knowing gleam in his crystal blue eyes. This was a game to him, and one he had no intention of losing.

"All right, cowboy." I looked at him like it was no skin off my nose. "Come on in. Make yourself comfortable in that rocking chair over there."

I got to it before he could, swinging it around so that it faced the back corner by the door.

"Now you can keep your eye on the door."

My heart was starting to pound along with my head as I watched him walk across the room. I was remembering the first night I'd seen him, in his tight, faded blue jeans. This was not at all the way I'd pictured our future.

"Don't turn around," I cautioned.

"Don't give me a reason to," he answered. "Now start talking." He was off again, making me answer every little question he had about my movements the day before.

I stood behind him and slowly unzipped my jeans. He was talking and made no indication that he even cared that I was behind him, stripping down to my underwear.

"When did Vernell give you that pistol?" he said. I stepped out of my jeans and tossed them across the bed.

"I don't know. Six or seven years ago, I guess."

"Any particular reason?" I lifted my sweatshirt up over my head and threw it on top of the jeans. I was down to a pink satin bra and panties, Weathers was six feet away from me, and there was no more hope for romance in that room than there had been in the three years I'd been divorced from Vernell.

"He gave me the gun in a foolish attempt to save our marriage," I answered, as I pulled the black sequined dress off its hanger.

Weathers moved suddenly in the chair and I jumped into the dress.

"Save your marriage?" he said.

"Yeah, I dragged him to a marriage counselor and she said we ought to share a hobby. The gun was Vernell's idea of a hobby. He thought we'd go off in the country and shoot at tin cans or something. I just hope he hasn't been as foolish with his second wife."

Weathers laughed. "Target shooting?"

"Well, we've all got our notions of what's a romantic outing," I said, slipping my feet into spiky black heels.

Something in the husky tone of his voice made me look up and stare in his direction. Weathers hadn't moved a muscle and I could suddenly see why. From where he sat, if he stared just a little to the right, my every movement was reflected in the dresser mirror.

"Oh my God!" I shrieked.

"Something wrong?" he asked innocently.

I stared at the back of his head for a second. Could he really see from there? Maybe I was wrong. I walked up behind his chair and squatted down until I was at his eye level. All he would've needed to do was turn his head, just a little bit to the right.

"Lovely view, isn't it?" he asked softly. Before I could say a word, he was up and moving toward the front door. "You'd better get a move on, aren't you late?"

I stormed off after him, all sorts of snappy comebacks crowding into my head, but I couldn't say a word. Instead all I could feel was the heat that had suddenly filled my bedroom when he'd looked at me squatting down next to his chair. We had unfinished business, he and I, but now wasn't the time.

As we were heading out the front door of my house and moving to his car, he looked over at me and said, "What were you doing at the Mobile Home Kingdom after I told you not to go there?" The moment was broken, and we were back on familiar ground.

29

Weathers didn't want to let me go, but he knew he couldn't stop me. I'd answered all his questions. I told him all about my talk with Bertie Sexton. I told him in graphic detail how I'd been bashed over the head in the closet of a mobile home. I left out only one little thing—Sheila's revelation. That would just have to wait.

He rolled right up in front of the Golden Stallion, announcing to the world and Cletus, who was working the door, that Maggie Reid had arrived with a police escort. He could've just grabbed a megaphone and shouted, "Appearing live from the Greensboro jailhouse, Miss Maggie Reid!" But I didn't care. I was on time and leaving Weathers behind.

"Page me if you can't find a way home," he said, as I slammed the car door. If he were the last ride home, I wouldn't call him. If he were the last ride anywhere, I wouldn't call him. But I didn't say it. For once I kept my mouth shut. I was going to need him later, when Sheila decided to quit stalling and tell the police what she'd heard.

The band was warming up as I walked through the front door of the Golden Stallion. If Cletus was surprised to see me pull up in a police car, he didn't say a word. Instead he raised an appreciative eyebrow at my black dress and high heels, cocked his head to one side, and gave me his attempt at a wink. Cletus couldn't wink. It looked more like a squint accompanied by a lopsided leer.

Sparks took the band into my theme song when he saw me standing at the back of the house. It was show time. I cut through the crowd, greeting a few of the regulars, and walking like I owned the place. This was where I belonged. For a few short hours, life was going to be uncomplicated, just me and the music and the boys in the band.

Jack was blowing on the harmonica when I stepped up to the mike, dancing across the stage in his loose-shouldered, knee-lifting dance style. Sparks had his head bent to the pedal steel, ferociously playing a lead. And Sugar Bear was slowly leading the boys off the intro and into the song. I looked out on the floor, flashed my biggest grin, and started singing about lonely cowboys.

The house was unusually full for a Tuesday night. Carvette, the line-dance instructor, had a large group of fat ladies stumbling across the floor behind her. Had to be a promotion with the weight-loss clinic, I figured. Carvette was big on working the public relations angle. The Young Bucks dance team took up the side of the floor closest to a table of young secretaries who were celebrating and impressed by what the farm boys had to offer. It was going to be a swinging night.

"Where have you been?" Jack had snuck up behind me, and I hadn't even heard him.

"Home and chasing up after my young'un," I answered. "Gettin' my head half bashed in and driving on the sidewalks of Greensboro." Jack laughed; obviously I had to be kidding. Sparks frowned at him, thinking we were going to mess up, and I slid into the last verse.

Jack stood right by my side, playing softly and shuffling in place. His jeans were wrinkled and he still looked as if he could use a good hot meal. The boy needed a mama.

"Can I catch a ride home with you?" I asked between songs.

"Sure." He looked surprised. "Need a place to stay?" He looked hopeful and a little lonely. Where was that Evelyn of his? Then I remembered him crying the other night, and realized what must've happened.

"Sorry, sweetie," I said, the same way I'd talk to Sheila, "I'm going to sleep in my own bed for awhile. Those water beds make me seasick." He laughed and went back to his harmonica. When this current crisis was over, I was going to have to find that boy a good woman.

It was a good night for making music, but as the first set came to an end, I realized that Mama Maggie wasn't too happy. By the end of the second set, my mama instincts were going haywire, and I could no longer deny that Sheila might be in trouble. I'd tried to believe that she'd gone off when Keith came by, and probably she had done just that. He'd probably come to the front door and carried her out to dinner and then driven her back home to Vernell's. But what if she hadn't?

I tried to call her just before the last set started up, but there was no answer at the Spivey castle, only the answering machine with Jolene's tinny little TV voice instructing me to leave a message and "have a nice day." I hung up and ran up the steps to the stage. Where was that girl?

"She's probably asleep, Maggie," was Jack's theory. "It's almost one o'clock in the morning. The whole house is sleeping, if you ask me."

"But she just took off."

"All teenagers just take off," he said, turning back to his harmonica for a brief moment. "It's what teenagers do."

I didn't feel better. Instead, I felt more and more apprehensive. Deep inside my bones I could feel it. Something was not right with Sheila.

I kept scanning the door all through the last set, half expecting to see uniformed officers, or Weathers. It was the McCrarey gift of second sight, I could feel it, tingling my scalp and running down my arms. Even Jack sensed my unrest, sticking close by me as I sang the last few songs.

"All right," he said, when the last number drew to a close and the house lights came up. "It's last call. We can leave. I'll take you home, or wherever else it is you need to go."

"Home. I can feel it, I need to go home."

Jack looked at me, looked deep into my eyes, and locked onto my fear. "All right, Maggie. We're leaving now." He spun around, blew a kiss to a young girl with curly brown hair who'd been watching him from the dance floor, and started heading for the back door. "You coming?" he called over his shoulder.

"Yes," I yelled, running to catch up.

"It's a good thing that dress has slits up the side," he said. "But you're gonna be cold."

I didn't really pay any attention to him, that is, not until he walked up to a small motorcycle and unfastened the two helmets that were tied to the seat.

"I always come prepared," he said, handing me a helmet.

"Jack, what happened to your car?" I asked. I knew the answer before he even said a word.

"Evelyn has it," he said softly. "I figured she needed it more than me."

I stared at the lonely little motorcycle and back at my kindhearted friend. When I finally met Evelyn, I was going to give her a piece of my mind. Who would leave this sweet man and take his car?

The early morning air had turned cold, and I knew it would cut through my flimsy dress like a million tiny knives. For a brief second, I thought of calling Weathers and taking him up on his offer of a ride, but I had my code of ethics and Weathers was not an option. Jack offered me his suede jacket, but I wouldn't take it.

"You'll be up front," I said, "I'll just hunch

down behind you. Let's go." The anxiety I'd felt inside was reaching the panic stage now. It didn't matter how I got home, I just had to go.

As we pulled out of the Golden Stallion and onto High Point Road, it began to sprinkle. By the time we hit Holden, it was pouring. Water slid down my neck, running the length of my back and sliding down my legs. I leaned as close as I could into Jack, but it didn't help. We were both soaking wet. Jack was working to stay focused on his driving, slowing down to an almost-crawl and braking carefully as we came up to a red light.

"Sorry," he called back to me.

"Hey, it's not your fault it rained. I'm just thankful you're taking me home." I was shaking with the cold and wishing like anything for shelter. Why did I ever agree to let Weathers drive me to work? What kind of a deal had that turned out to be?

By the time we pulled up in my backyard, I was numb. I half fell off the back of the bike. My dress was ruined and water squished out of my shoes in noisy little gushes. I looked like a black-and-red drowned rat and I felt a hundred times worse.

"Thanks, Jack!" I called. "Do you want to come inside and dry off?"

He shook his head but all I could see was the tinted glass of his faceshield. "Might as well go on home. I'm soaked through anyway," he said. He backed the bike out into the yard and swung around. I was up the steps and inside as he gunned the engine and tore off down my back alley.

"Sheila?" I called into the darkened house.

No answer, but I hadn't really expected one. I checked the answering machine, water dripping down my legs and forming little puddles at my feet. No messages.

"All right, baby girl," I said to my empty bedroom, "Mama's coming after you. If you're not in trouble, you soon will be!" But my heart wasn't in it. I knew my girl was in trouble, the same way my mama always knew when I needed her. It was a gift and a curse, but it was certain knowledge. My daughter needed me and that fact was all I could think about.

30

As I saw it, I had only one option. My daughter was missing, at least to me, and I needed to go over to Vernell's New Irving Park palace, wake everybody up, and assure myself of her safety. If that was an inconvenience to Vernell and the lovely Dish Girl, well, so be it and I hated it for them. Parenthood was not without its tribulations and rewards. Maybe old Vernell needed to be reminded of his parental responsibilities.

If Sheila wasn't home, he needed to be up and by my side until we found her. If she was home, then the lovely Jolene needed to answer the phone when I called looking for my daughter and not leave it to the answering machine. The way I saw it, people didn't call your house at one A.M. unless it was a total, life-threatening emergency. I always answered my phone when it rang in the middle of the night.

Armed with this justified way of thinking, and warmed by dry clothing, I set off across town. I hadn't gone two miles when I realized I had trouble. My car, always reliable, seemed to have caught cold. It was coughing and wheezing, and when I hit the light at Green Valley and Battleground, it died and almost didn't start up again.

"Don't do this," I pleaded. "Not now." But my little VW, Abigail, couldn't help herself. She was struggling to keep going north on Battleground, but we made the split onto Lawndale, with Abigail choking and dying out unless my foot was constantly tapping the accelerator. By the time we wound our way through to Vernell's street, I knew she wouldn't make it home again. Abigail waited until we were on the downhill slope of Vernell's little cul-de-sac to die. I lifted my foot off the accelerator, slipped her into neutral, and coasted to a halt just inside Vernell's cobblestoned driveway.

"Oh, well, that's that." I sighed. I was not a Triple A member, a fact I deeply regretted at that moment, and one I promised myself to rectify just as soon as I got back home.

"Well, girl, at least you got me here." My voice sounded loud in the stillness of Vernell's dignified street. There was not one light on inside any house in the circle, including Vernell's. We'd slid to a stop just behind Sheila's black Mustang convertible, but that meant nothing. She'd been driving Keith's truck that morning.

Vernell's Day-Glo orange panel truck stood next to Sheila's little car. Too large to fit in his garage, I was certain status-conscious Jolene had plenty to say about Vernell bringing the revolving Jesus home to rest in her driveway.

"Glad that's not my problem," I muttered and headed up the drive to ring the front doorbell.

As I pressed the brass button, I noticed one little light on in the back of the house. Someone might be up. I pressed my face to the cut-glass oval that took up half of the heavy wooden door, and tried to see into the house. At the same time, I kept my finger continuously pressed on the doorbell. Someone was moving toward me, shuffling slowly, half bent over, and weaving from side to side. Vernell.

"Where's the fire?" he called. He swung open the door and a loud voice startled both of us.

"Intruder! Intruder! Front entrance. You have twenty seconds to disarm!"

Vernell looked momentarily confused and worried, then disgusted. "Dag-blamed security system!" He turned away from me and began stabbing a pudgy finger at the keypad by the front door. "If it ain't one thing it's another with this place," he grumbled. He was wearing his blue polyester leisure suit, rumpled and stained from what looked like continuous wear without benefit of washing.

"Come in! Come on in!" Vernell's dark hair stood up in tufts across the top of his head. "I was just talking to you, anyway," he said. Vernell's breath and body smelled of liquor and I could see a bottle of Wild Turkey sitting out on the kitchen table.

I followed him into the kitchen, tempted a few times to reach out and grab him as he threatened to do damage to a fancy doodad or knock into a framed picture with his drunken body.

"Vernell," I said, "do you know what time it is?"

"You come all this way to ask me the time?" Vernell looked genuinely puzzled. "Well, I reckon it's coming up on ten o'clock."

"Vernell, it is two-thirty in the morning."

"Well, if you knew, why'd you ask?" Vernell eyed me suspiciously. "This is some kind of test, isn't it? You just want to know how much I been drinking. Just like Jolene—hellfire, just like any woman. That's the trouble with you people, always asking questions. Wanting to talk about your feelings." Vernell was on the verge of a sermon.

"Vernell, hush! Where's Sheila?"

Vernell's eyes cleared for one second. "Why, ain't she with you?"

"Vernell!"

"Well, honey, she called hours ago. Told Jolene she was going to stay at your place tonight on account of you had a headache."

My heart jumped up into my throat. "Where's Jolene? Let me talk to her! Wake her up!" I jumped up from the table and stood staring down at Vernell.

"Can't do it," he said slowly. "Jolene ain't here either. She's over to her mama's on account of her mama being sick. She's helping out." Vernell looked morose. "Well, that and maybe she got a little hot because I was drinking."

"Come on," I said, grabbing the shot glass out of his hand.

I was off, heading for the stairs, looking for anything that might tell me where Sheila had gone. Vernell puffed along behind me.

"Up at the top of the stairs to the right," he said. "When's the last time you talked to her?" Vernell's voice had changed. He sounded almost sober and definitely worried.

"About four or five this afternoon. She lay down in her room to take a nap. Vernell, last time I checked on her, she was sleeping." *It's my fault,* I thought. I shouldn't have fallen asleep. I should've done something, everything, differently.

I ran down the hallway, knowing without being told which room was Sheila's. I'd been sitting across that street for so many nights, watching that little light over her desk, trying to catch a glimpse of my girl, hoping to know for sure that she was home where she belonged. Where was she now?

Vernell pounded right behind me, stopping at the entrance to Sheila's room as I ran inside. I stood still and looked around. It was every teenage girl's dream. A beautiful brass daybed, piled high with lacy pillows. White carpeting and pink walls, thick crown molding, and a walk-in closet crammed with all the latest fashions from Sheila's favorite stores. A lot of the clothing still had price tags hanging from the sleeves. Sheila couldn't possibly have worn all those things.

"Vernell, my God, did you let her buy all those things?" I asked.

Vernell seemed as puzzled as me. "No, I guess Jolene must've done it. You know how she likes shopping." He peered deeper into the closet. He sighed. "Women. I don't recall you ever having that many outfits. Jolene says we gotta look the part. She says image is everything."

I could just hear those words dripping off her lips.

"Vernell," I said, "it don't matter if you paint the barn black or white, it's still a barn. Now let's get to it."

"To what, Maggie? She ain't here. Let's start calling her friends."

"Vernell, unless you've been spending a lot of time around her new school and know some things I don't, we don't know any of her friends. And think about it, Vernell, if your best friend ran off, would you tell where he was?"

Vernell spent too long pondering his answer, and I couldn't wait. I pulled open the drawer of her nightstand, looking for her phone book or anything that could help us.

"What about her boyfriend?" he asked. "Keith."

"I don't know his phone number," I said, tugging at Sheila's crammed bedside drawer. "We'll have to ride by, but I doubt she's there. He lives with his parents."

Sheila's drawer was full of letters and photographs, some of which spilled over and fell onto the floor as I wrestled to get the drawer all the way open. It was stuck on something, and I couldn't quite reach it with my fingers.

"Well, least we can do is ride by," Vernell huffed. "Let me get that." He pushed me aside, reached for the drawer, and gave it a mighty tug. The crystal lamp began to topple, the pink princess phone slid, and the drawer came flying open. Papers rained everywhere and a small clothbound book fell out onto the floor, its cover scuffed and bent from its tussle with Vernell.

"There it is," he said.

"This isn't her phone book," I said, picking the small journal up and flipping through the pages. "This is her diary."

I sank down onto her bed and started leafing through the purple ink-covered pages, looking for the last entry. I'd never gone through Sheila's things before and I felt slightly guilty for doing it now, but a crisis was a crisis.

I will carry flowers on the beach, she wrote in large loopy script. My heart froze. *Red ones. And Keith says he knows a guy ordained by that mailorder Universalist Church of Higher Love that's gonna do the ceremony.*

I read the words aloud as Vernell sank down beside me. "No," he moaned softly. "No."

It won't be that church wedding my mama wants, Sheila wrote, *but at least we'll have the beach. Keith says our lives will be bonded together forever. We will share our future. What's his will be mine, and what's mine will be his. We won't ever get like Mama and Daddy did. Our love will last. True love forever.*

Tears rolled down my cheeks, dripping onto the purple ink and leaving blotches of pale purple tears. Vernell, reading over my shoulder, reached out and put an arm around me.

"I'm sorry, honey," he said softly. "I really am sorry."

"We can't get into all that right now," I said, looking up and folding the book shut. "We've got to stop them."

"You wanna ride by Keith's place?"

I stood up and pulled a pale pink tissue from the box on Sheila's nightstand.

"Yeah, just to make sure," I said, "but then we'd better get a move on."

Vernell looked puzzled, and still sad. "Get a move on?"

"Vernell, don't you realize where they've gone?"

"To the beach?" he said. "Maggie, they could be anywhere. Hell, they could be in Daytona with all them bikers and—"

I cut him off. "Vernell, they're at your parents' place. That's the only beach house Sheila knows. That's where she'd go. She knows nobody'd be there this time of year."

Vernell just stared at me for a moment, as if reading my lips and hoping to make sense out of what he saw and heard. His little girl, marrying a skinhead on the beach outside of his parents' beach house. It was all more than he could imagine. Then something else happened. Vernell returned. Not the Vernell I'd seen drunk and out of control, but Vernell the self-made man, Vernell the survivor, Vernell the man who wasn't about to let a boy ruin his daughter's life.

"All right," he said, his voice strong and filling the frilly bedroom, "let's ride." He moved past me, down the hallway, down the stairs, and over to the hat rack by the front door where he grabbed his white straw cowboy hat. He stopped by the front hall table, scooped up a set of keys and his cell phone. We were outside in the cold morning air, heading for my car, before I remembered that it wouldn't run.

"Vernell," I said. "Wait. My car died in the driveway. Let's take Sheila's car."

Vernell stopped on a dime and looked over at me. "Can't," he said.

"Why not?"

"I don't got a key. Sheila has it."

"Well, where's your car?" We were taking too long. We needed to be leaving. For all I knew, the wedding could be taking place first thing in the morning. It would take four hours to reach Holden Beach, and we'd have to be flying to do that.

"Calm down, honey," he said. "My car's at the office. We gotta take the truck. Let's go!"

Vernell had opened the door, hopped up in the cab, and started the engine before I reached the passenger side. *So much for keeping a low profile*, I thought. The satellite dish groaned as it began to turn, and we were off, backing down Vernell's driveway, and out into the street. "Rock of Ages" bellowed out into the silent cul-de-sac, and one by one lights began coming on. Vernell's neighbors had to hate him.

"Vernell, can't you cut that down?"

"Say what?" he yelled. "I can't hear you with the music on."

"Turn it off!" I screamed.

Vernell calmly reached up under the dash and hit a toggle switch. "You don't have to yell," he said.

"Just drive, Vernell." I sighed and looked out the side window. He was impossible.

"Where to?"

"Keith lives three doors down from my place. I suggest we ride by, see if his truck is there, and if it isn't, check my place. Maybe she came back after I left." But I knew it was pointless. Sheila was in Holden Beach.

Vernell drove the truck like a sports car, careening around corners, sliding up on curbs, and running the truck flat-out and wide-open. If our mission hadn't been so serious, we might've enjoyed ourselves. It was like the old days, in high school, when we rode around the Virginia country-side, whooping out the windows and feeling the air fresh in our faces. Back then, we were reckless and carefree. Back then we would've done anything on a dare. Now our daughter had replaced us, and it was up to us to save her from herself.

"He's not there," I said. We were running down my street at fifty miles an hour, narrowly squeezing past cars parked on either side of the street. Vernell was either one hundred percent sober, or a very skilled drunk driver.

"Stop in front of my place and I'll run in and check."

Vernell stood on the brakes and skidded to a stop. "Hurry it up!" he said.

We both knew it was pointless. I ran up the

steps, slammed the side of my fist into the front door, and stepped inside my darkened house.

"Sheila?" I called, switching on the light and moving rapidly toward the back of the house. No answer. "Sheila?"

Of course she wasn't there. Her room was undisturbed, except for the slight rumpling of the quilt where she'd lain sleeping the last time I'd seen her. I moved on to my room and glanced at the answering machine. No blinking red light. No messages.

"I'm having a bad feeling," I said aloud to the empty room. I picked up the phone and dialed the number that had stuck in my head, unwanted, since the first and only time I'd called it. "A really bad feeling," I said again.

"This is Corporal Marshall J. Weathers of the Greensboro Police Department," a familiar deep bass voice said. I sucked in my breath, about to answer him, but he went on. "I am away from my desk or out of the office. Please leave me a brief, detailed message and I will get back to you as soon as possible." There was a pause and then the familiar beep.

"Detective Weathers, this is Maggie Reid. Sheila's run off with her boyfriend, to Holden Beach, and I think she intends to get married, maybe in Myrtle Beach. She's underage, as you well know, and I don't like this guy. He's been arrested before, but I guess you know that. Can you call down there? Do you know anyone? I'm heading down there, but I don't know if I'll make it in time." I was running out of time and breath. "Oh, shoot, I know what. Never mind, I'll page you."

I hung up and dug deep in my jeans pocket for his card. "If you need me, page me," he'd said. I needed him. I punched in the number, waited for the series of beeps, and then punched in Vernell's cell phone number. I hesitated for a second, then punched in 911. "That oughta get you," I said to the lifeless phone, and ran out of the house.

Vernell was still sitting in the middle of the street, the Jesus satellite dish spinning around like a dancing girl on top of his truck. When he saw me, he gunned the engine and motioned for me to hurry.

"What'd you take so long for?" he asked.

"You got your cell phone on?"

Vernell gave me a "Do you really take me for an idiot?" look, and pointed to the cell phone that lay on the seat between us. A green light winked on and off. "Of course," he said. "I am never out of communication." He meant he was never off Jolene's leash, but I didn't say a word.

Lying under the phone was an assortment of papers and junk. A thick white envelope with a Flatiron and Scruggs, Attorneys at Law, return address caught my eye.

"Vernell," I said, pulling the envelope out from under the phone. "Aren't these Jimmy's lawyers?"

Vernell looked a little uncomfortable. "Well, technically, they're the attorneys for the business, but he used them to do his estate stuff, too."

"So, is this about Jimmy's estate?" I asked.

Vernell looked over at the envelope and changed the subject. "Let's not talk business," he said. "Not at a time like this. Times like this make me remember what we had, Maggie."

"Vernell," I cautioned. But it was too late. We were headed out of town on Highway 220, in a fluorescent orange panel truck, with Jesus dancing on top of our heads, trying to save Sheila from a fate worse than death, and Vernell was choosing this moment to get nostalgic.

"Maggie, face facts. Jolene don't love me. She thinks I'm a withered up old man, made of money." I looked over at him, and was surprised to see that Vernell Spivey was actually crying. Tears ran down his weather-toughened cheeks.

"Oh, Vernell," I said, "now that just can't be so. She married you. She chased up after you for years." The words were hollow comfort, and I knew it as well as he did. Vernell had driven his ducks to bad market and they were coming home to roost.

My fingers picked at the envelope in my hands, bringing my attention back to it.

"Is this a copy of Jimmy's will?" I asked.

"No." He moaned. "She never did love me. Even Jimmy knew that. He tried to warn me right before he died." Vernell was milking this act, I could tell from the way he kept casting nervous little looks over at the envelope. He was trying to lead me away from the envelope, like a papa bird leading a cat away from the nest.

"Well, is it?" I asked.

"Is it true?" he said. "I don't know. I only have what Jimmy said to go on, and Lord knows he was jealous to beat the band."

"Vernell, answer me. Is this Jimmy's will?"

"Jimmy always said she wanted me for my money. Said she'd crawl up my back with spikes to get to the next best thing. Bleed me dry, is what he said. Jimmy done told me, I walked out on the best woman in the world and I—"

"Vernell, I'm gonna look for myself!" I lifted the flap and pulled out the sheaf of papers that filled it.

"Maggie! I'm trying to talk to you!" he said. "Don't you have a lick of respect for other people's privacy?"

I didn't listen; instead, I read the enclosed letter. Vernell had asked for a copy of the will. He wanted to contest it, the snake!

Highlighted in yellow were all the parts of the document pertaining to the business, including my name and Sheila's. Roxanne had been given a life insurance policy and set up with a trust fund which would dole out money monthly. Jimmy had signed over his portion of the satellite dish business to Vernell, so the lawyers seemed to feel Vernell couldn't do a thing about it. It was signed and witnessed, all legal and binding.

"Maggie," Vernell said, "it wasn't nothing personal."

I didn't even look at him. I was afraid I'd hit him if I saw that pitiful look he always wore when he knew he was in deep trouble with me. I stared at the will, forcing myself to concentrate on the paper. Signed and sealed, all good and proper. Bertie Sexton had notarized it, and Sheila's Keith and Don Evans had witnessed it, so Jimmy must've signed it in his office.

"Now, Maggie, honey, don't be mad."

I looked up at him. "Why should I be mad, Vernell? Because you want me to believe that you think you've made a terrible mistake leaving me? You can't break the will, so you want to con me into coming back to you? I don't think so, Vernell. I really don't."

"Honey, Jolene's the one started this whole mess. She called the attorney. Said we needed to make sure of our rights, and little Sheila's, too. I mean, what if Roxanne was to contest the will? And what if something was to happen to you, God forbid? I'd have to look out for Sheila's interests. She'd inherit the whole forty-nine percent. Lord." Vernell whistled. "Cain't you just see her, eighteen and loaded? You think that closet's full now!"

"So Jolene's behind it, huh? I don't buy for a New York minute that she had Sheila's best interests at heart." In fact, little pieces of the puzzle were all starting to come together in my head.

"Maggie! I can't believe you would think such a thing as that!" Vernell said, but his words were wasted. The cell phone began to chirp and we both grabbed for it.

Vernell snatched it out of my hands. "Give me that! What if it's Jolene?"

"What do you care, Vernell?" I said sarcastically. "She's just a big mistake!" Vernell put the receiver to his ear and leaned away from me, causing the truck to lurch across two lanes of highway.

"Vernell!" I hissed. "Pay attention!"

"Hello, sugar," he cooed into the receiver. "Hey, who is this?" he said, his voice shifting angrily. "Oh!" Vernell was all cooperation now that he knew it was the cops. "Yes, Officer, she's right here. I'll put her on. You have a good evening, now, y'hear?"

Vernell glared over at me as he shoved the phone into my hand and whispered, "Why didn't you tell me you gave a cop my number?"

"And when could I have gotten a word in edgewise?" I hissed back.

"Hello?"

"Maggie Reid?" I didn't recognize the voice and my heart lurched. Where was Weathers?

"Yes," I answered.

"Maggie, it's Bobby, Marshall Weathers's partner."

"Oh, hey, Bobby." His voice was tinny and far-away sounding.

"Listen, Marshall got your message and your page, but he's out of town. He asked me to call and see what you needed."

Well, I wasn't going to tell him. It was one thing to ask Marshall Weathers for a favor, but it was another thing again to ask an almost total stranger.

"When's he coming back, Bobby?"

"Well, I don't know for sure." Bobby's voice had taken on a formal, "I can't talk about police business" tone that I knew all too well from Weathers.

"Well," I hedged, "it can wait awhile, Bobby. I didn't mean to trouble him."

"Well, Maggie, you punched nine-one-one in after your number. . . ."

I decided to play dumb. "I'm sorry, Bobby. My daughter ran off to Holden Beach with her boyfriend, and I panicked. But I know where she is now and I've got it all under control. I'm on my way there with her daddy. We've got it covered."

Bobby was not at all sure, but he had no choice. "I'll be calling him back," he said. "Do you want me to give him a message?"

"No," I said. "It can wait. Good night."

I hung up the phone without waiting for him to end the call. I didn't want any more questions. He'd already given me the one piece of information I needed: Marshall Weathers was not available. Taking care of my daughter would be entirely up to me.

I stared at down at my lap, my eyes slowly focusing on Jimmy's will. Sheila and I stood to inherit a large amount of money. Of course, we couldn't inherit if we were dead; Vernell would cash in then. I looked over at him; his roughened hands gripped the wheel, and he bit into his lower lip like a kindergartener. Vernell was not a murderer. He was foolish and bad to drink, but he wasn't a killer.

"Vernell?" I asked softly. "Think back a second. Jolene sure didn't seem too upset when I got that threatening phone call about Sheila. Remember that night? Jolene doesn't care about Sheila." *And she doesn't care about you, and she pure-T hates me.* "How sure are you that Jolene's with her mother?"

"Well, God, Maggie, where else would she be?" He looked across at me and saw the frightened look on my face. "Maggie, you don't think. . . ."

Vernell's face crumpled for a brief moment, then hardened.

"Vernell," I said, my voice shaking, "hit the gas. I think Sheila's in a world of trouble."

31

Vernell took the bridge over to Holden Beach doing eighty-five miles an hour. It was life-threatening and I attempted to tell him so, but Vernell was in full panic mode. When he nearly lost it on a curve near the top of the span, he got in touch with our mortality.

"Now, will you slow the hell down?" I yelled. "We've got hard thinking to do here."

Vernell scowled. "That's your problem," he said. "Ever' last one of you women's gotta think. Act!" he said. "Actions speak louder than words, remember? I'm gonna grab that young sport up by his dog collar and shake his ass loose of my daughter. Then I'm gonna haul her butt into this truck and drive my baby on home. That's when I'll think!"

"Pull over," I said, as we neared the bottom of the bridge. "Just pull over right now, Vernell." I reached for the ignition, like I was going to snatch the keys out, so he'd know I was serious.

"All right, all right!" Vernell whipped into a realty company parking lot, slammed on the brakes, and turned to face me. "I hope you know you're wasting precious time," he said.

"Vernell, has it not occured to you that Keith and Sheila may not be alone?" Vernell frowned, but I continued. "Have you thought that Jolene might be down here, too?"

"How would she know to come here?" he said. "And why would she?"

The man was dumber than dirt sometimes. "Because, Vernell, she has just as much of a reason to stop this wedding as you and I do. She wants all that money to stay in your family. And she could've found out where they were headed the same way you and I did. So let's be on the safe side. Let's scout the situation out before we go bursting in." Vernell was working hard to listen.

I reached over and took one of his weathered hands in mine. "Vernell," I said, "I want you to listen to me. I'm gonna say something that we both know is a home truth, but it's gonna break your heart." Vernell looked at me, his eyes pooled-up brown spots of pain. He knew. "You were right a while back when you said Jolene don't love you and Sheila. She's in this for the money, just like Jimmy tried to tell you. I think Jolene killed Jimmy and I think she killed Jerry Lee. I think she could be aiming to kill Sheila and you, and maybe even me."

Vernell's head dropped to his chest and a sound escaped his lips, half-sigh, half-moan. Then he lifted his head and looked straight into my face. "Oh, God, I think you're right," he whispered. "Let's go get our little girl."

I squeezed his hand, leaned over, and rested my head on his shoulder for a brief moment. "Okay. But let's be smart about this. If she's down here, she could already be at the beach house. She's killed twice, Vernell. We don't want her to panic."

"What are you thinking?" he asked.

"I'm thinking we park the Day-Glo Jesus, walk along the beach until we're level with the house, and scout it out."

Vernell nodded. "Yeah, that's good. But if she ain't there, I'm goin' in and kickin' that young skinhead's hairy behind!"

"Vernell! All right! But first, we do it my way."

It was kind of strange, walking along the Spivey beach with my ex-husband. It was still early morning and the sun was just beginning to edge its way over the horizon. Vernell and I were moving fast, his thick black work boots kicking up sand as we made our way closer and closer to the Spivey house.

Vernell and I had covered this beach every summer of our youth, hand in hand, laughing and cutting up. Then we'd lost it, and times had turned hard. We weren't talking about the future anymore, or looking at the past, we were here to save our daughter.

Vernell was the first to spot the car. He stopped in his tracks, holding me back with one muscled arm as he pointed up the beach. Jolene's white Cadillac was parked underneath the house, next to

Keith's shiny red truck. As we stood staring, the sliding glass door leading to the deck slid open and a man walked out onto the deck. It wasn't Keith the skinhead.

"Who's that?" asked Vernell.

I reached up and spun Vernell toward me, away from the beach house, using his body to shield my own.

"It's Don Evans, and I don't want him to recognize us."

When I saw Don Evans, the last pieces suddenly flew into place. What was it Bertie Sexton had said? *A high-dollar, married girlfriend with a white Cadillac . . . comes running whenever she calls.*

Vernell wrapped his arms around me and I stood huddled inside them, peeking out every now and then to take stock of the situation. Don Evans smoked a cigarette, then lit another one right after it. There was another flash of color at the door as Jolene stuck her head outside and seemed to be saying something to Don. A moment later, she emerged with Keith and Sheila. The sunlight glinted off an object in Jolene's outstretched hand.

"Vernell," I said, my voice shaking, "she's got a gun and they're all heading for the car."

Vernell was transformed into action. "Come on," he yelled, "run!" He was off, moving down the beach, away from the beach house and back to the parking lot where he'd hidden the Dancing Jesus. I lit out after him, my heart pounding in my throat. Now what were we going to do?

Vernell sprinted the distance back to the truck and had the motor started by the time I caught up.

We were less than a quarter of a mile from the beach house in one direction and almost a mile from the bridge in the other.

"They're gonna have to go through me to get off this island!" Vernell yelled over the sound of "Amazing Grace" that suddenly blared out over the loudspeaker.

"Turn the music off!" I yelled back.

Vernell flipped the switch, but nothing happened. Instead I could hear the grinding of the satellite dish as it started moving faster. Vernell's truck seemed to be developing a mind of its own. Vernell flicked switches and dials, but still the music screamed out into the early morning air.

"Vernell, do something!" I screamed. "There they go!" Jolene's white Caddy shot by, speeding down Beach Road.

Vernell put the truck into gear and laid rubber out onto the street. "Don't worry!" he yelled over the "Hallelujah Chorus," "we'll catch up to them! I had this baby custom-built. She'll flat fly!"

Vernell stomped on the gas pedal and the truck lurched into a screaming acceleration, just what we needed to catch up to Jolene and my baby. We didn't have a plan, we didn't even have a weapon, but we were going to, by God, save our little girl. And we might have done it, too, if Vernell had just been watching the road up ahead.

"Look out!" I shrieked. "Slow down!" But it was too late. Up ahead the traffic had come to a halt, backed up by an accident that seemed to eat up the foot of the bridge.

Vernell tried to react, but the Dancing Jesus

had other ideas. "Onward Christian Soldiers," it blared, the music coming so fast, it was sounding like Munchkins on a holiday from Oz. Vernell reached for the emergency brake, stood on the brake pedal, and slammed the truck from one low gear to another. The tires squealed, the brake lining smoked, and the Dancing Jesus mobile turned sideways in the street, slid off the edge of the road, and bounced into a telephone pole with a mighty thud.

Vernell flew forward as I was thrown to the floor. His head banged up against the windshield and his body fell back against the seat. There was a mighty hiss as the radiator sprang a leak. For once the Dancing Jesus was silent.

"Vernell!" I said, pulling myself up off the floor. "Vernell, are you all right?"

Motorists were leaving their cars, walking toward us with concerned looks on their faces. After all, it wasn't every day that Jesus took a flying leap into a telephone pole. Vernell lay sprawled on the passenger seat, moaning softly, a big goose egg rising up in the center of his forehead.

In the distance, I could make out Jolene's Cadillac, locked into a queue of cars. Every emergency vehicle in the world, or on the island, was congregated at the foot of the bridge. They wouldn't get to us for awhile, if ever. In the meantime, Jolene might get away with my baby, and if she did. . . .

I looked back over at Vernell. He was out of it.

"Honey," I said to his prostrate body, "stay here. I'll be back." I reached down on the floor, among the fast food wrappers and other trash that littered the Dancing Jesus, and pulled out a baseball cap and a tire iron. I crammed my hair up into the cap and pulled the bill down low over my face. I pushed the tire iron up into the sleeve of my sweater.

Vernell moaned again. "Wait," he cried weakly. "Sheila."

"It'll be fine," I said softly. "I'm done thinkin'. It's time to act."

With that I left Vernell to the ministrations of strangers and took off to save Sheila.

As I walked swiftly up the line of cars, I tried to develop a plan. Short of reaching into the car and hauling Jolene out by her hair, I was not having much success with the tactical aspect of my mission. The closer I got to Jolene, the closer I came to the scene of the accident. It was a nasty one. Two victims lay on the ground, tended to by EMS workers. The fire trucks obscured the crash vehicles, but from the amount of glass on the highway, I knew it must've been bad.

I crept up behind Jolene's car, trying to peer inside without being spotted. Don Evans sat in the driver's seat with Sheila next to him. Jolene sat behind her and Keith sat next to Jolene. It was a perfect setup. If Sheila or Keith caused a problem, it would be easy to shoot them. The windows were rolled up, the air conditioning was running full-blast, and the outside world went by in front of them like a movie.

I waited two car lengths back, hidden by a family passenger van, looking for my moment, waiting for the element of surprise to be on my side. Up ahead, volunteer firemen were slowly moving down the line of cars, stopping at each one, talking about the accident. People were everywhere. I waited, sweating under my cap and sweater, the tire iron eating into my armpit. Then, just as the volunteer started for Don Evans, gesturing for him to roll down his window, I made my move.

I loosened my grip on the tire iron, letting it slip down my sleeve and into my hand. Like Mama always said, *opportunity is not a lengthy visitor*. I took a deep breath and jumped out from behind the van, ran up to Jolene's side of the car, the tire iron held high over my head. I brought it down quickly, smashing into Jolene's window with all my might.

The glass shattered into a million little diamonds, and Jolene screamed as the tire iron grazed the side of her head. I don't know how I did it. I don't remember doing it, but somehow I pulled her scrawny little body out of the window. Unfortunately, the gun came with her.

Jolene stood for a second, dazed, the gun trembling in her hand, and then she seemed to come back to life. Her eyes focused, her lips curled into a snarl, and she started to bring the gun up in front of her. I slashed out with Vernell's Dancing Jesus tire iron, knocked her hand out of my way, and then lunged at her. Sheila was the only thing on my mind. The woman wanted to kill my baby.

This was not a woman you wanted to fight with for a sale item at the semiannual Dillards' clearance sale. I charged her and we went down, hitting the asphalt with a bone-rattling jar. The shock finally loosened the gun from her clawlike grasp, sending it skittering across the road. I was beating the crap out of Jolene, and it felt so fine. I tangled my hands in her bleached blond hair and yanked so hard, she screamed. She brought her knee up and attempted to disembowel me with the sheer force of her adrenaline. But I banged her face against the gravel.

"That's for Sheila!" I panted, and proceeded to pull my fist back. I had never been in a fight, not in all of my life, but it came natural and easy. My fist connected with her pretty little nose, and to my surprise, it cracked. "And this is for Jimmy!" I screamed. "And Jerry!"

I don't even think I felt the police officer pull me off her. I know I didn't feel any of the blows she landed. I kept trying to get to her, even as she was surrounded by uniformed officers and led away.

"Maggie, let up now, girl." I heard the familiar voice, talking right into my ear. "You want to see your daughter or not?" he asked. "'Cause I can't let go until I know you're in control."

I had to be hallucinating. He couldn't be here, but he was. Marshall Weathers held me fast, his mustache brushing against my ear as he pulled me tight against him.

"Let me see Sheila." I quit moving and stood still, waiting for him to let go.

"All right," he said. "That's it. That's better."

"Jolene killed Jimmy and Jerry Lee," I said, trying to catch my breath.

"I know," he said calmly.

"You know? How do you know?" I couldn't

stand it. Always in control, never surprised, Detective You-Can't-Tell-Me-A-Thing Weathers. "And what are you doing here?" I asked.

"Maggie, we recovered a tiny piece of a partial print when the crime lab processed your gun." I nodded slowly. "It took a while, and the lab used a pretty advanced technique, but we found one. That's why I'm here."

"Jolene's print, huh?"

Weathers shook his head. "No, Don Evans's. It wasn't until we started surveillance that I knew about Jolene. She picked him up yesterday and we followed them here. That's when we started to figure out what was going on. Then Bobby called and told me about Sheila. That started making the pieces fall into place."

"So you knew."

"Well, let's say I had a pretty good idea," he said. "I didn't have the Jolene piece and still wasn't sure."

"She and Don were ripping off Jimmy, and he found out."

Weathers nodded. "We were working on getting them out of the beach house when you and Vernell arrived. I had the realty company call and say they were sending in workmen. We had this all staged," he said, gesturing toward the accident scene. "We wanted them out in the open, so we could control the situation." There was that C word again.

"Where's Sheila?" I said, looking around. "I need to see her."

"You can see her, but then we'll get on to the hospital."

"Why? Oh God!" I said. "Vernell! Is he at the hospital?"

"No, he's all right. He's with Sheila. You're the one who needs a hospital."

"I don't need to go to the hospital!" I said, and started to walk away from him.

"No, that's right, you don't." He reached up and touched the side of my head, his hand coming away covered with blood. "You can just bleed all over yourself until you die." He was getting worked up again. His jaw twitched angrily. "You don't need a damn hospital. What you need is a little time in jail for obstructing justice!"

The sight of blood, my blood on his hand, suddenly made me feel a little woozy. Weathers sensed this and softened a little.

"It ain't gonna kill you, but you'll need some stitches."

I looked past him and saw Sheila walking toward me with Vernell on one side and Keith on the other. Sheila was clinging to her father's arm, her head on his shoulder. Keith seemed to have been forgotten, and, if I knew my ever-changeable daughter, that probably meant he was already a fading memory. True life-and-death trauma can take the thrill out of young-love romance. Slowly, the world seemed to come back into focus, and I realized how tired I was, and how scared I'd been.

"Is it really over?" I asked Marshall.

"Yeah, honey," he said gently, "it's really over."

32

It was good to be back, doing the one thing that seemed to come natural to me: singing. When I walked into the Golden Stallion, for the first time in days, the boys fell all over themselves. Was I sure I wanted to sing tonight? Was I really all right? They didn't know how badly I needed this time, how much I wanted to feel normal again. Harmonica Jack knew. He didn't say a word, just smiled and took my guitar from me.

"I'll put it out on its stand," he said. "You go puke or whatever it is you do in the ladies' room."

I wanted to say something to him, but it wasn't necessary. Whatever might have passed between us was best not examined. We had a connection that bridged the usual man-woman type stuff, and I'd never had that before. So, I walked away.

Just before the band got started, Jack walked up again. A tall, very thin woman with short silver hair stood by his side, smiling expectantly. She looked like a floating angel, barely touching the ground, her skin a translucent white. I knew in an instant who she was, and I also knew something else. She was very, very ill.

"Hey, Maggie," he said. "This is Evelyn. Mom, this is Maggie."

Evelyn reached out and slipped a thin hand into mine. "I've been waiting to meet you," she said, her voice escaping in a delicate whisper, "but my body doesn't seem to want to cooperate these days."

My eyes met Jack and finally I understood his sadness.

"Evelyn's gonna stay for the first set," he said softly. "I'll go get her settled in."

Evelyn and I looked at each other and smiled.

"I really like your son," I said. "He's always talking about you."

Evelyn smiled and slipped her arm through his. "I'm right fond of him myself," she said. "But he needs to eat more." She looked from him back to me, her head moving quickly, like a little bird. "Maybe you can make sure he eats now and then?" she said.

"There's nothing I like better than laying on a home-cooked meal," I said. "Maybe I can get you both over for a Sunday dinner."

"Maybe," she said, her face suddenly wistful.

Sparks looked over and gave us the high sign; it was time. Jack steered Evelyn away and I walked off-stage to wait for my cue.

The first set went off like clockwork, not a missed note, not a harmony out of place. I was back and it was good. Even Sparks was happy, his ten-gallon, white straw Stetson nodding over the pedal steel. But I should've known it wouldn't last. In the middle of the second set, while I was singing a particularly slow ballad, I saw Sugar Bear look offstage at something I couldn't see, nod, and walk over to Sparks.

This was all accomplished while Sugar Bear was picking out his solo, but he never missed a note. Jack didn't see the conversation between Sparks and Sugar Bear because he was trying to put a riff behind Bear's solo. I came back in for the last few lines, but not before I saw Sparks look over at me, frown, and then give the nod to Sugar Bear.

Before the next song could start, Sparks beckoned me over.

"Maggie, sit this one out."

"What do you mean, sit this one out? I'm the singer. I don't sit out!" If there was going to be trouble, I wanted in on it. If Sparks still had an axe to grind with me, he'd soon find out that I was no longer a pushover.

"Calm down, Maggie," he sighed. "Bear's just been working on something he wants to try."

"Oh," I said, still suspicious, but relieved that it wasn't a problem with me.

"You can put something behind it if you want," he said.

I looked over at Sugar Bear, who was adjusting my vocal mike to his height. He looked like a frightened teddy bear. To my knowledge, Sugar

Bear had never sung the lead on a song. He was too bashful. In fact, I couldn't recall ever hearing him hum, let alone sing.

"What's he going to do?" I asked.

Sparks shoved his hat back on his head. "Some request. A Clint Black tune. 'Our Kind of Love.' You know it?"

Know it? It was my favorite cut off my favorite CD. Before Jimmy'd died, I'd listened to it almost every day. I'd sung the harmony along with Allison Krauss so many times, I could probably sing it in my sleep.

"Great! No problem. I'll do the harmony."

Sparks wasn't listening. He was counting off the intro and giving Bear an intense glare that said, "You'd best not mess this up!"

I walked to the side of the stage and brought Bear's mike down to my level. Jack was all the way across the stage, blowing his harmonica with his eyes closed, dancing in place. I started nodding, tapping my foot in time to the bass. When Sugar Bear began to sing, I stopped short. His voice rang through, rich and deep and very pure.

"Long ago, with a younger partner. . . ."

"Now they hold their own, out on the liner. . . ."
I came in with the harmony, goose bumps raising up on my arms at the sound of our voices blending together. Out on the floor, the two-steppers swung into action. It was the perfect two-step tune.

As I watched, my eyes were drawn to a tall, lanky cowboy wandering through the dancers, his intense blue eyes staring into mine, his thick cowboy mustache twitching with a smile that I knew only too well. He walked right up in front of the stage where I stood and crooked his finger at me. He was asking me to dance!

I started to shake my head, my knees trembling just as they had that first night during my audition.

Down on the floor someone shouted, "Go on, Maggie, do it! Dance with him!"

Jack wandered across the floor, still blowing his harmonica while Sugar Bear sang.

"Go, Maggie, we got you covered," he said. He was smiling, and I looked behind him at the others. They were all smiling, and Sparks was actually motioning me off the stage. This was planned. Weathers had set me up again. Only this time I didn't mind at all.

I walked to the edge of the stage and down the steps and into the arms of my blue-eyed cowboy. I looked back at the stage. Jack was mouthing something I could just make out: "Breathe."

Marshall's arm slid around my waist, one firm hand pressing gently against my back, the other resting on my shoulder. We moved off onto the floor. I was dancing, floating in his arms. The boys chimed in behind Bear, blending their voices to make a perfect three-part harmony.

"I've been waiting a long time to do this," he said, his eyes reaching into mine.

I looked up at him and smiled. "A girl could do a lot worse," I said. He laughed and pulled me closer.

Mama's voice floated across the years, taking the place of the music for a brief moment. "Oh, you'll know, honey," she'd said. "You'll just know."

Acknowledgments

In its own wacky way, this book is about the importance of family. I would like to acknowledge mine. Without their love and support, this book would never have become a reality and Maggie Reid would never have gotten her shot at stardom.

I am also very grateful to Cpl. J. F. Whitt of the Greensboro Police Department. His assistance was invaluable. His mustache, unforgettable. He put up with me on a regular basis for the months it took to write this book, and always, always came to my assistance and answered my questions. My thanks, also, to the officers of the Greensboro Police Department who rode me around town for hours and told me their stories. In particular, I would like to thank Cpl. Stan Lawhorne for the tour of Greensboro at dawn.

Harmonica Jack and the Boys in The Band provided the backdrop for Maggie's music. We shared a special time in our lives. We grew up together. I will never forget those days, nor cease to be grateful for the friendship and loyalty I found at the Ranch.

I set this book in Greensboro, North Carolina, the town that I have called home for four years. I have moved and created landmarks and streets. I have taken liberties with a beautiful city. All the mistakes and creations are mine alone and none of the characters are meant to resemble anyone, living or dead.

I want to thank my loyal critique group: Nancy Gates, Wendy Greene, Chris Farran, Carla Schwarz-Buckley, Ellen Hunter, Charlotte Perkins, and Renee Gilleao. I also wish to thank Irene Kraas for saying, "Write it, kid!" I am deeply indebted to my editors: Jeffery McGraw for his tolerance, kindness, and nutty sense of humor, and Carolyn Marino for adopting Maggie into the HarperCollins family.

Perhaps the biggest thank-you belongs to those who have to live with me: my husband and my children. They gave me wings and let me fly. They rarely complained about cold suppers or eating among the manuscript pages. They believed in me even when I didn't believe in myself.

I am so fortunate to have such an unconditionally loving family, both immediate and extended, in-laws and out-laws. They read my works in progress, they forgive my oversights and forgotten birthdays, they brag about me, even when I am most outrageous. This large, eccentric family of mine has taught me the most important lesson of all: Family is everything. Treasure it. Scoop up your babies and hold them tight. Listen, even when you disagree. We have only each other, and only this one moment. Thanks, guys. I love you, too!